MARKED BY SHADOWS

ALSO BY LAUREN DAWES

The Cat McKenzie Series

Bad Vampire
Bad Witch
Bad Fae
Bad Wolf
Bad Kitty

The Helheim Wolf Pack Series

Fate Revealed
Truth Untold
Denied Revenge
Destiny Concealed
Love Unbound

Gods & Monsters Trilogy

Torment
Revenge
Downfall

Shadow Shifers Series

Marked by Shadows

MARKED BY SHADOWS

SHADOW SHIFTERS
BOOK 1

USA TODAY BESTSELLING AUTHOR

LAUREN DAWES

Cover design by Deranged Doctor Design
Edited by Heather Long
Proofread by Bookish Dreams Editing

For Phil and Evie
...always.

1

DRAKE

Drake leaned over and turned up the music. The bass thumped through the subwoofers, making the table the sound system was sitting on jump like it was having a seizure. It was a rare day off for him and the rest of the Revenant, and it was one they'd all been looking forward to.

There was a shout, and he turned his head to find Mateo and Jett both leaping from the couch at the same time, the controllers for their gaming system dropping to the floor. He wasn't surprised when the swearing started, nor was he happy. The fuckers tended to make a mess when they got into these dick measuring contests. The pair were always competing against each other, though, whether it be in the gym, in the field, or chasing a female they both wanted to bed. The only saving grace was that they were better at sharing the latter.

Barely.

Drake shifted his gaze over to the other side of the room where quicksilver-eyed Sasha was brooding in her corner. She was the only female in their team, but underestimating her would be a fucking mistake—probably the last one you'd ever make. The woman had ice in her veins and a heart made of stone. Her ruthlessness made her the perfect soldier, the perfect member of the Revenant. They were, after all, the ones responsible for policing the other Shadows, for protecting the Trinity's interests.

Her brooding was understandable. She'd been saddled with the fucked up ability to see what was going to happen in the future. From what he understood, knowing when you and everyone you'd ever come into contact with was going to die wasn't a picnic, but to Sasha's credit, she never flapped her gums about what she saw unless it was pertinent to the situation.

He glanced to his left as Grayson sidled up beside him. A tumbler was in his left hand, the clear contents cozying up to the two ice cubes still floating in there.

"You'd think they'd get bored of doing this every single time," the male murmured, his green eyes fixed on the two one-hundred-and-ninety-pound black jaguar shifters rolling around on the floor, trading punches and breaking furniture.

"I wish they'd take this shit outside," Drake growled. He and disorder were not friends.

Grayson grunted and ran a hand through his dark hair. At six-seven, the guy had a good couple of inches on Drake, but unlike Drake, he didn't have a hard, sharp edge to him. They referred to Grayson as the Gentleman because despite being a trained killer and protector of the species, he was from a pure bloodline and had impeccable manners and taste.

Drake bit back a curse when there was another crack as one of the side tables became a casualty of the brawl.

"Want me to break those two up?" His companion lifted his chin in the direction of Mateo and Jett. Grayson had the ability to read and manipulate emotions, which did come in handy when tempers ran high.

Which was about ninety-nine percent of the time.

"Nah, let them work this out with fists and blood. They need the release."

Grayson nodded. "Have you heard from the Trinity yet?"

Shifting to the side, Drake dodged a gaming controller sailing past his head. "Not yet," he replied, picking up his own glass of vodka and swirling the clear liquid around. The ice cubes bumped and skittered as far as they could within the confines of their glass prison, all destined to disappear and water down his drink. "But I expect to hear something soon. We're never left to our own devices for long."

The Trinity wouldn't allow it.

They were the trio of jaguars who controlled all the Shadow units, including Drake's team, doling out their assignments and which pride they were to serve. Two hundred years ago—long before Drake's time—the Trinity didn't exist. It was only after a Leo—the most dominant male who ruled an individual pride— tried to overthrow multiple prides by using all the Shadows to do his bidding that they were established. By removing direct contact between the Leos and the Shadows who served them as security and protection, they eliminated the possibility of a coup happening ever again.

And the Revenant existed to make sure all the other Shadows and jaguars alike toed the line. They were the Trinity's attack dogs—every other shifter's Bogeyman.

Grayson smiled, revealing his slightly elongated canine teeth. "Well, wherever we're going, let's hope it's something that requires us to take a vacation."

Drake nodded curtly. His team called Wyoming home, but the weather was cooling off, and the chill of winter was setting in earlier than expected. Soon, their compound would be surrounded by snow and they'd be balls deep in it, too. He looked out the set of French doors at the ass-end of the room, the twenty or so small panes of glass revealing the endless forest that hemmed them in. Darkness swathed the branches, the moon barely making its mark on the leaves that swayed gently in the breeze.

Their place was remote, and that was just the way he liked it. Security was tight, and if someone so much as came within a mile of their front gate, he'd know about it. Drake emptied his glass, taking what remained of the cubes into his mouth and biting down.

"Another?" Grayson asked, tipping his chin in the direction of his glass.

He contemplated it for a moment. Getting drunk enough to forget would've been difficult, but the idea of numbing out was fucking tempting. Ten years ago today, he'd received the worst news a twin could possibly receive. Ten years of regret. Ten years of self-loathing.

Against his instincts to get so polluted he wouldn't remember his name in the morning, he shook his head. "No. I'm going to bed."

Grayson's eyes flashed with his cat as he no doubt got a bead on Drake's grief.

"Come on, D, don't be a fucking pussy," Mateo called from the ground, blood dripping from one nostril. Drake looked to Jett. The guy was not leaking fluid, which meant he was the victor.

This time.

Drake flipped Mateo off then clapped palms with Grayson. "I'll catch you tomorrow." As he left the rec room, he glanced over at Sasha, finding her looking out at the dark forest. He worried about the female sometimes, worried about what lurked around in her gray matter and made her so introspective. She turned her head toward him, her black hair falling over half of her face. Her eyes, though—those haunting gray eyes—latched onto him and made the blood in his veins run cold. The hair at the back of his neck prickled in awareness, but he wasn't ready to hear the details of the premonition she'd just had. Not tonight.

Turning, he left the room, the feeling of dread sliding from his shoulders as he jogged up the stairs to his room. Pulling the black T-shirt over his head, he dumped it on the ground on his way to the bathroom connected to his room. Crisp white marble was on every surface, from the heated floor beneath his bare feet to the countertop that housed twin sinks. The walk-in shower was much the same with an oversized rain shower head stretching across the top.

Leaning in, he got things started before stripping out of his sweats. While he waited for things to get good and foggy, he stared at his reflection in the mirror, running his index and middle finger over the mark over his heart. The Shadow Mark—the one he'd been born with—had rerouted his life. It was a simple 'X' with a circle inserted between the two upper arms and it was this that set him apart from other shifters and Shadows.

Stepping into the shower, he quickly ran through the whole wash-rinse routine, ignoring the triple-milled sandalwood soap Grayson ordered by the crate and stocked in every bathroom, sticking to his usual bar of Dial. After he rinsed off the suds, he shut off the water and stepped out, wrapping a towel around his waist.

As he turned to leave the bathroom, he caught a glimpse of the tattoo on his back. Stretching from the base of his neck to the bottom of his spine, the Grim Reaper stood sentry, its hollow eyes and wicked grin making a sense of dread uncurl in his stomach. Wrapped in his arms was a woman, her face turned toward the personification of Death, her expression one of surrender.

He liked to think of death in this way—something you go toward willingly.

Without hesitation.

Without regret.

Without fear.

Stalking into his room, he swiped a clean pair of sweats from the straight-backed chair in the corner of his room and pulled them on. His legs suddenly felt like they'd turned to Jell-O, and he collapsed into the seat. He rubbed at the spot over his heart, wincing. Time didn't seem to care he was still hurting from the loss of his twin sister. Sometimes, though, he could swear he still felt her, like an apparition that followed him around, tethered to his soul.

His phone started to vibrate on his nightstand, and he got up to answer it.

"Zed," he drawled in a bored tone, hoping to mask his real feelings.

Which was fucking off-kilter, unhinged, and off-balanced.

"Drake. How are you?" Zed, one of the Trinity, asked.

He sat on the edge of the mattress. "Good, although I have to tell you, I'm not one for social calls tonight."

"Blunt as ever, Drake."

"Nah, just no time for bullshit."

"Fair enough," the Shadow Elder replied. A weighted pause crawled over the line, one that lasted long enough to make Drake's eye twitch.

"What is it?" he demanded, planting his feet onto the thick

carpet. He flexed his toes, needing to feel grounded because he had a feeling he was about to be put through the wringer.

A heavy sigh, and Drake could just imagine the male rubbing his eyes like he was goddamn tired. Yeah, well, that made two of them. "Something's happened."

Drake's hand tightened on the phone, but he forced himself to relax. "Talk to me, Zed." Christ, he almost didn't want to know.

"A female has been reported missing."

Impotent rage suddenly burned through his veins, and he stood up to pace, his legs mimicking the speed of his memories from a decade ago. He hadn't been home when his twin sister went missing, and he punished himself for it every damn day. The fact that this news was reaching his ears today, of all days, was a bad, fucking omen.

With fingers tightening around the phone, he barked, "Who? Where?"

"A female called Elsie Fox. I don't know much, but what I do know is she was taken sometime between her classes at UC Berkeley yesterday. Her roommate reported her missing to her parents."

"Is Specter on this? Does Lewis know?"

"They're taking care of it," Zed replied in a slow, calm voice. "I just wanted to give you a heads-up since…"

"Thanks," he bit out, cutting the guy off before he could say the words that would strip him to the bone.

There was a pause, then…

"Don't get involved, Drake," Zed warned with a soft snarl. "Let us handle this."

"But—"

The Elder cut him off. "I mean it. Stay out of this. Your judgment is clouded right now."

Drake's free hand tightened into a fist. Every single instinct he had started firing, bucking against the shackles that had just been placed on him. He bit his tongue. Hard. That sweet, salty taste of copper flooded his mouth, and he swallowed it down.

Without another word, Drake hung up, his phone slipping from his fingers and thumping to the carpet beside his foot. Zed's words lapped his conscious thoughts until all he heard was the reality of the situation.

The walls of his room felt closer than before, pressing against his skin. Smothering. He gasped, trying to choke down another breath of air, trying to get more oxygen into his lungs to stifle the sensation of drowning. Beneath his skin, his cat prowled like the caged beast that it was, snarling and hissing at him, baring his fangs. Drake had to get out of there. Practically ripping the bedroom door from its hinges, he ran down the stairs and yanked open the front door.

Behind him, Grayson yelled something, but Drake didn't stop. Couldn't stop. Stripping out of his sweats, he thought about the cat who inhabited his body, sharing his blood, his instincts, and his brain. He thought about him coming to the surface of his mind. Between one breath and the next, Drake's vision changed from color to muted shades of blue and gray. Throwing his head back, he roared and let the beast out.

For three hundred agonizing seconds, his bones broke and reset. His muscles and tendons were torn and reformed to fit his cat's sleeker, more lithe body. His jaw throbbed as the larger incisors took up residence, his whole face elongating and flexing. Finally, fur started to sprout.

Like all Shadows, his coat was solid black. There were no hints of rosettes beneath the solid swallowing color—he was all oily darkness. All fluid grace.

When the pain finally subsided, he flexed his whiskers forward and stretched out his new body. There were a few pops and groans as his new bones slid into shape, and he finally felt like he was seated in his new skin properly.

Sensing eyes on him, he threw one last look at the house. Grayson was standing in between the jambs, his eyes cycling between human and cat. The guy eventually nodded, having gotten a good enough read on Drake's emotional grid—which was, BTW, fucking screwed up—and retreated back into the house.

Drake huffed.

Turning, he started pawing through the underbrush, his fur getting tangled in burrs as he passed. He didn't know where he was going—all he knew was he had to keep moving. This news had shaken him to the core, and although he didn't know the female, he knew the feelings her parents and siblings must be running through because he had suffered through them too.

Regret.

Fear.

Anger.

With a small snarl, he picked up the pace, not bothering to dampen his footsteps as he went. He had no intention of hunting, but if a deer was stupid enough to get in his way right now, he'd be sure to show it a good time.

He ran until his lungs burned like they were laced with shards of glass and his muscles ached, but still the same thought was banging around in his head.

It had happened again.

2

NEVE

Neve inspected the nail she'd just painted and blew gently over the Smith & Cult polish. Palace in Wonderland was the name of the color, but all she saw was a horrible shade of metallic fuchsia. Even if she bothered with painting her nails, she wouldn't have been caught dead wearing that color. Her cousin, on the other hand…

Katie squealed when she saw the shade of pink on her fingernails and clapped her hands together excitedly.

"Katie!" Neve said. "You're going to ruin the finish. Let the damn things dry."

But Katie being Katie, only ignored her. It was par for the course really. With only six months separating them in age, she was more like a sister than a cousin, and with the amount of time they spent together, they may as well have lived in the same house. Katie's dad was Neve's uncle, and thankfully, they only lived a few miles up the road.

She was Neve's closest, and perhaps only, friend.

"Neve? Hello?"

She refocused her attention on Katie and smiled. "Sorry. What were you saying?"

"I was saying you need to find yourself a mate."

She barely kept herself from rolling her eyes. "Why does every conversation come back to this?" Katie sounded just like Neve's mother.

"Because this is what we talk about," Katie replied. The *duh* was implied. Neve placed the lid back on the bottle of polish and sucked in a deep, calming breath.

"No, Katie, this is what *you* talk about."

She got up and walked to the window, her sore muscles protesting with the movement. The self-defense training she'd done with Roman and Tailor that afternoon was brutal—a session involving hand-to-hand combat and disarming an attacker. She'd have bruises on her forearms by tomorrow. It was just one more thing for her mother to disapprove of. If it wasn't the fact she wasn't mated yet, it was the way she unashamedly wore her bruises and shallow cuts like badges of honor.

Neve peered out at the night sky, the slowly ascending moon mesmerizing her with its potency. Unlike weres, shifters weren't subject to the whims of the lunar cycle. They were free to shift whenever they wanted and run through the forest at the drop of a hat. And right now, that was all Neve wanted to do…

Escape.

Escape from her responsibilities, from the expectations.

"So," Katie began softly, almost hesitantly. "What do you think about Charles?"

Neve took a moment to smooth the disgust from her expression before she turned around. She couldn't understand why Katie was still hung up on the male, since it wasn't like he even knew she existed. "What about him?"

Her cousin's face got all dreamy, like she was picturing their mating ceremony. Outside her door, Neve's mother was getting busy with the Dyson, which given the time, wasn't weird. Any spare minute was spent vacuuming the expensive wool carpets that covered most of the house, and right now, she had about half an hour to kill while the roast lamb she'd cooked for dinner was resting.

"Don't you think he's just perfect?"

Perfect for a human shield in a zombie apocalypse.

"Uh-huh," she replied without meaning it at all. Katie had been crushing on the male for months now.

The *whir* of the vacuum got louder as Mom worked her way up the hallway. "Can't you see it, though? Us getting mated…"

Yeah, she could see it. She could totally see her cousin doing exactly what Neve's mother wished she'd do. The thing was, Neve wanted a little more from life than becoming someone's mate and popping out the next generation of shifters. What she wanted she couldn't articulate because it would mean letting down her father and disappointing her mother. She had to keep her aspirations to herself like some kind of dirty little secret.

"I think he's perfect for you," she said instead. It wasn't a lie. Charles would make her the perfect mate, and her cousin would make the perfect wife, and they would make the perfect children.

But all of that wasn't for Neve.

Katie glanced at the door, the high-pitched whine reaching its zenith outside. "Why is your mom vacuuming now? I thought she hired a housekeeper not that long ago."

Neve couldn't help but laugh. "Seriously? You've known me my entire life, and you're asking that question?"

A beautiful smile graced her cousin's lips. She had the same dark hair as Neve, but her eyes were the blue of a clear spring day rather than Neve's watery green. "Fair point. I guess she had a lull between cooking and serving dinner."

"You got it," she replied, folding her arms over her chest and leaning against the wall beside the window. "Are you staying?"

"Are you kidding? It's roast lamb Friday. I'm definitely staying." She wiggled her fingers back at Neve. "So, are you going to finish these for me? You know you want to," she added in a singsong voice.

With a small smile, Neve pushed off the wall and picked up the bottle of godawful fuchsia, making sure the top was screwed on properly before giving it a little shake. Katie put out her hand, spreading out her fingers and grinning like she'd won an argument Neve didn't even know they were having.

The sound of the Dyson cut and there was a knock on the door.

"Katie?" Mom called. "I take it you're staying for dinner, hon."

"Yes, please, Aunt Rose!" Katie called, not taking her eyes off her Palace in Wonderland nails.

"All right, well, it'll be ready in ten."

The vacuum started up, and Katie sighed. "I hope Charles calls me one of these days."

Neve did roll her eyes this time, but kept them down on her work. They were back on this topic again? "I'm sure he will," she replied, her voice hollow. "Do you think…" She paused, undecided whether she should even be bringing this up.

"What?"

She shook her head. "Nothing."

Katie snorted. "It's never nothing with you, Neve. Spill it."

Jogging the little brush into the polish bottle over and over again, she said, "Do you think you'll ever want more?"

A small frown appeared between her cousin's eyes, marring her otherwise perfect features. "More than what?"

Neve looked toward the window, toward the black expanse that hovered just outside the glass. "More than this life? More than what your parents expect of you, of what the pride expects from you?"

Her frown deepened. "Why would you want more than this? You're the Leo's daughter. You have everything you could possibly want." She leaned forward as if the words she was about to speak were going to change the world. "You could have *any male* you want."

But what if that wasn't what she wanted? Katie couldn't understand because she never wanted anything more than the life she had. All she had to look forward to was mating some male who would dote on her—and they would because her cousin was just too sweet not to—and have five or six children.

Blowing out a frustrated breath, she screwed the lid back onto the polish bottle. "Just forget about it." Neve had the distinct feeling Katie was slipping through her fingers. They'd grown up together, laughed together, crushed on the same guys together. They'd navigated puberty and their first shifts together, but this right here, tonight, this was where their journey together ended. She could see it as clearly as if she was standing out in the forest. Before them were two paths, but their hearts were divided for the first time.

Katie, however, didn't seem to notice. She was too busy inspecting her nails and cooing over sparkles that caught the light.

"Girls! Dinner!" Neve's dad called out.

"Come on," Neve said to Katie. "Let's eat, then we can watch a movie before you have to go home."

As they walked into the dining room, Neve found her dad sitting at the head of the table, a glass of amber liquid at his elbow. Dropping a kiss to his cheek as she passed, she took her seat to his left.

"Hi, Uncle Greg," Katie said with a warm smile.

"Katie, what a surprise to see you here," he said dryly, his mouth curling up in a grin.

Neve shook her head. "It's not her fault our house is more exciting."

Her dad threw his head back and laughed loudly. "My brother was always the boring one growing up."

"Greg!" her mom admonished as she swept into the room, all Martha Stewart graceful. She placed the roast lamb onto the table with a flourish and stood back, waiting for the praise to roll in.

"It looks wonderful, my love," her dad said, holding out his hand to her mom. She stepped into him, and he snaked his arm around her back, pulling her closer. Her parents had always been this loving, but then again, they'd been lucky and had an actual love match—he had found his true mate.

"All right, all right." Her mom waved her hand to dismiss the compliment she'd so easily teased from her mate. "Let's eat before it gets cold."

3

JETT

Jett tipped back his head and emptied the contents of the glass into his mouth. The tequila burned on the way down, and he chased the bitterness away with a lemon wedge jammed between his teeth. He and Mateo had given up on the Xbox an hour ago, choosing to switch out their entertainment to one of the *Fast & Furious* movies.

Mateo refilled Jett's glass before taking a swig directly from the bottle.

"You're an animal," Jett told him, tossing back his drink.

Mateo laughed and flipped him off. "That's because I am. You are too, dick."

Jett eyed the red tattoos on the other male's right arm, his golden skin warming the ink and turning it a deep shade of sienna.

"Fuck, what time is it?" He picked up his phone, focusing his eyes on the digital numbers at the top of the screen. It was a little after midnight. He dropped his phone back onto the couch, only to have it beep at him like it was bitching him out for the rough treatment.

"Are you going to get that?" Mateo asked, his voice sounding like he hadn't been drinking for the past six hours.

"How are you still sober?" Jett asked sourly. Mateo only laughed and pointed to the tattoos snaking along every inch of the skin on his arm. The symbols were all the same—healing, protection, health. Over and over again. The guy was a walking health retreat, able to heal himself passively. The ability was great when it came to healing his own injuries—including flushing all the alcohol from his system when he drank. The only drawback was if he wanted to get really polluted, he had to drink triple the amount of alcohol in a fifth of the time. Maintaining the buzz was just as difficult.

Picking up his phone again, Jett squinted at the screen, trying to focus on the small writing. His eyes widened when he saw who had sent him the message—Luce. Standing up, he left Mateo to slam back the tequila by himself and climbed the stairs, weaving in the direction of his room.

Collapsing onto the edge of the bed, he stared at the screen before sliding his finger over it to read the whole message. When he was done, he took in a deep breath, let it out, then hit call.

"Jett," Luce whispered, keeping her voice low.

"Hey, Luce," he said, his voice softening. Luce was fifteen years his junior, a sweet-faced, softly-spoken little girl who loved the color pink and drawing fat rainbow-farting unicorns on any flat surface she could find. "What's going on?"

In the background, the sound of the TV blaring told him their mom's boyfriend was there. The fucker had gone deaf from working in construction for his entire life.

"Luce?" he asked when she was quiet. He made himself loosen his grip on the phone. "Come on, baby, tell me what's going on."

"It's Mom."

"What about Mom?" he coaxed gently. Her message had been cryptic at best, so he had no idea what was actually going on.

"What about Mom, huh?"

"She won't wake up."

As those words were spoken, Jett's whole body began to shake. Not from fear—rather, it was rage. This was an emotion that was always simmering in the background of his life, and all of it was firmly directed at his mother and whichever dickwad male she was dating at the time. He'd like to say this was the first time he'd had to field a call like this from his innocent little sister, but it wasn't.

He suspected it wouldn't be the last time either.

Drawing in a deep breath through his nose, he let it out and asked, "Where's Richard?"

"Lying beside her. On the bed." She added that last bit in a squeak.

Jett licked his lips, indecision playing him like a fiddle. "Is she still breathing?" He kept his voice low, soothing. He shouldn't have even been talking to her. The cut from his family was supposed to have been a clean one when he joined the Shadows. The past was no longer his past—the future was the Shadows.

"I don't know."

Fuck. "Where are Katya and Mila?"

"Katya had a shift at the cinema. Mila is with her boyfriend."

He sucked back a hiss. Katya had to work to keep the damn household above water, but Mila didn't need to leave Luce in that goddamn trailer with *her* and the male she put above her own family. Katya would be home soon—the last showing would have been at around eleven, but she had to lock up afterward. Jett wasn't willing to leave Luce alone for that long, though.

"I'm coming home," he told her, making sure to keep the hot, crawling rage out of his voice. It scorched his veins, emanating from his fingers. As he unclenched one hand, his palm glowed red, heating up yet not burning. "Go and hide under the bed, Luce." He paused, the rustle of her moving around followed by the dull thump as the phone was placed on the floor. There was a hush then her breathing over the line.

"Are you there now?" he asked, needing to focus less on destruction and more on Luce's safety while he traveled to get there.

"Yes," she whispered. He could just picture her hugging her favorite stuffed unicorn to her chest, her big blue eyes wide and guileless. She was too young to see such ugliness.

"Good. I'm going to hang up now, but I'm coming to get you, Luce. Promise me you'll stay where you are."

"I will."

He was suddenly exhausted. He was sobering up now too, but probably not sober enough to drive just yet. Picking up the leather jacket hanging on the back of the wing chair in the corner, he slid his arms in and yanked open the door. Grayson was standing there, his hand raised as if he was about to knock.

Jett was careful to arrange his expression into cool indifference, although he didn't think he'd fooled the other male.

"Hey, man," Jett said, staring hard at his boots. "Can I ask you a favor?"

"Yeah. Anything." Grayson's voice was calm, like a trickle of a stream over rocks. But that was Grayson. Rock-steady and always cool in a crisis.

"Could you take me somewhere?"

"I'll take you anywhere you need to go," he replied. "Let me go and get my keys. I'll see you downstairs in a few."

Jett exhaled loudly, suddenly aware he'd been holding his breath.

"Thanks, man. I appreciate it." He took a moment to collect

himself, ready to accept that his mother could actually be dead this time. He wasn't quite sure how he'd feel about it if it was true. She hadn't been the role model he'd looked up to for so long now. Drugs were such a defining part of her life that he really couldn't have one without the other—they were a package deal.

He made his feet move and walked down the stairs, the knot in his stomach getting tighter and tighter as he went. What if she was dead? Luce would have to deal with that shit for the rest of her life. It wasn't fair to her, and it sure as shit wasn't fair to him. He'd gotten out of there at sixteen, the lifeline of training with the Trinity taken with both hands, even though he hated leaving his sisters behind. He would've taken them with him if he could, but training had been mandatory, the cutting of family ties absolute.

But still, he hadn't been able to sever the bonds, even if that broke one of the Trinity's cardinal rules. Now he just had to make sure he kept it secret.

Outside in the courtyard, Grayson slammed the door of his cherry red Mustang GT and started the engine. It came to life with a growl, and Jett slid into the passenger seat, bracing himself for the questions he didn't want to answer.

"Where are we going?" Grayson asked softly, playing with the dials on the radio rather than looking at him.

"Head toward Thayne," he replied in a hollow voice. "I'll tell you where to go from there."

Grayson moved the car slowly down the drive, going through each of the security checkpoints carefully. The GT prowled down the small country lanes until they reached Highway 89 where Grayson opened up the engine, giving his baby her head. They shot down the quiet road, farms and fields passing them by in a blur. They turned off just before they hit the town proper, and if it had been daytime, Jett would've seen the Wyomings in the background, all snow-capped and postcard perfect. As it was, all he could see was black, and it totally fit with his mood.

"Take the next left," he croaked a few miles down the road.

As the car slowed and turned into the lot of the Flat Creek RV park, Jett directed him to the last trailer on the left.

"What is this place?" Grayson asked.

He turned to his fellow Shadow. "My childhood home."

If Grayson was shocked by the admission that Jett still had contact with his family, it didn't show. He peered out at the structure, his cat's vision taking over as the small light on the mobile home he'd grown up in came on. There was trash littering the front along with a pink bike lying forgotten in the dirt.

Grayson turned off the engine, and they both sat there until only the *tick, tick, ticking* of the cooling engine could be heard.

"Want me to—"

"No," Jett replied. "Thank you, but no. Stay here. This won't take long."

The warmth rushed out as he opened his door. He took in the double-length home with beige siding and cinder block supports. How in the hell it was still standing? Rust red shutters had been added to the windows, probably to give it a homier look, but the flaking paint and rotting wood failed. Glancing up, he saw the low-pitched roof had sustained some damage last winter and would need to be repaired before this season's dumping of snow came.

Taking the two steps up to the door, he looked in through the diamond-shaped window, but couldn't make out anything other than a beat-to-shit couch and a TV that had been new back when he was a kid.

Turning the knob, he eased the door open, then stepped inside.

His nose crinkled at the instantaneous and unrelenting assault on his senses. It smelled like a dump. In the kitchen, he found the reason why. Stacks of dirty plates filled not just the belly of the sink, but also on either side of the counter. Cupboard doors hung at strange angles, like they'd been ripped off and reattached with Silly String. The trash can overflowed with refuse, roaches and ants swarming the all-you-can-eat smorgasbord.

Down the hall, he went into the first bedroom on the left and got down on his hands and knees to look under the bed. Luce's deep blue eyes seemed to fill the space, her fear taking up the rest of the room.

"Jett," she breathed, clutching that unicorn of hers closer. "You came."

"I said I would." Scooting back a little, he said, "Why don't you come out of there, baby?"

She darted her eyes from side to side, terror filling them.

"Hey, it's okay. I'm here. I'm not going to let anything hurt you."

Slowly, she shuffled out from under the bed frame. She had dirt on her face and little clean tracks where the tears had slid down. Wrapping her in his arms, he buried his nose in her hair and thanked whatever god was up there that she was okay. This time.

"What are we going to do?" she asked softly.

"How about you come and visit me for the weekend? Would you like that?" He had no right to invite her, of course, but there was no way he was leaving her here.

Her eyes lit up, just as he'd hoped they would. "Really?"

"Of course, Luce," he replied softly. He looked around her tiny room. "Have you got a backpack?" At her nod, he said, "Pack enough clothes for three nights, okay?"

"What about Mom?"

"I'm going to go and ask if it's okay now. You pack, and I'll be back in a few minutes."

She nodded, placing her unicorn down onto the stained and ripped comforter, and got to work pulling clothes from her drawers. Leaving her to her work, he ducked back into the hall and stared at the closed door at the end of it. He inhaled deeply, trying to sift through all the scents already bombarding him. He didn't smell death, but it didn't mean it hadn't just happened.

He stalked to the door and shoved his way inside. His steps faltered at the sight of his mom lying still on top of the comforter. Her mousy brown hair was fanned out around her shoulders. She'd almost look ethereal if it wasn't for the track marks up her arms and the syringe still stuck in her vein.

On her other side was Richard, the cock-sucker who had introduced her to H. Jett personally blamed the asshole for his mom's rapid decline as he always kept her supplied. He didn't bother to check if said asshole was still breathing. As far as he was concerned, whether he lived or died was not his fucking problem.

His mother, on the other hand…

Holding his finger beneath her nose, he confirmed she was still breathing, and the weight of his own guilt lifted from his shoulders. Removing the needle, he bent the shaft over the hub so it couldn't be used again and threw it into the corner of the room. Pulling out his phone, he dialed the number for the pride's doctor and left a message. Help would come, but he had no plans to be there when it did.

Turning around, he froze. Luce was standing in the doorway, her wide blue eyes taking in everything. Gently, he ushered her back into the hall.

"Is Mommy going to be okay?"

"Fine," he replied, shutting the bedroom door behind him. "I just called the doctor to come and see her." When she said nothing in reply, he added, "Hey, are you ready to go? Do you have everything? Mr. Unicorn?"

As if by magic, she produced the stuffed toy and jammed it under her arm.

Scooping up her backpack, he said, "Come on, Luce. Let's go have an adventure."

As he walked her out to the car, he wondered what Grayson would say. He opened the door of the GT and flipped the seat forward so his sister could get in.

"Hi," Grayson said warmly. "What's your name?"

Luce remained quiet, her gaze darting between Grayson, him, and the still open door.

"It's okay, Luce. This is Grayson. He's a very good friend of mine. He drove me out here tonight."

"Where's your car?" she asked in a squeak.

"I have a motorbike now, so you see, I wouldn't have been able to bring your bag back with us," he lied. There was no reason to tell his kid sister he was so fucking drunk he could barely see straight—or at least he had been. Being told your mom was out cold and maybe dead from using drugs by a ten-year-old had a way of sobering you up real quick.

To Grayson's credit, he didn't push Luce with more questions, nor did he glance in Jett's direction as he got in and buckled up.

"Home?" he asked, already turning the car around.

"Home," Jett replied, bone-weary and in so far over his fucking head, he didn't know how he'd make it out the other side.

4

DRAKE

Drake rolled over, blinking at the drapes barely keeping the sun from his room. He hadn't slept much, his dreams haunted by the ghosts of his past—ones he'd tried so hard to forget. Leaving the bed, he padded into the bathroom to relieve himself, before he splashed water onto his face, but the cold and wet stuff did nothing to wake up his brain and drag it from the nightmares still lapping inside his frontal lobe.

Pulling the small towel from the rail, he dried his face and got moving. He didn't need to look at his reflection to know he looked like shit. Christ, he wanted an assignment today. He needed to take the edge off on someone else's ass.

Shrugging into his leather shoulder holster, he checked over his forties before he slid them into place under each arm and then grabbed his phone from the nightstand on the way out. Sasha waited for him on the landing, and he bit back a curse. She lounged casually, but her mournful stare cut him to the bone.

"What's up, Sash?"

"I have a message for you."

Oh, shit. He braced himself, both physically and mentally, crossing his arms over his chest. "Am I going to like it?"

She shrugged her slender shoulders. "A sapling needs protection from the oak."

He frowned. "I hate the cryptic ones." Before he could ask any more questions, she walked away, leaving him holding his proverbial dick. *A sapling needs protection from the oak.* What the hell did that mean? Whatever it was, Sasha had never been wrong. Ever.

Still puzzling over the message, he walked down to the kitchen. The place was decked out for a gourmet chef, not that any of his team could cook. The extent of their culinary prowess was limited to steak and dialing out for takeout food, but Grayson was known for whipping up pancakes on occasion too. The one thing they did pride themselves on, though, was that the fridge was always stocked. The behemoth was a Wellkart double glass-door fridge that, when completely filled, held just enough food to get them through a couple of days.

On the commercial white wire shelves were cans of energy drinks, hotdogs, and cold cuts. Another shelf was completely dedicated to fruit, but Sasha was the sole user of that. Cartons of eggs, milk, and juice were scattered throughout, and the freezer looked much the same, except it was frozen meals and an emergency supply of hotdogs in there.

Drake popped the seal and grabbed out the open carton of milk and placed it on the counter. In the pantry, he peered inside the box of Frosted Flakes. He was in luck, the other bastards hadn't eaten them all yet. After pouring himself a bowl, he added enough milk to submerge those delicious flakes, then took a seat at the island bench.

He was about four spoonfuls in when Grayson entered. The guy was usually as chirpy as a bird in the morning, but today, his eyes were dull like he'd seen some shit and no amount of mental scrubbing was going to remove it.

Resting his spoon on the side of his bowl, he said, "You look like shit."

The male's mouth flexed into a tight smile. "Thanks."

Drake's internal alarm clanged, his whole body going taut as if waiting for the kick in the balls to come. "What is it?"

Whatever it was, surely it couldn't trump what he'd found out last night.

Grayson shook his head. "It's not my place to say."

Forcing himself to stay in his seat, Drake curled and uncurled his fingers resting against his thighs. The urge to get into the other male's head and read his thoughts was nearly irresistible, but he wouldn't violate his brother in that way.

"Whose place is it then?" If there was an issue in his unit, he damn well better know about it. "Grayson?"

"Jett, man," he said warily, scrubbing a hand over his face. "Speak to…speak to him." Grayson wandered in the direction of the Krups, getting himself a solid cup of hot wake-the-fuck-up before leaving the kitchen. In his pocket, Drake's phone rang.

"Yeah?"

"Drake," Zed drawled.

"Fuck."

A chuckle boiled up over the line. "Nice to speak to you too."

He didn't want to know what the guy had to say to him. He only hoped it wasn't worse than what he'd dropped on his ass last night. "How would you feel about playing host?"

"Host? To who?"

"All of the captains of the Shadow units, the Leos, and us."

Christ. Fifteen type-As in one room? If he was honest, it sounded like a powder keg waiting for a spark. That many alpha males in one space would be an exercise in restraint. For everyone involved. Given the Revenant's position, though, it made sense. Their place was neutral ground—they were Switzerland.

"I'm listening."

"We need to meet—"

"Is this about what you told me last night?" he barked out. Looking down, he noticed his free hand pumping, a white-knuckle fist he wanted to punch through a wall. A steel door. The gates of fucking Hell.

"I didn't tell you anything last night," Zed replied in a confident drawl. "We never spoke."

Drake read between the lines. Zed's call had been made in an unofficial capacity. It was a courtesy. Whatever was going to be brought up at this meeting had the potential to leave him a fucking incompetent puddle on the floor, and in a roomful of alpha types, that was never a good thing.

He ground his teeth together. "Understood."

"Good. Now, back to my question. Feel like playing host?"

"Fine. When?" Great. He was so ticked off he was monosyllabic.

"Monday."

He sucked back the curse sitting on his tongue. "Monday," he agreed. "I'll make sure we're ready with a basket of muffins and a fucking fruit platter."

"Good man," Zed replied lightly, but his next words chased that levity away. "Keep your shit tight, Drake. I have a feeling this thing is going to get a whole lot worse before it gets better."

"Thanks," he muttered, ending the call. Before pocketing his phone, he punched out a text to Mateo, who replied a moment later with just one word. *Done.*

Dumping what was left of his cereal in the sink, he left the kitchen and climbed the stairs, Zed's words bouncing around in his head. This was just another scoop on his shit sundae right now. It was also something out of his control. He hated not being in control, but there was one thing he could do something about now.

Determined to find out what was going on in Jett's head, he stopped outside the male's room. With his fist, he pounded on the wood.

"Jett? We need to talk," he barked.

A moment later, Jett pulled open the door and slipped out into the hall, firmly shutting the door behind him. Drake watched his jaguar's movements with shrewd eyes. What was he hiding?

"Drake," Jett said, not meeting his gaze. Drake inhaled, the scent of his anxiety like a punch to the gut.

Folding his arms, he leaned against the wall, keeping his body and expression relaxed. "What's doing, Jett?"

"Nothing. Just getting breakfast." Stepping around him, Jett made a beeline for the stairs. Drake was about to give chase when he thought better of it. Unless his attitude endangered him or his team, Drake wasn't about to chase down a male who clearly wasn't in the sharing mood. And the last time he checked, he wasn't the Dr. Phil type. Hell, even speaking about his own shit made his skin twitch and his stomach revolt.

Needing to expend some of his pent-up frustrations, he debated between a punching bag or a willing female. A noise behind him made him spin around, and he reached for one of the forties under his arm, before leveling the muzzle at the threat. He was definitely a shoot now and ask questions later kind of male.

He reared back when he realized what he was considering

pumping full of silver. Staring at him from between the door and the jamb was a young girl probably no older than ten or eleven. Her fear was a tangible weight against his skin. Pushing into her mind, a barrage of images hit him. Jett, someone shooting up in a cramped bedroom, holes in walls and door, an empty fridge, hiding under a bed, a dilapidated trailer home. He pulled out of her mind with a snarl, holstering his gun.

Rage curled around him as he stormed down the stairs and into the kitchen, drawn by the sound of even more cursing.

Misery likes company, right?

"What the fuck, Jett?" he demanded as soon as he walked in.

Jett was fighting with the toaster, trying to get two Eggos into the belly of the metal beast. The guy didn't even look away from his battle.

"I don't actually have the mental capacity for this, Drake, so why don't you chew my ass out for whatever I've done wrong this time, then leave me in peace?"

Drake bit his tongue until he tasted blood. "Who's the girl?"

The other male's head popped up like it was on a string. He said nothing, but then again, he didn't have to. His chest was pumping too wildly for Drake's question not to mean a thing.

"She doesn't have anywhere else to go," he replied, staring at the tiled backsplash.

"Who is she?" His words were a calm, deadly crawl.

Jett turned around, his blue eyes tired, his sandy-blond hair sticking up in a hundred different directions like he'd had as good a night as Drake had.

"She's my sister, Luce."

Breathing in deeply through his nose, he let it out. "Why are you still in contact with your family?" What was he thinking? It was forbidden to have any ties with their parents or siblings after training began with the Trinity. If they knew…

"Shit at home is bad. And before you ask how bad, just know I'm not going there." Jett looked down at the Eggo box in his hand. "But… Luce needed me last night, so I brought her here."

"You know the rules. The cut is supposed to be clean."

"*I know*," Jett replied vehemently, his eyes flashing. "Jesus, she couldn't—" He ground his teeth as he fought the urge to say more.

Drake scrubbed a hand through his hair. "Tell me she's not staying long."

"She has school on Monday. I was going to spend the weekend with her, then take her home on Sunday night."

"You know I can't allow that," he replied.

Jett glanced up at him, the scent of disappointment leaking from his pores. He didn't have to get in the male's head to know he was hurting right now. "Please, Drake. Cut me some fucking slack for this. *Please*."

He was about to shake his head, when Sasha's words drifted through his mind.

A sapling needs protection from the oak.

"Goddammit," he cursed. *Sasha better know what she's fucking doing.* "She needs to be gone by Sunday, Jett. I'm not fucking around with this. We have a big meeting scheduled for Monday, and guess who gets to play host."

The toaster popped, spewing out its cargo. "I swear it, Drake. Thank you." He turned to retrieve his waffles. "Who's coming and what do they want?"

"All the Leos, all the captains, and the three big bosses, and no idea. Whatever it is, I'm not looking forward to it. It's got TARFU written all over it."

5

NEVE

If Neve believed in hell, this would be it. Sitting in the dining room, she was opposite her mom, and her dad was to her right like always, but it was the person at her other elbow that was the oddity.

"More potatoes?" her mom asked politely, but the question wasn't directed at Neve. It was directed at the stuffy, over-cologned male beside her. His name was Bradley Winchester. The *third*. The only son of the Pride's good doctor, he was a fifty-year-old living in a twenty-three-year-old's body. With short, neat hair and flawless skin, he was very pretty to look at, but there was no substance there.

"Thank you, Mrs. Bolton. This is all delicious," he added, gesturing to the spread in front of them. Mom had really gone all out tonight—caviar for an entree, roasted quail with rosemary baked potatoes, and enough steamed vegetables to feed half the pride. Honestly, Neve thought it was a bit of overkill, but Mom liked to play matchmaker.

It was a pity it was such a bust, just like all the other times.

"Would you like some more wine, sweetheart?" her dad asked. She looked at him, seeing the pity in those green eyes of his. Hers were the exact same shade, a mint green so pale, it was almost white.

Although tempted to drink herself into a stupor, she politely declined. Bradley, however, was all up for it. Maybe he needed a little bit of liquid courage. There were plenty of rumors floating around about her, about how she was an ice queen, frigid, *and* a whore. She wondered if anyone realized all those attributes were contradictory. Either way, she never gave the *whispers* much airtime. Maybe Bradley here hadn't heard what was being said, or he had, and thought he'd try his luck anyway.

"So, Bradley," her mom started sweetly. "Tell me what you've been up to."

Neve did her best to seem attentive, as if she actually gave a damn about what was being said, but she was failing. Her mom hung on the male's every word, though, so it had to be something she deemed as an example of *exemplary breeding*. Nothing roused her mom more than strong blood and a good family line.

"You were going to take that up, weren't you, Neve?"

She glanced at her mom, trying to figure out what she'd missed. Her mom's eyes darted over to Bradley, but really that didn't help her in the slightest.

"Umm…"

"I was just telling your mother about my hobby of arranging flowers."

She covered her mouth, even though the smile she was sporting was practically beaming through the gaps in her fingers.

After clearing her throat too noisily, she swallowed twice before saying, "Floristry. No kidding? Yep. That was right at the top of my *hobbies I want to try* list."

"Maybe you should, Neve," her mom interjected, her gaze fixed on the bruises on Neve's arms. "It's a much better use of your time than *training* with the males." Her mom said 'training' like it was a personal insult. "A female of your position should act with more decorum."

The smile Bradley gave her was warm, if a little vacant. "You should come to one of my classes," he invited. "Perhaps I could set something up?"

"Thanks, but…" Jesus, how was she supposed to get out of this?

"Right, who wanted some more quail?" her dad asked, breaking the awkward silence apart with a metaphoric sledgehammer.

"I'd love some!" Neve replied a little too brightly. Her dad was straining to keep a straight face as he served her, but the slight pull of his lips gave him away. He thought this was hilarious.

"Excuse me, sir?" the housekeeper said hesitantly.

Everyone turned to where Emily stood in the entryway of the dining room. Why was the woman there on a Saturday night? Maybe to help clean up after dinner?

Her dad took the linen napkin from his lap and placed it beside his plate. "Emily?"

"Sir, there's a phone call for you."

Nodding, he turned back to the table. "If you'll all excuse me." He rose before heading in the direction of his office.

"Neve? What are you doing?"

She turned to see her mom… still seated. Bradley was too. Neve had stood without realizing, driven by instinct. Looking back in the direction of the study, an unsteady feeling began to unfurl in the pit of her stomach. Pride business was not conducted on weekends. Pride business was not conducted after six p.m. unless there was an emergency.

Glancing back at her mom, she said, "Would you mind… err… would you mind excusing me? I need the restroom."

She shoved the seat back and hurried down the hall. As she passed her dad's office, she slowed. He was talking in a staccato rhythm, like machine gun fire.

"Christ… no… how long?... Hmmm…"

She edged closer to the entry, the floorboards beneath the wool carpet her mom had no doubt vacuumed twice today creaking under her weight. Her dad snapped his head up, their gazes met, and she held her breath. She expected him to dismiss her, so when he crooked his finger at her, she slid inside the room and shut the door behind her.

She took a seat on the old leather lounge her mom had refused to keep in the living room, bringing her legs up under her body. As his phone call continued, she stared ahead at the wall of books. Her dad collected first editions, often paying ridiculous amounts of money for some he'd attempted to acquire for decades. The scent of rich, earthy leather filled the whole office, the sweetness of it reminding her of home and the male she'd idolized since she was old enough to realize he would protect her with his life.

Silence suddenly fell on the room, and she turned to find him slouching in his chair, clutching the receiver of the old rotary phone to his chest. She sat forward. He looked grave, like he'd aged ten years in ten minutes. She eyed the phone, wondering what could've possibly happened.

"Dad?" she asked, her voice as loud as a gunshot in the still room.

His unfocused eyes shifted to her face, and for just a moment, he studied her.

Sliding to the edge of the sofa, she clasped her hands together so tightly her knuckles turned white. "Just tell me."

"Katie didn't make it home last night."

6

KATIE

Katie woke with a groan. Everything hurt, from her head to her shoulders, her hips and her legs. When she realized she was lying on her side, she tried to sit up, but cried out when her spine and the muscles surrounding it recoiled like a dagger had been plunged in there and twisted.

The hiss of clothing against something hard filtered through the room, and she stopped moving, her breathing coming out in short, sharp pants. Something else was in there with her. She blinked into the swimming darkness. Where was she, and what happened? Above her head, a small amount of murky light filtered through, illuminating a few feet ahead of her. A roughly poured concrete floor. She shifted her gaze up again and saw…

Bars.

Panic squeezed her throat with invisible fingers, choking the air out of her lungs with each exhale. Sucking in a breath, she tried to get more oxygen into her body, but fear choked her and tears burned her eyes. She moaned, the pitiful sound echoing around the room.

"Shut up," someone hissed in the darkness. With short, sharp jerking movements, Katie rubbed away the tears quickly, facing the direction of the voice.

It was so dark.

She swallowed past the lump in her throat, fear squeezing her lungs in her chest. Blinking, she waited for her vision to stop undulating like a boat on the open sea. The last thing she remembered was getting out of her car because she had a flat tire. Cradling her head, she tried to sift through her hazy memories, but each time an image coalesced through the fog, it slipped through her fingers like a wraith.

"How did they get you?" whispered a faceless voice, and Katie froze, holding her breath. She blinked a few times, her eyes slowly adjusting to the limited light. That was when she saw the woman huddled against the opposite wall, her face hidden by lank hair hanging down like a shield across her face.

Katie's heart was thundering in her ears, and she bit her trembling lip. "Who are you?" she asked in a croak. "Wh-wh-what is this place?"

The woman turned her head, her hair, matted and dirty, shifting to reveal a bruise that stretched from her cheekbone to her temple. Her eyes flashed a dull yellow, signs that whoever this woman was, she was also a shifter. She lifted her nose and sniffed. She was a black jaguar too, but not from the Black Claw pride.

"What happened to you?"

The other female's chest expanded with a shallow breath. "The same thing that happened to you," she replied, wrapping her arms around her legs more tightly. "The same thing that happened to all of us. Drugged. Captured. Brutalized."

Katie's brain only clung to one word—*brutalized*.

Panic threatened to take over, clawing up her throat, and tears burned the back of her eyes again.

"Don't cry," the female warned. "If you cry, they hurt you. If you scream, they make you bleed."

A whimper bubbled up her throat, kept at bay behind Katie's tightly-pressed lips. Her pulse was still fluttering too quickly in her chest, the scent of her fear mingling with the acrid stench of urine and unwashed bodies.

She tried to focus on something else, anything to take her away from this horrific scene. She wished Neve were here with her, to guide her. Squeezing her eyes shut, she tried to think about what her cousin would do.

Stay calm. Take in all the details. Try to figure out your location.

Neve's voice whispered like a phantom through her mind, and Katie swallowed, trying to pay attention to what was around her. Turning her head, she let her senses roam. The air was damp, a chill coming up from the rough concrete floor. The room felt like it was subterranean, a basement maybe?

She tried to sift through the sounds and scents, her cat coming forward in her mind. There were a number of females and women in the room with her, maybe half-dozen not including her and her cellmate.

Your first instinct is usually correct.

She let out a shuddering breath, her throat clogged with panic and abject terror. Her fingers slowly curled up, as if trying to get a grip on reality. The thing was, her reality looked a lot like abduction and imprisonment on a mass scale.

Turning back around, she whispered, "How long have I been unconscious?"

The female shrugged. "I'm not sure. Time moves… differently here."

"What do they want with us?"

Shaking her head, the other female tightened her arms around her legs.

"What's your name?" Her voice was barely a whisper on the damp air, but there was the shuffle of feet behind her.

"Elsie," her cell-mate replied.

Edging a little closer, she asked, "How many of us are down here? Shifters?"

"At least two more."

"And…" Katie swallowed, trying to ignore the pressure building in her chest. "What do they want with us?"

"It's better that you don't know." Elsie buried her face into her arms, shutting down the conversation.

Katie shuffled back on the concrete pad until her back hit the metal bars. Strips of frigid steel transferred their chill into her body, making her shiver. She was still dressed in a light sweater and jeans with her favorite silver glitter Keds on her feet. The cold was seeping into the backs of her calves, her thighs, her ass. She shivered, and the cold started to make her drowsy. Like hypothermia. Maybe she really wasn't here. Maybe she'd crashed her car, and the cold she was feeling was just the night air kissing her skin. Katie fought to keep her eyes open, but in the end, her body won out. Her lids closing, she shut out what she prayed wasn't her new reality.

Katie woke up to the sound of an anguished scream that chilled her down to the marrow. The broken sound barely had a chance to start before it was quickly muffled.

"If you know what's good for you, you'll know not to do that again," a male voice hissed. Katie remained still, barely breathing, as she cracked open an eye and saw what was happening to Elsie.

"Get up," the guy said, yanking at her cell mate's arm and dragging her to her feet. Tears streamed down Elsie's face as she tugged against her abductor's hold. His hand was wrapped tightly around her upper arm, and even in the murky filtered light, Katie made out the bones of his knuckles standing out in stark relief. The peaks and troughs of those bones reminded her of the Wyomings. Would she ever get to see home again?

Gather information and use it to your advantage, Neve's voice whispered through her mind. Shoving the fear away, she focused on what she could see, what she could smell and hear. The man was only human, so he shouldn't have been able to handle Elsie so easily, which meant she was compromised in some way—that maybe *all* of them were compromised in some way.

She inhaled, tasting gun oil and metal, her eyes skimming down his body to find the weapon he was carrying. His jacket flapped open, revealing a gun on his hip. He wasn't using it to threaten Elsie, though, so he was either too cocky, believing she wouldn't hurt him, or he was confident she couldn't. The guy dragged Elsie toward the cell door, grabbing a hank of her lank hair when her knees buckled. With a small cry, she was yanked from the cell, the door slamming shut behind them.

Katie's throat burned as tears threatened to fall, and she bit her lip to stop herself from screaming. She flinched when the sound of clothes tearing rent the nearly silent air. Pain tore through her chest as she realized what she was about to witness. Elsie began to beg, pleading with the man not to do it. A *crack* fractured her litany, followed by a snarled, "On your knees, or next time, I break your jaw as well as your nose."

Blood perfumed the air, and Katie squeezed her hands into fists, keeping them locked down under her body. She didn't want to listen. She wanted to cover her ears, but she was terrified of moving, of drawing attention to herself.

She didn't want that to happen to her, too.

9

DRAKE

"**I** don't care. I want her home with me, now."

Jett held the phone away from his ear, wincing at the volume of his mother's voice. He'd picked up Luce on Friday night, and it was only now—thirty hours later—that his mom had sobered up enough to notice her youngest daughter was gone. He shuddered to think how much she'd snorted in an attempt to maintain the high—at least every six hours, according to what Luce had told him. If she were human, she would've been long dead by now. A decade of abuse. A decade of slipping. A decade of self-loathing and punishment.

"She's *my daughter*, Jett, and you will return her to me."

He laughed derisively. "If you gave a damn about Luce, it wouldn't have taken you this long to demand to have her back."

In the background, Richard ran his mouth, filling her head with words and ideas that were only meant to be used to intimidate him. The thing was, he'd seen it all, heard it all. Hell, he'd lived through it all himself too, so there was no way the threats worked.

He glanced away when he felt eyes on him. Luce sat on his bed, the piece of furniture dwarfing his little sister until she looked like a doll propped up against the pillows. He didn't want to send her back to their mother, back to that trailer with the drug paraphernalia being used as decor, but Drake had been very clear that Luce couldn't be at the compound when the meeting went down. Returning her home, though, didn't sit well with him either.

"Jett, you *will* bring her home, or I'll call the authorities."

He smiled grimly. "*I am* the authorities," he snarled. "Human police have no jurisdiction here. We do."

There was a sound like the phone being passed to someone else, and he braced to go for round two with Richard. He opened his mouth, ready to spit words so vile that he'd have to see a priest after, but stopped when he heard Katya say, "Jett?"

"Katya." He ran a hand through his hair. "Fuck. Thank fuck you're home, Kat."

"I'm home," she whispered.

"How are you?" Apart from a brief text chain, he hadn't spoken to his sister since he'd picked up Luce. All he knew was that Kat was happy Luce had gotten a break from the toxic environment.

"I'm okay," she lied.

Like hell, he thought.

"I'm sorry you're playing intermediary."

"I know. But…" she hesitated. "Mom is okay now. You can bring her home."

Jett's free hand curled into a fist at his side as a pounding headache started between his eyes. "What if this shit happens again?"

"I promise it won't."

"How can you make that promise? You work nearly fifty hours a week to support Luce and yourself."

"I've asked for my vacation time. I get two weeks of paid leave."

"And after that?" he asked, desperately looking for a way out of the fucking hole his mom and Richard had dug with their drug habit.

There was a pause, and then a door was shut. When Katya spoke again, her voice was a bare whisper. "I have some money saved up."

Jett's stomach twisted. He hoped their mom didn't hear that. "How much are we talking, Kat?"

"Enough to get us into an apartment somewhere, enough for the first and last month's rent. It'll be enough to get out of this depraved shithole she's forced us to live in for ten years."

He was stunned. His sister never swore. Like ever. He clutched the phone more tightly in his fist, looking at Luce when he said, "If you swear you'll be there, I'll bring her home."

"I swear it, Jett. I… God, I wish this wasn't our life."

Didn't he know it. He would've sprung them himself, except training to become a Shadow meant giving up everything from his former life. That aside, the stipend the Trinity gave them was barely two hundred and fifty bucks a month. At first, he'd sent it home, but after his mother used it to feed her habit, he started depositing it direct into Katya's bank account. It wasn't much, but it was something to support his three sisters.

He rubbed at his Shadow Mark under his shirt, wondering—not for the first time—why he'd been given the out. He supposed it was thanks to his father, since the genes for Shadows were carried on the Y chromosome ninety-nine percent of the time, but he didn't even know who the bastard was to thank him.

"I know. I wish it were different, too."

There was a creak as she sat down on her wrought iron twin bed, the one that had belonged to him before he insisted she take it after he moved out. "When will you bring Luce back?"

He stared into his little sister's blue eyes, seeing how she pleaded with him not to let her go. "This evening," he replied in a hollow voice. "I'll bring her back this evening, but I want to spend the day with her first."

"Okay. Okay. Good. I'll let Mom know."

"Just do me a favor, Kat? Make sure she's sober when I get there."

"I'll do my best."

The line went dead, and Jett lowered his arm, defeated.

"Do I have to go?" Luce asked in a small voice.

He sat down beside her, putting his arm over her too slender shoulders and pulling her closer. "I'm sorry, baby, but yeah."

He smelled her tears before the soft sob reached him.

"Don't worry, though. Katya's going to be home with you for two whole weeks. She'll take you to and from school, and make sure nothing happens to you or Mom."

"What about her job?"

"She's taking some time off just for you, Luce, and as soon as I'm able, I'm going to be helping out more." He didn't know how he'd swing it, but he'd find a way.

"Do you promise?"

He pulled away a little to look in her eyes. "Don't I always keep my promises?"

She nodded and wiped away the tears.

"Now, we have the whole day to spend together, so what should we do?"

Her eyes lit up like only a little girl who'd just been given a reprieve from a shitty home life could. "Ice cream," she started, holding up her fingers and ticking things off as she went. "Mini-golf. The cinema. Pizza."

"Whoa, whoa," he interrupted with a laugh. "How about we start with the ice cream and see how far we get?"

———

The sun was already dipping below the horizon when Jett and Luce finished off the last of their pizza. They'd spent the day doing everything Luce wanted to do, which meant mini-golf, ice cream, a movie, and a trip around the mall to get her some new books. Escapism shouldn't be the coping mechanism of a ten-year-old, but she did what she had to do.

"Jett?"

He turned to look at Luce, who was studiously looking through the front passenger side window of Grayson's car. "Hmm?"

"Why does Mom do drugs?"

He let out a breath and wondered how to answer that loaded question. He didn't know for sure why she'd turned to the chemical relief, but he could take a guess.

"That really is a question you'll have to ask her, but I think she does it because she's mad at your dad for leaving her, she's mad at herself for letting him go, and I think she's just mad at the world."

Luce took a minute to digest all that before saying, "Maybe she needs to forgive herself."

Jett was stunned by the wisdom of his little sister. It was funny how the view of someone who didn't have as much life experience could resonate so much. Reaching across, he patted her on the knee and said, "You know what? I think you're right."

Silence settled around them again, Jett praying that she didn't fire any more moral questions his way. He was hardly a role model for clean living, but he knew without a doubt he would never, *ever* touch drugs.

"Do you think she'll stop?"

His jaw tightened. He'd thought about this question a lot, had *asked himself* this question a lot. He couldn't bring himself to tell Luce that he thought their mom was a lost cause. There was only one way she would stop using, and that was when she was in the grave.

"I think she'll know when the time is right."

When he slowed the car and turned into the driveway of the trailer park, he gave himself a mental pep talk. He *hated* the idea of leaving Luce here again, but with Katya around, he'd made peace with his reality. He stopped the car outside the worn out mobile home and killed the purring engine.

He glanced up when the door swung open, slamming into the siding that would no doubt leave yet another dent in the place. Richard was standing in the doorway, backlit so his face was in shadow. But Jett didn't need light to see the rage held in every tense muscle of his body.

"Stay in the car, Luce," he said, not taking his eyes from Richard. Jett popped open his door, rotating his neck until the vertebrae popped in submission. He was going to fucking put this bastard on the ground.

"You have some nerve, *boy*," Richard drawled, all confident swagger of a man fighting on his home turf. Well, fuck him and the drug mule he rode in on.

"I was just protecting my sister," he snarled back, his hands curling into tight fists. He was more than ready to throw down. In fact, he'd been waiting for this for a decade.

"She doesn't need protecting. I'm here now. *I'm* the head of this goddamn family. *I* protect this family."

"I wouldn't trust you to protect the dirt under my shoes."

Richard stepped down onto the hard-packed earth, going toe to toe with Jett. Jett had at least four inches and fifty pounds on him. It wasn't an even match, and the urge to just pummel him into the ground was nearly irritable. He needed the guy to swing first though. He *needed* it like he needed his next breath. So he waited. And sure enough, the fucker obliged. He telegraphed his move so all Jett had to do was duck, before slamming his fist into the guy's stomach. He was rewarded with the sound of all the air rushing from his lungs as his body gave the evac order. Richard fell to his knees in front of Jett, his place of supplication totally at odds with the anger and rage polluting the air between them.

"Jett!" his mother screamed, though she made no move to help her partner. She simply stood in the door, weaving as the drug haze funneled out of her body. He gave her a fleeting look, but that was all Richard needed. He head-butted Jett in the groin, dropping him like a stone.

A heartbeat.

That's all it took for Richard to get his bony ass off the ground and onto Jett. Straddling his waist, Richard started to rain punches on him, hitting him over and over again. The problem was—well, his problem at least—was that all the drugging had left him with terrible stamina, so after a minute of throwing fists, the guy was exhausted, sagging off to one side as he tried to catch his breath. With his opponent taking a little breather, Jett flipped the script and clasped his hands together, slamming them into Richard's sternum.

The bastard tilted backward, falling into a heap on his back. The world became silent then, all except for the ragged gasps of air being sucked back into barely functioning lungs. Jett got to his feet and walked over to where the male flopped around like a dying fish. Winding back, Jett kicked the guy as hard as he could, a satisfied smirk forming on his mouth when Richard spat out his teeth. Jett lined up for another kick and another, snarling when Richard rolled over onto his front, tucking his legs in and covering his head the best he could.

It was a shame that not all the vital organs were in the front.

Jett took to kidney shots before making sure the fucker's spleen was wrapped around his spine. His swimming vision shifted from full color to muted grays, his gift firing through his blood like a high-octane engine being flooded with gasoline. His palms tingled, the need to burn an irresistible pull.

His legs began to ache as he continued to kick and stomp on Richard's motionless body. Blood decorated the ground around his head, a gruesome halo, a grotesque mockery of an angel. The scent of copper got stuck in his nose, and he recognized he was getting lost in the bloodlust, a feral need to punish Richard for everything he'd done to Jett's family. He was prepared to dig the grave himself, right here, right now…

"Jett."

He spun around to find Luce standing there, her stuffed unicorn held to her chest, her blue eyes wide and without judgment. Her gaze traveled down, taking in the sight of Richard's blood on his shirt, on his fists, on his face. His breathing was even, modulated, as if he'd barely broken a sweat beating the ever-living shit out of a male jaguar.

"Take me inside?" Such an innocent question, but as she hugged her unicorn even tighter, he saw the white-knuckled grip she had on it. He looked down at Richard, who was still curled up in a ball. He barely resisted the urge to spit on him. He hoped the guy stayed out here all night and froze his fucking balls off.

Putting his arm around Luce, he started in the direction of the door and ushered her to go up the stairs. His mother stared at him like he was a stranger.

"Are you coming inside?" his sister asked.

Jett looked down at himself, finally seeing how much blood was on his shirt. On his arms. On his fists. "I'd better go, Luce. I think I've caused enough trouble here tonight."

He took one last look at her, then his mother, before getting back in the car. He did a three-point turn to get out then crept up the dirt and gravel road. At the entrance, he stopped, a figure standing in the darkness catching his attention.

Katya stepped up to his window and stared. "Jesus, Jett, what—" He could practically see the pieces fall into place, the proverbial shoe dropping. "Is he still alive?"

"Unfortunately."

Her face tightened. "Please tell me you didn't start it. If Richard—"

"I didn't start it," he replied. "I'm smart, Kat. I know how to draw someone into a fight."

She looked relieved.

"Where were you?"

She held up her hands, revealing groceries. "I thought some ice cream might smooth things over with Luce."

He smiled. "She already milked me for two today. That kid has some sort of super persuasion power."

"Yeah, she does. Just like her brother."

His expression sobered. "Where's Mila?"

"Still at her boyfriend's place."

He rankled. "Have you met the male?"

"Man," she corrected. "He's human."

"Fuck me," Jett replied, the words popping free of his mouth without warning. Of course shifters dated humans, but the little problem of turning furry at will was always something that was a hindrance. "What's he like?"

Kat shrugged, peering down at her feet. "He's okay. He treats her well. He doesn't do drugs."

"All redeeming qualities," he mumbled under his breath. He inhaled sharply and smelled his sister's indecision. "There's something you're not telling me. Kat?" he prodded when she remained tight-lipped.

"Maybe you should talk to her."

Okay, now he was getting pissed. "Maybe *you* should talk to me. What's going on? I'm trying really hard to keep this family together, breaking all the rules by staying in contact with you. Do you know how much shit I'm in now?"

Katya's eyes widened, and she shook her head. "Will they kick you out?"

"They can't," he lied. "But I've already come this far. There's no point stopping now. So why don't you tell me about whatever is happening with Mila."

Katya sucked in a breath, and the scent of her resignation filtered through the air, like burning wood in a pine forest. "She's moved out. Mila is living with the guy."

Jett blinked, still trying to piece together the meaning of the words he'd just been told. "Isn't she too young?" It was a fucking ridiculous thing to say, but his words had escaped him.

"She's twenty-one, Jett. She's old enough to drink legally, and she's old enough to choose who she lives with."

"I know this," he replied through gritted teeth. What he didn't know was why Mila hadn't even bothered to share this information with him. They'd been tight—tighter than him and Katya had been growing up. She was only four years younger than him. He'd looked after her at school and watched out for her growing up. What the hell had happened?

"You left, Jett," Katya said sadly, reading the anguish on his face. "You didn't just leave the house, though—you left us behind, too. And I know you had no choice, but Mila didn't see it that way."

He ran a hand through his hair, well aware he was rubbing Richard's blood into it. He'd fucked this up, hadn't he?

"Christ, Katya."

His sister only stared at him with sad eyes and shrugged.

"Are you really going to get out of there? Take Luce with you?"

"Yeah. I've been looking for apartments for months now. I just haven't found the right place yet."

He felt like a fool for not seeing it before now. He'd failed them, hadn't he? "I have to go, Kat. I just…" He stared at her, praying she'd understand. "I have to go."

Jett put the car in gear and pressed on the accelerator. He watched her silhouette disappear in the rearview mirror, the truth of her words buzzing around him. He felt like his skin was vibrating, like he needed to get out of it for a while. Pulling the GT over to the shoulder, he killed the engine and shut off the lights then got out, locked the doors, and pocketed the keys.

He stepped off the road and walked into the forest that hemmed in Highway 89. When the pine needles beneath his boots crunched, he began stripping off. Leaving his clothes folded neatly beneath a lodgepole pine, he let his cat out to prowl in the hopes that purging his skin would also purge his guilt for not doing more.

8

NEVE

Every breath Neve drew settled in her lungs with a tangible weight, like concrete being poured down her throat, choking her. She stared at the chess set sitting on the small end table in her father's study, her focus had not moved for…

God, she had no idea how long.

All she could think about was Katie, her brain throwing up all sorts of scenarios that ended with Katie's body being recovered, or not even found. She was stuck in an endless loop of grief and anger and feelings of complete hopelessness. She loathed the impotence.

After the phone call her father had received, after he'd told her all the details of her cousin's disappearance, she'd snuck out of the house and shifted, running to the spot only a mile and a half from her house. Katie's car wasn't there anymore, but she sniffed around, using her cat's senses to try and piece the puzzle together.

The night had closed in around her, the moon partially obscured by a long thick stretch of cloud that didn't budge. The lack of light wasn't necessarily a problem until the cloud cover fully blocked the moon for a moment. Keeping alert, she swept the area, pinpointing where the car had stopped. Motor oil and Katie's scent still lingered on the dirt shoulder of the road, but there was something else…

Neve had taken more of that foreign scent into her lungs, trying to place it. It was vaguely familiar, a tapping on her memory, but no matter how hard she tried, she couldn't figure out what it was. As she'd paced back and forth, her paw struck something metallic, the sound of it bouncing across the blacktop amplified by the dark, silent night. Swiping out her paw again, more of those metal objects tinkled into life—dozens of them. More. The cloud drifted away then, the moon revealing a hundred dull-gleaming stars across the road's surface. Not stars…

Screws.

Hundreds of screws were strewn all over the road.

She ran back the way she'd come for half a mile, finding more and more screws along the road.

Not an accidental flat tire…

But an engineered one.

One of those screws was now in her jeans pocket, the weight of its secrets pressing on her. She stared at the hearth where a fire was burning happily, throwing off heat she barely felt. Was Katie cold where she was? Was she hurt or afraid, or had she somehow managed to muster some courage from within her sweet, gentle heart?

Flipping her gaze over to the phone on her father's desk, she willed the thing to ring, to get some sort of news or just a hint as to where her cousin was. Wrapping her arms more tightly around herself, she curled her hand around the only piece of evidence they had so far, placed her chin on her knees and waited some more.

"Has she slept?" her mom's voice crept in from the hallway,

her anxious tone sliding over Neve. Her mom didn't need to be worried about her. Neve was at home—safe.

"I'll get her to eat something," her dad replied before her mom's hushed footsteps receded and the Dyson fired up. Trust that female to turn to cleaning in a time of crisis.

"How are you doing, kitten?" her dad asked a few minutes later, kneeling in front of her and swamping her periphery. Blinking, she looked at him, finding tension branching out from the corners of his eyes. Even the lines that bracketed his mouth seemed to be deeper.

"I can't sit around waiting. I… *can't.*"

He squeezed her knee and placed a sandwich on the table beside the couch. "I know."

"So what's been done? Is anyone out looking for her? She's been missing for almost twenty hours already."

He let out a tired breath. "The Shadows have been notified."

Hope flared. "What are they doing?"

"Speaking to your uncle and—Neve! Where are you going?"

She was already out the office door when she called over her shoulder, "I'm going to help, dammit." There was no way she could sit around idly while her cousin was out there. Snagging her coat from the hook by the door, she palmed the keys of her 1980 F-150 and strode out the door. The sound of the Dyson trailed out after her, cutting off as she slammed the door of her truck. She drove as fast as she dared, taking the turns much quicker than her truck could really handle and gunning it to her cousin's house.

She tore up the driveway, gravel pinging against the undercarriage, the rear tires losing traction and sliding into a fishtail as she took the curved driveway with too much gas. She slammed on the brakes at the apex, narrowly missing a black Escalade already parked there.

She threw the truck into park, left the keys in the ignition, and ran up to the front door.

"Neve?" her aunt Celeste asked when Neve barged through the door without so much as knocking. Her aunt stepped out of the kitchen to her left, her hands clutching a dishtowel too tightly. With the light shining behind her head, it was like looking at an older version of Katie, and a crushing sadness fell over Neve. What if Katie never made it to middle age? What if her life was destined to be cut short now?

Neve shook her head and cleared her throat, her lungs working overtime to get more oxygen in. "Have you heard anything?"

"Nothing."

The little flare of hope that had sprung to life in her chest guttered and died just as quickly as it had formed. She tilted her head in the direction of her uncle's study at the low rumble of two voices—one that belonged to her uncle Peter and another that sounded like crushed glass—raw and sharp and dangerous.

"Who's that with Uncle Peter? One of the Shadows?"

Celeste shook her head. "The captain of the Revenant."

Neve's eyes widened, her heart lurching in her chest. "The Revenant are involved?" she asked in a whisper.

"I don't know what's going on. The Phantom Unit captain was here, talking to your uncle, but as soon as the other male arrived, he was dismissed." Aunt Celeste worried at the dishtowel in her hand again, her knuckles white. Clearly the idea of having one of the most lethal shifters ever known in her house was terrifying. "He said he's come to help at your father's request."

Bile bit the back of her throat. If the Trinity sent the Revenant, Katie's disappearance couldn't be an isolated event. They were taking this very, very seriously. Her hand slipped into her pocket, and she touched the head of the screw.

Determination flooded her body. She was going to find her cousin, terrifying male or not. Walking down the hall, she stepped into the study without knocking, her desperation for information overriding her basic need to be polite. As soon as her foot hit the expensive NASIRI rug, she stopped and fought the urge to recoil from the giant male sitting in front of her uncle. Despite having his back to her, she felt the weight of his stare even without having his attention on her.

Her uncle Peter looked up, his expression a reflection of her own. He hadn't slept, but she couldn't blame him. Katie was his only daughter, and male cats were very possessive of their females.

"Neve." Her name was barely out of his mouth before he was out of his chair and rounding the desk, wrapping his arms around her. She hugged him back, clutching at his shoulders as she sensed the grief rolling off him in waves.

Pulling away, she said, "We'll get her back. *I'll* get her back. I swear it."

Her uncle turned around then, motioning to the mountain of a man sharing the same air as them. "Neve, this is Drake, the leader of the Revenant."

Drake rose to his full height, and Neve's gaze went up, up, up. Fuck, he was tall. And big. And lethal-looking. She eyed the breadth of his shoulders and the way his body tapered down to his narrow hips before flaring out to muscular thighs. Her gaze made its way back up his body, settling on his harsh face and cutting citrine-yellow eyes.

He was watching her too, his gaze licking down her body before coming back to her face. As their eyes met, she could've sworn a blast of heat came off his body.

"Drake, this is Neve—Katie's cousin—and also the last person to see her last night."

His eyes narrowed on her, and she shifted uncomfortably, not knowing what to do with her hands. She settled for folding her arms, closing herself off to his scrutiny.

"You saw Katie last?" Drake asked, his voice a rolling bass.

Neve nodded and let out a breath. "Yeah, she had dinner at my place, and we watched a movie."

"What time did she leave?"

Feeling her legs go weak, she sat on the couch against the wall. "It was probably around midnight."

"And did she say anything about going somewhere else before going home?"

She shook her head. "No, and Katie wasn't the kind of female who'd take off without telling someone."

Drake peered over his shoulder at her uncle. "Would you mind giving us a minute?"

Her uncle left without hesitation, and when the door was shut behind him, Drake pinned her in place with a hard stare. "Neve? Does Katie have a male she's seeing?"

She stared at him. "A male? Like a boyfriend?"

"Or a lover. Do you think she would've gone to see him?"

"No," she replied quietly. Craning her head back, she looked into his eyes and said more firmly, "No. Katie wasn't dating anyone. And she'd never have a casual lover." Her hands balled into fists. "Ever."

He began to pace. "You're sure about that?"

"One hundred percent. I know my cousin."

"How do you know she wasn't keeping this from you?"

Irrationally, her anger flared. "Why are you so brutally cynical?"

He bared his too-sharp teeth. "Just answer the question."

She touched the screw in her pocket, the only clue she had. "Because I *know* her. There wasn't anything we didn't share with one another. We're closer than cousins. We're blood."

Whether it was her tone or her words, Drake rolled to a stop in front of her, his citrine eyes serious. "What's his name?"

She blinked, trying to keep up with the topic change. "They weren't a couple," she blurted. His brows rose, and she cursed. "She had a crush on him. That's all."

A pressure started to build in her head, a slash against her skull like claws digging their way in. She squeezed her eyes shut tightly and let out a shaky breath, breathing through the pain. It disappeared just as quickly as it came, and when she opened her eyes again, Drake frowned.

"What's the kid's name?"

It was a demand, and it rankled. "I don't understand what he has to do with it. They weren't a *thing*."

He lowered himself down until his face was level with hers, his eyes hostile and his mouth pulled into a sneer. "You don't have to understand, *sweetheart*. You just have to answer my question, or maybe you don't want to get your cousin back."

"Of course I do."

"Then answer my goddamn question." His words came out in a quiet drawl, but behind them, there was a male who was used to getting his way.

"Charles," she said. "Although I don't know what he has to do with any of it."

"Do you know where he lives?"

"Up on Greenacre Avenue."

His cunning eyes darting to her pocket. "What's in there?"

Exhaling sharply, she pulled out the screw and held it out to him on her palm. He studied it like it was a viper about to strike.

"Where did you get that from?"

Her hesitation was met with a growl, and even though she wanted to not tell him a goddamn thing just to spite him, she wasn't stupid enough to let this opportunity for help to slip past her.

"I found it."

"Where?"

"I went looking for clues. I found it where Katie pulled the car over to change the flat."

"How do you know that's where she stopped?"

She lifted her chin and squared her shoulders, planning on knocking that mocking smile right off his face. "The smell of engine oil and gas was the strongest there. Plus I smelled Katie."

Drake gave a barely imperceptible nod like he was impressed with her, then picked up the screw carefully from her palm and brought it to his nose, inhaling. He frowned.

"I couldn't place the smell either," she said.

"How many of these did you find?"

She shrugged. "Hundreds. All along the road for a half mile before the spot she stopped."

His jaw tightened. "Fuck." Turning on his heel, he left the office.

"Wait!" she called, jumping from her seat. She burst out the front door behind him. "Hey! Where do you think you're going?"

He wheeled around at the bottom of the porch, his eyes practically glowing. "Stay here."

"I'm coming with you."

"No," he growled. "This is my business now."

His business. Not *Revenant* business. "We need to check out the scene of the abduction again. Her car too."

"Not *we*, sweetheart. Me."

Ignoring her, he prowled into the direction of the garage tucked up against the side of the house. Opening the side door, he went straight to where her uncle Peter had parked Katie's abandoned car. Neve followed, wanting to get a better look at the vehicle, to see if it would reveal any more of its secrets.

Drake glared at her over his shoulder, and she stopped at the door, leaning against the jamb and folding her arms. She watched him open all the doors, including the trunk, and go through it all, using his nose to catalogue the different scents. Finally, he inspected the flat tire, sticking his finger into the hole that the screw had made. Surging to his feet, he left the garage and started down the driveway.

She caught up to him, but only because he let her, and dragged him to a stop—also because he let her. She jerked back when a hiss escaped his lips and his eyes glowed more brightly. Planting her hands on her hips, she said, "Still think it's Charles?"

"Most victims know their attackers."

His words sliced at her, and she recoiled, one word echoing around her head.

Victim.

Victim.

Victim.

"Do you think she's dead?"

"I never said that. I just said if she's been taken, then she was probably familiar with the person who did it. I didn't scent blood or any other fluids in the car, which tells me what?"

"She probably wasn't forced from the car, that she got out willingly."

He held up the screw, its matte grey surface absorbing what little light was coming from the house. "She got out of the car because she had no choice. This was a deliberate act with an intended victim in mind."

Neve swallowed past the lump in her throat, realizing who the real victim had meant to be—her. Katie wasn't the Leo's daughter, she was. She was definitely the bigger prize.

"If you're going to speak to Charles now, I'm coming with you."

A muscle in his jaw feathered. "No."

"You don't know where he lives."

"Sure I do," he replied in a casual drawl, walking toward the Escalade. "On Greenacre, like you said."

"Greenacre Avenue is nearly six miles long. Are you going to drive the whole length of it, just randomly knocking on doors until someone named Charles answers?"

He kept walking.

Not even a pause or a *Hey! Why didn't I think of that?*

Asshole.

With a small growl of frustration, she jogged ahead of him and put herself in his path, making him jerk to a stop before he ran into her. And judging by the size of him, she would've been the only one hurt.

"What are you doing?" Amusement colored his words, making a spark light up his yellow eyes.

Neve squared her shoulders. "Dragging you to my car. I'm driving."

"*Dragging me?*" he retorted with a dark chuckle. "Do you think I can't find out his address? Because I can assure you, I can."

She snorted. "This would be a lot faster."

"I work alone, *female*. You're not coming with me."

Female? Neve crossed her arms. "Don't be a dick. You have no idea where you're going. And I gave you that screw. Without me, you'd never have found out that the puncture had been caused on purpose."

"Conjecture," he retorted. "A truck could've dropped a box of screws from its flatbed and the driver didn't realize."

"Fact," she shot back. "That road isn't used by anyone other than me and Katie. It's our private route to and from our houses."

"It doesn't mean someone else couldn't have used it. You know, you don't own the fucking world, *sweetheart*."

She bristled. "Why are *you* fighting *me* on this? Katie is *my* cousin. It's my right to help you."

His nostrils flared, and his eyes narrowed to slits. "You're used to getting your own way, aren't you?"

She gave him a sweet smile, edged with malice. Jerking her head toward her truck, she snapped, "Get in. I'm driving."

Nothing but silence for a beat before a laugh rumbled out from his chest. "You're a tough female," he told her once the laughter had evaporated as quickly as it had started.

Folding her arms over her chest, she shrugged one shoulder. "My father calls me obstinate."

"I have no doubt." His words were nothing but a soft murmur. He studied her, almost as if he was sizing her up, but for what?

She turned slowly, her cat's instincts to not give him her back screaming. He was a threat in every way—his size, the thick ropey muscles covering his bones, the shadow of danger that hung from those broad shoulders.

She resumed her path to her truck, her footsteps the only ones disappearing into the night for a few excruciating seconds. But then she heard him.

Walking.

Following.

Opening up the driver's side door of the cab, she got in and waited for him to stuff himself inside. When both doors were shut, she felt like she couldn't breathe. There was so much raw power in him that it pressed against her skin like a lover. Letting out a long breath, she started the engine and performed a three-point turn, before traveling back down the drive and out onto the street.

9

DRAKE

Drake shifted in his seat, trying to ignore the way his body reacted to this female. She shouldn't be getting to him like this. She shouldn't be eliciting this reaction from him.

But she was.

She'd challenged his authority and ordered him to her truck. Of course, he could've said no and gone back to his own car, but he hadn't, because this female intrigued not just him, but his cat as well.

He drew in a deep lungful of her scent, and her shoulders tightened. Fear mixed with annoyance tickled his nose, but there was one other scent mixing into the duo, and it was the female flush of arousal.

Long, dark hair fell over her shoulder, and although she was petite for a female, she had all the right curves, as well as some definitions in her arms like she worked out regularly. When he'd first smelled her in her uncle's office, he'd gotten hard then too, but he beat the bastard back with thoughts of what was happening to these females ghosting from the pride's territories.

"So, what do you know about old Charlie-Boy?" he asked to distract himself. He'd found out about the call out for the

Shadows only a couple of hours ago after Mateo texted him with an update. Drake had had the Trinity's phones tapped for a while now, gleaning information when necessary, since the ancient bastards could be as tight-lipped as a virgin on her wedding night.

He didn't give a fuck what they did or said, though. This was something he was taking personally.

Her hands tightened on the wheel, hands that would look great wrapped around his cock. "Not a lot—just general female chatter."

"You say that like you aren't included in the chatter."

"I'm not," she shot back, keeping her pale green eyes on the road. "I've got better things to do than listen to gossip."

He twisted to look at her, jamming one knee up against the door. "What do they say?" He smiled when she rolled her eyes at him.

"He's one of the pride's most eligible males."

"Why?"

She was silent for a moment, her eyes on the darkened road ahead of them. The old truck's headlights were weak against the pushing blackness, but her cat's eyes would've been picking up the slack. "Honestly? I couldn't tell you. I think he's an asshole. He's arrogant and entitled and—"

"So, not the kind of male you'd go for?" He clamped his mouth shut as soon as the question came out. A) What the fuck was he thinking? And B) why the fuck did he care? It seemed when it came to this female, his brain took a little TO. He glanced over at Neve when he realized she hadn't answered his question. "Neve?"

Her head jerked toward him, her eyes unfocused for a moment. "Sorry. What was the question?"

He would love to take a peek inside her head, but for some reason, he hadn't been able to break past her mental shields when he'd tried before. "I asked if Charlie was the kind of guy you'd go for."

She shook her head. "No. Katie, on the other hand, is a female more after the traditional lifestyle."

"Traditional, as in…?"

"She wants to get mated and start having kids right away."

"Jesus," he muttered. "Is this guy even down for that?"

She shrugged. "They aren't a couple, so why would it matter? But that's why I'm sure she wouldn't have a lover. My cousin isn't wired for casual sex."

"Does Charles even know she exists, that she's interested?"

"They've been introduced," she replied with a shrug, and Drake shook his head. Shifters had a very antiquated way of looking at things. It had a lot to do with the older generation being born in the last century and passing down those ideals and restrictions to their offspring.

"She thinks she's in love with him," Neve said quietly, glancing over at him.

"And you don't?"

She held his eyes for a long minute before turning her attention back to the road. "She's in love with the idea of him, of what his status would mean for her."

"You make her sound like a gold digger."

A growl filled the cab. "Katie is *not* like that." Neve practically spat the words at him, and the gleam in her eye was murderous. "You know the hierarchy that exists in the prides. You know that females are expected to act in a certain way, to follow a certain path."

He didn't actually. He hadn't been born into one of the 'elite' families in his pride. "Your parents expect you to do the same?

Get mated? Become the obedient female?" He didn't know why, but the thought of Neve bowing to any male made his thoughts violent. He'd literally only known her less than an hour, but her spirit was so strong. He didn't want to see it snuffed out by some male on a power trip because of daddy's money.

"Something like that."

Drake chewed the inside of his cheek and looked out the windshield. The road ahead of them started to curve and wind between the sheer faces of the mountains. Letterboxes appeared like specters from the darkness along the side of the serpentine road. They ascended for a few minutes before Neve slowed the car.

"It's just up here," she murmured to herself, pulling the car off the road and turning down a long driveway not unlike her uncle's. Darkness swallowed the car briefly before the light pollution from the large house in front of them cut through his vision.

The house was huge—a literal McMansion built into the sharp ridges of the Wyomings. He peered out at the thing.

"Jesus Christ."

"Yeah, you could say that," Neve replied dryly. "His is one of the original elite families, and they're richer than Trump, hence the house."

Fuck. "What kind of business are they in?"

"I'm not exactly sure. Something in the human world, though."

Well, whatever the hell they did to earn bread, it only meant one thing to him—these fuckers were going to close ranks and threaten legal involvement as soon as he showed his face. Rich shifters, a lot like rich humans, did exactly that. Whether it was to save face or just to prove they have enough money to waste on hiring a legal team, he didn't know. All he did know was that his job was getting exponentially harder by the second.

The driveway in front of them broke off into two paths. Neve took the right, swinging around to the front of the house until she was under the porte cochère. An honest to God butler opened his car door like he was expected. He got out, and one inhale confirmed the guy in the penguin suit was human.

The Homo sapiens's eyes drifted higher and higher, and when they reached his yellow eyes, he didn't seem confused or startled by the unnatural color—well, unnatural to their species at least. For jaguar shifters, it was one of maybe a handful that were native to their DNA.

"Good evening, sir," the suit said. "Is the master of the house expecting you?"

"He is not," Drake replied, sizing up what little of the house's interior he could see through the narrow windows at either side of the front door. Neve joined him a second later, and he tried to ignore that lovely scent of hers. It was like night-blooming jasmine—delicate yet with an unreserved strength to it too.

"I'm afraid you'll have to come back—"

Drake pushed past his mental shields and fed him some memories of his boss telling him they were expected. A moment later, the butler bowed to them and said, "Follow me, if you will."

"Thank you," he replied, ignoring the look of surprise on Neve's face. He took the lead, doubting there'd be any danger inside the house, but old habits died hard. He reached inside his jacket, keeping his hand on one of his forties under his arm just in case someone sneezed in their direction.

His boots hit the polished marble floors just as the interior styling hit his retinas. It was a sea of white and gold. The marble was veined with gold striations, but instead of seeing neat squares of pattern, he saw huge slabs of it, like they'd forgone the tile option and gone straight to the kitchen counter size route.

Columns in that same marble rose above their heads, drawing his eye to the gold ceiling. Jesus, how much money did this family have?

"Please?" a stiff voice prompted, and he saw the butler had paused at a doorway. Drake entered the room with Neve hot on his heels. The space was filled with books at one end and had a quartet of plush armchairs clustered around a round table at the other. On the adjacent wall to the seating area was a marble fireplace, a fire burning brightly in its hearth.

"Please wait here. My master will be with you shortly."

Drake nodded and moved toward the fireplace, inspecting the details carved into the marble face. He glanced over his shoulder to find Neve lowering herself into one of the pale blue striped armchairs.

"We need to speak to Charles," she told him. "Alone."

"We will." But they needed to address the motherfucker who wrote the checks first. He knew exactly how it was going to go down too. They'd talk to senior, whose name was no doubt also Charles. He would then stonewall them before the junior got all hopped up about not being able to defend himself and give his side of the story. They'd be ushered out before they could witness the seams of a very wealthy machine popping and they'd be right where they were now—waiting for information.

"Why are you doing this?" she asked.

He frowned. "I'm not sure I follow."

"Why are you taking this job yourself? I mean, you're the captain of the Revenant. Surely this is something the Shadows could do, or you could send another one of your team in your stead. You could've waited until tomorrow to do this." She looked down at her hands folded in her lap. "I guess I just want to know why *you're* taking this so personally."

He kept his face neutral, but on the inside, he was reeling. He couldn't tell her the real reason—that was his cross to bear—but the reality was, he felt as if this was his chance to make amends, to atone for his sins.

"I'm just doing my job," he told her.

The doors to the room opened with a flourish, and an older shifter strolled through. He was dressed in a tailored suit, his shoes polished to a high shine. Although he carried a cane, Drake knew it was more for show. Black jaguars aged incredibly well, their bodies keeping up until they were well into their mid-four-hundreds.

"Watts said you were here to see me," the male said, taking a seat.

"Yes, sir," Drake replied, leading with good manners. You caught more flies with honey than vinegar, after all. "We're here to speak with Charles."

"Well, *I* am Charles."

Bingo.

"We need to speak to Charles Jr.," Neve said, shocking Charlie Sr. that a woman was in the room, let alone addressing him directly.

Charles Sr. brushed her off easily, his eyes narrowing on Drake instead. His easy dismissal of Neve made Drake's hackles rise. It looked like Drake didn't have to bother with pleasantries now.

"And who are you?" he demanded imperiously.

"I'm the captain of the Revenant."

Well, *that* got his attention.

The male suddenly looked as if he'd been goosed with ten

thousand watts, his body becoming rigid as the scent of his fear wafted out from underneath that expensive suit. "There must be a grave situation if you're involved."

"There is. Females are going missing."

Charles went the color of pea soup, but Drake didn't give a damn about his sensibilities.

"So, where's your son?"

A frown appeared on the other male's brow. "I can assure you my son has nothing to do with this."

"That's not the answer to the question I just asked you."

"Now you listen here," Charles began, surging to his feet. Drake stared at him impassively, uncowed by the display of bravado from the wealthy male in front of him. "You can leave with those accusations right now."

"What accusations?" Drake countered, his voice calm—in complete contrast to the rising pitch of Charles Sr., who had shed the green tinge and was rocking into red territory. "All I said was that I needed to speak to Charles Jr."

"He didn't do it," the guy blustered. "And if you continue with this line of inquiry, I'm going to have my lawyers sue you for slander."

Drake gave him a cold smile. "Didn't do what, exactly?" he asked. "Hmm? Is this not the first time Charlie-Boy has gotten his nose dirty?" He wondered how many times he had to clean up after his son, wondered how much money he had to flash to get things taken care of *discreetly*.

The other shifter's lips pulled back, baring his teeth in a snarl. "Get out of my house."

Drake shook his head slowly. "Not going to happen, Charles, so why don't you be a good little subject and run along and get your son."

"Drake?" Neve asked anxiously although her voice was still soft. He glanced her way, but made a motion with his hand for her to stay there.

Drake opened his mouth again, but Charles just steamrolled right over him. He wasn't used to that. He was used to fear and capitulation, but the rich-ass, tailored-suit wearing male wasn't pulling his weight here now, was he? Drake had had enough, though.

Moving quickly, he grabbed the guy by his lapels and lifted him off the ground. His cane clattered dully to the area rug, and Drake kicked it out of the way. The quick levitation act got Charles's mouth to stop working, and Drake took the opening.

In a low hiss and speaking very close to his face, he said, "Get your son's ass in here right now, before I do something I might regret."

The color drained right out of the other male's face, his mouth opening and closing like a drowning fish. Drake dropped him to the floor, then made a little waving motion with his fingers. "Go on. Time's wasting."

Charles hot-footed it out of there, slamming the doors behind him.

"Do you think that was necessary?"

He turned at Neve's question, finding her standing up, her hands hitched onto her waist. He inhaled the smell of her irritation, but there was no fear. Odd.

"We're getting to speak to Charlie-Boy, aren't we?"

She huffed. "We'd be lucky if he doesn't return with a shotgun aimed at your chest."

"Concerned for my safety?" he simpered. "I'm touched."

She mumbled something that sounded a lot like *jackass* under her breath and sat again. Drake smiled. Just then, the double doors were thrown open, and Charles Sr. returned with a male who was nearly identical to him. Dressed in cream-colored khakis and a black turtleneck sweater, the guy stank of preppiness and privilege.

Charles Jr., he presumed.

"Sit," Drake said, pointing at the chair the elder Charles had vacated. The younger male parked it like he was battery-operated and Drake had the controller. Raising his gaze to the door, Drake pinned his father with a hard stare. "You can wait outside."

The guy looked like he wanted to argue, but wisely shut his mouth as well as the double doors. When he turned back, he found Neve's peridot stare fixed on Charles like she was trying to scoop information out of his brain herself with sheer will alone.

"Charlie-Boy," Drake started, his booming voice startling the poor guy. He looked at him, his gray eyes hardening as he remembered they were in *his* house and his lovely world of wealth.

What a dick.

"What do you want?" he asked, his voice surprisingly strong. Well, what do you know? It looked like the bastard had balls.

"We're here to talk about Katie Bolton."

His face got all vacant, but Drake wasn't biting on the *who-are-you-talking-about* game. The thing was, he didn't have the damn patience to play with this asshole.

Leaning in, making sure to get his face in real tight, he snarled, "Don't play dumb, Charles. I have it on good authority that Katie Bolton and you were involved with each other." Which wasn't exactly the truth, but he needed the right bait. If he refused to talk, Drake could always burrow into his head and find the truths he may have been hiding.

"Okay, okay. I know *of* her, yes. We were introduced a couple of years ago."

Drake turned to stare at the fire. "Where were you last night?"

"Last—? Here, at home."

Drake placed his hands on the mantle and leaned in, letting the heat of the fire become almost unbearable before stepping back and turning back around. "All night?"

Charles frowned like he was trying to figure out a math problem. "Yes."

"Can anyone corroborate that?"

"Why would I *need* anyone to corroborate that?"

"Just answer the question," Drake snarled softly.

Charles's attention drifted over to Neve briefly before snapping back to his face. "No. My father was out."

"Your mother?"

"She died years ago." Drake raised a brow. "Old age."

Damn. His mother must have been well into her four hundreds when she'd had him—not unheard of, but definitely not common.

"What about the butler?" Drake asked, wandering over to the book-lined cases at the back of the room. Angling his body so he could see the other male, he pulled out one of the tomes then slid it back into place when Charles's shoulders hitched up to his ears. His father probably didn't like anyone touching his collection. "Where was he?"

"He had the night off."

"And there was nobody else here? You didn't speak to anyone? Share part of your affluent life to your followers on Instagram Live? What's your handle? @richdouche? Nah, it's probably @HighballerBiebtard."

Charles glared at him, his contempt burning as hot as the fire in the hearth.

That's right. Get angry. Slip up, you bastard.

"I just had a quiet night. Here. Alone. No phone calls. No social media."

"So what were you doing?" Drake grabbed another book, pulling it all the way out and flipping through its pages noisily. "Here. Alone. On a Saturday night," he added in an antagonizing tone.

"Drake," Neve said in warning.

"Neve," he replied. That was when he noticed Charles's head jerk in her direction, staring at her. He put down the book and stepped closer to the male.

"You're her cousin?"

She nodded stiffly.

Charles licked his lips, suddenly nervous. "My father doesn't know."

Drake bit back the smile that wanted to flash onto his face. "Doesn't know *what* exactly?"

Charles let out a long breath. "She's told you about me?"

Neve didn't say anything—didn't move, hardly breathed.

"Doesn't know what?" Drake demanded again, snapping his fingers impatiently in front of the guy's face.

Charles exhaled noisily. "H-he doesn't know we're having a relationship."

"*What?*" Neve's voice crackled with something Drake had plenty of experience with—barely contained rage. She hadn't known. "She was your dirty little secret?"

"No! Never. I love her."

"Bullshit."

"It's true," he replied weakly.

"If it were, you'd tell your father about her," Neve replied. Drake made a point of stepping back and leaning against the mantle, the fire warming his back.

"I can't. Please, believe me when I say that."

Neve cocked her head to the side, studying him with an intensity that was straight up cold killer. And what do you know, Drake respected her a little more.

"It can't be a matter of bloodline," she said. "So what is it?"

He blew out a breath. "My parents have another female they intend for me to mate." When Neve remained quiet, Charlie-Boy started to fidget. "We're getting mated in the spring."

She rose from her seat in a surge of power. At her sides, her hands were balled into fists so tight that even from his position across the room, he could see the bones of her knuckles standing out. Taking advantage of the strength of her feelings, he nudged aside her mental shields and probed her thoughts, getting flashes of images like lightning strikes. He saw the scenarios playing out in her frontal lobe, mostly involving Charles choking on his cock after Neve shoved it down his throat. Drake smirked a little at that last one.

She paced in a tight line just like the jaguar she was before turning for the door. Drake righted himself, wondering if she was going to ask the six-million-dollar question. But as she reached for the handles, she casually said, "Well, don't worry yourself about cutting her loose in the spring." She peered at him over her shoulder, her eyes glowing. "She disappeared last night."

"What?"

"That's right, Charlie-Boy," Drake interjected. "Katie's gone, and guess who doesn't have an alibi?"

The kid blanched, his puss matching the color of his pants.

"Wait! Wait, what did you say? What happened to Katie?"

"She never came home," he replied flatly. "So, I'm going to ask you one more time, what were you doing last night?"

Charles's voice is barely a whisper, but he said, "I was here, alone. I have no one to corroborate my story."

He stalked toward Neve. He could feel her shock and anger simmering just below the surface, and in an uncharacteristic move, he placed his hand on the back of her neck, his fingers curling around the graceful curve of her nape.

"Let's go," he said softly into her ear, opening up the door and guiding her out. Charles Sr. was there, throwing questions at them like a yappy little dog. Drake blew him off, his focus on getting Neve out of there. The little truth bomb Charles had dropped had rocked her to her core, and even he had to admit he hadn't seen it coming.

He put her into the passenger side of her own truck, jogging around to the other side of the cab to get them out of there. They didn't speak, but somehow, he knew there was nothing he could say that would make her feel better. She was stuck in her own head, he could see it from the hard slash of her brows. She'd told him Katie only had a crush on the guy, that there was no relationship there, but that rug hadn't just been ripped out from under her tonight, it had been shredded and burned to ashes.

Betrayal by a family member was never an easy pill to swallow.

10

KATIE

Katie stared at the chipped nail polish on her fingernails, fighting the urge to cry. It seemed like a lifetime ago that she had sat on Neve's bed and had them painted. A lifetime ago that she'd talked about Charles with her, although she'd had to use veiled speech. Her cousin couldn't know that they were seeing each other. Despite his intended mating, she loved him and would take whatever he would give for however long he was willing to give it. Which was until next spring. Charles had told her that it was a political mating, something about solidifying a relationship between his family and his intended mate's, but it wasn't a love match. It was simply… business.

Thinking about Charles kissing another female made her chest hurt, and she focused on her nails instead, straining her memories, trying to remember everything about that night, every little nuance and detail and… She couldn't even remember what the color was called.

Stretching out her legs, she winced as the blood flow returned to her lower extremities and rested her head against the bars of her cell. How long had she been here? Flexing her fingers, she lifted one at a time as she counted along in her head.

Saturday night she was at Neve's.

She'd left around midnight, making her less than three-mile drive home.

She'd gotten a flat tire. Pulled over. Then…

She'd woken up here, in this cell.

Fixing her gaze on Elsie, who was huddled up in the corner, she found the female's haunted eyes focused on the floor in front of her. After the assault, her cellmate had said nothing, just covered her body as much as she could and retreated into her own head. Katie wondered whether it was any better in there, or whether her brain just kept replaying the event over and over—a horrible set of events cycling through on an endless loop.

Katie got busy counting again, lifting her fingers one at a time. Saturday, Sunday… Maybe it was—

"It's pointless," Elsie said in a hoarse whisper. "It's pointless to count, just as it's pointless to think we're going to get out of here."

Katie's lip trembled. "My father will be looking for me."

"As I'm sure mine is too."

"Do you know how long you've been here? I mean before I was stuffed into this cage with you?"

Elsie shrugged shoulders that were too thin. Shifters needed to maintain a high caloric intake, otherwise the weight just dripped off them. Even Katie was beginning to feel the strain of starvation on her body, even though it couldn't have been any longer than seventy-two hours.

"Maybe a few days before you. I don't… I don't really know."

Silence settled between them, making it seem as if everything was lost.

"How did they get you?" she asked in a whisper.

"I was walking back to my dorm from my last class for the day."

"Class? Like *college* class?"

Elsie nodded. "Yeah. I'm a junior at UC Berkeley. I'm getting…" She paused, frowned. "I *was getting* my engineering degree."

The use of the past tense told Katie a hell of a lot about her mental state. Pushing off the metal bars, she crawled over to Elsie and eased down beside her.

"You can't talk like that," she said softly, her eyes growing wet. "We're going to get out of this."

Elsie looked at her with a hollow stare. "No, we're not, and the sooner you accept that, the easier it'll be."

Katie opened her mouth to reply when the door at the top of the stairs opened with a groan. Everyone inhaled sharply, a fresh trickle of fear sliding like an insidious fog into the room. Burying her head into her arms, she hid her face, terrified to meet the eyes of their captor, but her head jerked up again when the smell of chargrilled meat wafted through the space, warring with the scent of fear pouring from every single female.

She watched, rapt, as one of their captors planted his feet at the bottom of the stairs. Complete with a Stetson, the guy looked like he'd stepped from one of the cowboy romance books Katie's mom liked to read when she thought nobody was around. Dressed in jeans and a plaid shirt, he strolled forward with a takeout bag clutched in his hand until he was standing in the middle of the vast room. He was able to see every cell—and wanted every*one* to see him.

The scent of the meat in that brown paper bag got stronger.

"Ladies," Cowboy said, his voice accented with a Texan twang, "it is your lucky day." He made a show of opening up the bag and pulling out two burgers, their paper wrappers transparent with grease. Katie licked her lips in anticipation. Her cat was starving.

Cowboy dropped one of the burgers back into the sack and placed it on the ground before proceeding to unwrap the other. He took a bite, making a show of chewing it slowly, savoring it. He wiped his mouth on his sleeve and continued to eat. Katie found her mouth moving along with his, mimicking his actions with each chew and swallow. When he was done, he wadded up the wrapper and dropped it into the open sack at his feet.

Cowboy licked his fingers slowly, knowing he had a captivated audience. "Delicious, but I couldn't possibly have the other one too, so I will offer it to one of you, *ladies*," he sneered.

Katie was torn between wanting to retreat and hanging on his every word. She settled for sitting forward a little bit, watching, waiting.

His boots made an odd hissing sound as he tracked back and forth in front of the cells. Cowboy walked closer to hers and Elsie's, peering in at them. He winked at Elsie, although this was not the man who had assaulted her before. Despite this, Elsie shrank back even farther against the cinder blocks.

Katie looked back at that brown paper bag, already tasting the burger on her lips.

"I'll give the extra burger to whoever lets me fuck them." He pointed down at the ground in front of him, a twisted smirk on his face. "Right here. Right now. In front of everyone." Silence filled the basement, and she wondered whether anyone would be that desperate. Selling their body for a semi-cold burger? It was unthinkable.

"I will," someone said.

Katie's eyes widened in surprise and beside her, Elsie buried her face in her arms. In the cell across from theirs, a young woman came to stand at the bars, her fingers clutching at the cold steel.

Cowboy cupped his ear, leaning closer. "I'm sorry, sweetheart, what was that?"

She sucked in a breath. "I said I'll do it."

Katie couldn't see from where she was sitting, but she assumed the bastard was smiling. Reaching into the front pocket of his Levis, he pulled out a key and opened up the cell. Crooking his finger, he invited her to come a little closer. When she was within reach, he yanked her out of the cell and shoved her face-first against the bars. He ground his hips into her ass and wrenched her head to one side to expose her throat.

Katie jammed her fist into her mouth to stop herself from making a sound, her hot breath streaming out from around her hand. The woman whimpered when Cowboy yanked her yoga pants down to her ankles and tore the underwear from her hips. At that point, Katie squeezed her eyes shut. Mirroring Elsie, she hugged her legs to her chest and buried her face in her arms. But just because she couldn't see it, didn't mean she couldn't hear it. The sound of it, the smell of it was something that was going to be branded in Katie's memories forever.

She tried to block out the ugliness she was powerless to stop by humming the tune to one of her favorite songs. She jumped when Elsie's hand snaked out and grabbed her own and together, they hummed.

When there was a groan that could've only come from Cowboy finding release, Elsie and Katie stopped humming in unison, but their hands remained fused together.

The rustle of clothes.

The crinkle of paper and a barely concealed sob.

The sound of the cell door opening and shutting.

It was only when Cowboy's boots receded that they both looked into the cell opposite them. The woman was holding the brown paper sack, trembling, her knuckles white as she stood motionless with her prize. For just a moment, Katie envied her. She was holding something everyone wanted, but she had paid the price none of them had been willing to pay.

She watched as the human opened things up, pulling out the burger and freeing it of the grease-soaked wrapper. Bringing it to her mouth, she took a bite and chewed, her eyes shuttering closed. When her lids popped open again, she stared down at the burger and turned around, holding it out to her cellmate. The jaguar she was sharing with took a bite then gave it back. Katie thought that was nice of her—to share what she'd rightfully earned—but then she was shocked when the woman actually went to the side of her cage and stretched out her arm as far as it could go, passing the burger to the others in the next cell over.

After each female took a bite, they passed on the rest of it until it finally reached Katie and Elsie. Katie was the one who'd taken it, nodding in thanks first to the woman who had given it to her, then to the human who had given up a piece of herself so she could feed them all.

"What's your name?" Katie asked softly.

The woman stared dully at her. "Bethany Scott," she replied before sitting down at the back of her cell, hugging her knees close to her chest.

"Elsie," Katie said, crouching down beside the other cat. "Take a bite. Here." She shoved the remnants of the burger under Elsie's nose, but her cellmate simply looked away.

"I don't want any."

"You have to eat," she pressed. "To keep your strength up."

Elsie said nothing else and still wouldn't look at her. Katie looked around, hoping for some guidance. When another one of the females made a gesture for her to eat, Katie brought what was left of the burger to her mouth and chewed.

Swallowed.

God, she felt so hollow inside.

11

ASHER

Asher studied his opponent's fingers as they clutched at his pawn. The glass piece had yet to be moved, but all its brothers-in-arms had left the relative comfort of home base and were falling quickly beneath Asher's sharp mind and even sharper tongue. He took a moment to look at the male who had wanted to have this audience with him, wondering why he'd chosen now.

All the pieces in the game were in motion, capturing their opponents' pieces as if he had orchestrated every move… wait, he *had* orchestrated every move, and it was a beautiful game to watch.

"You *do* understand what you're about to do, don't you?"

The male's hand paused over his pawn, hesitant for the first time since he'd walked into Asher's home.

"You aren't talking about my pawn, are you?" the male asked.

"I am not." Asher's voice was as smooth as the glass chess pieces—completely in control of the situation. Like everything in his life, he liked control.

The male's gaze darted to the side, taking in the grand fireplace and the marble mantel and the Manet painting Asher had paid a small fortune for three decades ago.

"I want in. I've seen what my brothers-in-arms have been able to do, and I want that power."

Ah, yes, more power. It all came down to that. The guy finally moved his pawn, as if his declaration had gotten him thinking about not just the square in front of him, but the whole damn board. The game that was already finished in Asher's mind.

"I understand. You know what I expect of you then, if I choose to give you this?"

While he waited, Asher made his next move, shifting his knight to capture the pawn his opponent had just moved. The male still hadn't answered, so he lifted his gaze up to find the jaguar staring.

"I need unwavering allegiance from you. In return, I'll give you what you need to stay riding high on the power you seek." Holding out his hand to the male, he murmured, "Do we have an accord?"

He had to tamp down his greed as he stared into the male's eyes, waiting for him to pull the trigger. His plan was foolproof, his synthetic enhancer guaranteed to bring them back time and time again. All it had taken was one—one jaguar to *drink the Kool-Aid* as it were, and he'd had them.

And then he would have his deepest desires.

"We do," the other male replied, shaking Asher's outstretched hand. "We do."

12

JETT

Jett was staring out the window, his gaze fixed on the way the morning sun played over the fall-ravaged manicured gardens at the front of their compound. Considering the rest of their place was traversed by lodgepole and cottonwood, the uniform plots of spindly rose bushes and the soft gray-green leaves of lavender were out of place, yet he found himself enjoying the symmetry and order. Maybe it was because his fucking life was so out of control…

Turning back to the boardroom-style table that had been set up in the dining room, he looked at Drake, Mateo, Grayson, and Sasha. None of them had parked it at the table yet. In fact, the only people sitting were Greg Bolton, the Leo of the Black Claw pride, and Callum, the captain of the Phantom unit Shadows. Greg was stock-still, his hands folded neatly in front of him. His body may have been motionless, but the turmoil behind his eyes was fucking off-putting.

Jett swung his attention to the front door, a combination of anxiety and barely restrained aggression battling with his self-control. They were awaiting the arrival of the Trinity along with the Leos of the four remaining North American prides and their Shadows.

Fifteen alpha males inside one room was like sitting with drums of gasoline beside a naked flame. All it would take was one nudge, and it would all go to shit.

Boom.

He took a mental tally of what could go wrong at this meeting.

Option one: one Leo takes offense over what another Leo says, and it ended in a bloodbath.

Option two: one of the Shadows looks at him wrong, and it ended in a bloodbath with him wielding the dagger.

Option three: they all got twitchy with their trigger fingers, and it ended in a bloodbath.

Whichever way, there was a high possibility they weren't leaving this thing without a colossal dry cleaning bill.

"Remind me again why this couldn't be a conference call?" he asked Drake.

His leader's mouth curled into a slight grin. "Because the Trinity don't know how to make that happen on a rotary phone."

A wave of laughter boiled up around the room, the levity much needed, considering they were staring down the barrel of a gun. Jesus, all this waiting was making him twitchy.

Jamming his hands into his pockets, Jett started to whistle, but when Drake threw him a ball-shriveling glare, he stopped. Right. Not cool. Dipping his chin, Jett got to tapping his feet instead. At least that sound was dampened by the deep nap of the carpet beneath his feet. Outside the room, the grandfather clock announced it was ten a.m.

As if the deep knells of the clock were the official announcement, the doorbell rang. Jett pushed off the wall to answer it. Any excuse to burn off the nervous energy, right? Strolling to the door, he tried to keep his emotional grid clear before he pulled it open.

Elian of Ghost Unit stood on the stoop, his green eyes serious. Behind him was Martin Worther, Leo of the Gray Fur pride. Jett stood back—his shoulders stiff and his aggression leaking—not bothering to close the door behind them. Out on the pea gravel drive, another three cars were pulling up. The Leos and Shadows of the White Fang, Yellow Eye, and Red Paw prides got out, and Jett's skin tightened in warning, his palm heating up. Flexing his hand into a fist, he let out a breath and allowed the wildfire that burned to be used extinguish.

He scrutinized the males who filed in. He didn't like any of them and having them in his house only cranked out his anger a little more. Slamming the door shut behind them, he walked back into the meeting room and took up position on the wall beside Sasha. The Leos were talking softly to their Shadows, their combined voices buzzing around the room, and Jett took to studying each of them—you know, just in case he needed to size them up for a casket or some shit.

Tavaris, captain of Shade unit, sat back in his seat, the wood groaning under his substantial weight. The guy was built like a linebacker and operated like one, too. Turning his head, he whispered to his Leo, Thomas Vecchio, who nodded once before resting his hands on the tabletop, palms down.

The front door opened once more, and then the Trinity strolled in like they had all the time in the world. Even though they were all pushing two hundred and seventy, the trio didn't look a day over forty-five. Ah, the beauty of shifter DNA.

Zed, Zepher, and Zeke took the three seats reserved for them at the head of the table, and Jett caught Drake staring hard at the trio, which was unusual. Their fearless leader didn't show his emotions so easily… unless it was anger, and then he was all over that.

Zed cleared his throat, calling the meeting to attention. "I want to thank you all for coming today. I know this meeting was arranged at short notice, but there's something of utmost importance to discuss."

Jett frowned. What it could be? Drake hadn't mentioned anything to them in the last couple of days, so whatever it was, it must've happened in the last twenty-four hours. He straightened and clasped his hands together in front of him.

"Females are going missing," Zepher announced, his voice a quiet rasp reminiscent of dried paper. With that announcement, there was a collective hiss. Male jaguars were territorial by nature, but if their females were threatened? They got downright murderous.

"Where? Who?" William Tallow, Leo of the White Fang territory demanded, his fist coming down hard on the table.

"Mine," the Leo of Yellow Eye, Tony Scheller, said. "They're disappearing from my territory."

The Yellow Eyes had the smallest territory compared to every other pride. With only the states of California, Washington, and Oregon to watch, Jett was stunned to hear *their* females were the ones disappearing.

"*Who?* Who are they?" Thomas asked.

"A female named Elsie Fox was reported missing by her parents about a week ago," Zed replied. "Another named Chastity Reynolds has also been reported."

"Are there any other prides that have been hit?" William asked.

Greg Bolton blew out a breath. "Yes." The Leo's voice was so low, it barely beat back the din of the other males voicing their objections to things that were completely out of their power. Zed slammed his fist against the table, quieting the room.

"A Black Claw female was taken on Friday night," the Leo said.

Friday night? Jesus. That was over forty-eight hours ago. Why the fuck had they been sitting on this for so long? Jett focused on Drake, finding the male's jaw tight as he stared straight ahead. Did he already know?

"Tell me you've got some solid leads on this, Tony," Thomas demanded. He leaned forward in his seat, jabbing his finger at the Leo. "Tell me you know what the *fuck* is going on."

Lewis stood up, a hand sliding inside his heavy jacket, his body jacking forward as a vicious growl rippled up from his throat. His eyes were laser-focused on Vecchio, ready to defend his Leo. Drake nodded to Grayson, who stepped forward and touched Lewis's shoulder, holding on tightly before the male could shake him off, and closed his eyes. Lewis retracted his hand and sat back down, glaring at Grayson over his shoulder.

With the situation diffused, the Leo of the Yellow Eye pride lifted his eyes, looking at each Leo in turn. "It's being investigated." Gesturing to the male beside him, he added, "Lewis is looking into all avenues and speaking to all the right people."

"Just trust that everything that can be done is being done," Zepher said before any other questions could be thrown out or blood drawn. "Now, the reason for this meeting wasn't to inspire fear, but to serve as a warning to all of you. Keep an eye on your female members. Besides them going missing under the cover of darkness, there doesn't appear to be any pattern or reason for the disappearances. Once contact has been made by whoever has committed these atrocities, then a plan to get our females returned to us will be put into place."

"What's been done in the interim?" the Black Claw Leo demanded. "What are the Trinity doing to mitigate against more abductions?"

"What do you mean?" Zeke asked, his eyes narrowing and his voice dangerously low.

Greg met his stare. "I mean, how are we supposed to protect our female members if we can't have a direct line to our Shadows? They're on the front line. They're the ones who can keep them safe."

Zeke's upper lip curled back from his teeth. "The rules we have are designed to keep us all safe."

Greg loosed a breath. "I understand the reason for the rules. I *understand* that you don't want to risk another insurrection among the prides, but surely if there was more communication—*open communication*," he stressed, "it would at least deter whoever's taking our cats, knowing that we aren't all walking around with blindfolds on here." Greg glanced around the table for support and found none.

"We're not here to discuss that particular matter, Greg," Zed said sternly, but not unkindly. "We need to focus on the more pressing issue here, and that's our missing females."

So they were treating the symptoms but not the cause?

"Do we have suspects at least?" Tavaris asked.

Scheller drummed his fingers on the tabletop. "Nothing. They've all been taken at night when they're alone."

A collective curse rose up from the table.

"Like I said before," Zepher boomed over the noise, "everything that can be done is being done."

Jett totally called bullshit on that one. If *everything that can be done was being done*, they'd be more than willing to relax their ridiculous laws and allow unfettered contact between the Shadows and their Leos. Jett's hands curled into fists as he thought about his sisters. This could so easily happen to Katya or Mila, and if it did? He knew he wouldn't be sitting in a meeting and discussing it. He'd be out nailing the sonofabitch who thought he could take from him to the wall and flaying the skin from his body.

He glared at the participants seated at the table, tuning out of the discussion as fire burned through his blood, licking at his self-control and turning it to ash. He had to get out of there. He couldn't be held responsible for turning the whole house into a wiener roast.

"I'm out," he said just loudly enough for everyone to turn and look at him. Like he gave a fuck. He stalked from the room, taking the stairs two at a time and making a beeline to his room. Pulling out his phone, he brought up Katya's number, hit send, and began to pace.

"Come on, pick up, pick up," he said.

"Hello?"

"Katya. Thank fuck."

The sound of squeaking hinges came over the line, the acoustics changing. "Jesus, what's wrong, Jett?"

Alarm bells began to blare in his head. "Are you outside?"

"Yes. Why?"

Oh, fuck no. "Get inside, Kat. Now!"

"Jett?" she asked in a small voice. "What's wrong?"

He blew out a breath when he heard the hinges squeak again. The sound of her footsteps moving along the linoleum was soft. And then it went quiet.

"What's going on, Jett?"

He wasn't sure how much he could tell her, but he also didn't want her to become alarmed with the truth. Instead he settled for something he should've run past Drake first.

"I want you out of that trailer. You and Luce. Now."

His sister sighed. "And where would we go? I haven't found a place to live yet. There aren't that many decent places in my budget."

"You can live with me."

"Excuse me?"

He sat down on the edge of the bed, his head hanging loose between his shoulders. "You and Luce. You can have your own rooms. I'll take care of you like I should've done when I first left."

"Jett… I don't even know where you live. I don't know anything about your life."

He sucked in a breath and then another. "I'll tell you as much as I can tomorrow." Massaging the back of his neck, he added, "I'll come and pick you up in the morning."

"I've been called into work tomorrow, and Luce has school."

Fuck. "Afterward then. Are you picking up Luce?"

"Yeah."

"Good. Go straight home afterward. I'll see you around four. And make sure you pack up all your stuff. You aren't going home after this."

A small sob escaped her mouth, the sound crushing him. "You're scaring me."

"I'm sorry." He pumped his free hand into a fist. "It's only a precaution. I've got it under control." He hung up before he said anything more and yanked open his bedroom door. Walking to the head of the stairs, he looked down at the foyer to see the last of the Leos leaving. Grayson shut the door, his head dropping as if the weight of the information shared at the meeting weighed as heavily on him as it did on Jett.

"Are you all right, my man?" Grayson said without glancing around.

Damn, Jett hated it when Gray did this. "Fine," he clipped.

The other male turned around and stared at him, calling a non-verbal *bullshit* on his statement. "You ran out of there pretty quick."

"I doubt there was much else they were going to say that I wanted to hear."

"True," Grayson replied, his eyes gravitating to the rec room on the opposite side of the hall.

"Where's Drake?" Jett called.

"In here," his boss called from the dining room. He took the stairs down, holding out his fist to Grayson as he passed. He walked in to find Drake still standing in the same position as when the meeting started, his expression vacillating between fierce anger and heart-wrenching sadness.

"Sorry for skipping out," he said, taking a seat opposite the imposing male. "All I could think of was my sisters."

Drake nodded. "I hear that. And honestly, if I could've walked out, I would have, too."

Jett stared at him for a moment. "You knew, didn't you? Before they announced it. That's why you took off yesterday."

Drake frowned briefly, like he couldn't believe he'd been found out by one of his team, then said, "I was given the heads-up by Zed over the weekend."

Jett tried to summon anger or indignation, but he knew the reasons why Drake had been told earlier. "Listen, I need to ask you something."

Drake's mouth thinned into a slash. "Is this about your sisters?"

He dipped his chin, ready to give him the reasons, knowing he needed to have solid explanations for what he was about to ask Drake to do. He figured he'd already fucked up enough with keeping in contact with his family. What was one more indiscretion? "I—"

Drake put his hand up and stopped him. "I already know what you're going to ask me."

He tried not to let his hope flare. "And?"

"And, what?" Drake jacked forward on his hips, jabbing a finger in Jett's direction. "You know we can't have anyone living here who isn't a Shadow. You aren't even supposed to be *speaking* to them. It's against protocol."

"I know, but—"

"Don't make me bring up that other shit either," he warned, talking over Jett. "You've been in contact with your family not on one occasion, but for fucking *years*."

"I know," Jett ground out. "But given what's going down right now, they'd be safer here than where they're currently living."

Drake folded his arms across his massive chest. "But I wouldn't know anything about that now, would I?"

Jett's hackles rose. "Forgive me for not being a Chatty Cathy about my less than stellar childhood."

"I get it, I do, but without knowing more, how can I make a decision about what you're asking of me? If I agree to this, it opens a can of worms we'll never be able to close."

So Jett had two choices. Spill his fucking guts about what his life was like—what it was still like for his sisters—with the possibility that Drake *might* allow what he was asking of him, or pucker up tighter than an asshole and risk his sisters' safety.

"Fuck." Looking around, he said, "I'm going to need a drink if we do this."

"It's not even lunchtime yet."

"And?"

A smile flashed onto Drake's face. "After the morning we've had, I'm down with that."

13

NEVE

Neve rolled her head to the side, her unfocused eyes not tracking anything at all. Katie was still missing, and her cousin had lied to her about her relationship with Charles.

He doesn't know we're having a relationship.

As she lay sprawled on her bed, those words ran on repeat in her head, and all she could see was Charles's stupidly arrogant face as he denied, denied, denied. Katie *was* his dirty little secret, one he was hiding from dear old dad.

As Drake had put her in the passenger seat of her own goddamn truck, she wanted to disappear, to just get sucked up by the shadows and spat out somewhere where she could think and digest the revelation. Betrayal, because that's *exactly* what it was, wasn't something she'd ever expect from Katie. The thing was, she'd seen Charles with her own eyes, had seen the anguish in his face as he learned the news of Katie's disappearance, and she believed it was all true.

Downstairs, she could hear her mom fire up the Dyson and start her twelfth pass of the house. Dust didn't have a chance in this house when there was a crisis. She'd started the first round this morning, right after her dad had left the house to attend a meeting with the Shadows—all the Shadows and the other Leos. It was the first time he'd ever had a meeting with all of them in the whole fifty-seven years he'd been Leo, but she knew the exact reason they were meeting—Katie wasn't an isolated incident.

Why would they call a meeting for one missing female cat? Short answer? They wouldn't. There had to be something huge going on.

Christ, she felt like she was going insane. Stuck in her skin. Stuck in her head, her mind taking her to places where Katie had been beaten, raped, or worse…

Killed.

Neve jumped off her bed and yanked open the door, rushing down the stairs to her father's office. He was sitting behind that solid oak desk she associated with power and love and protection. His cologne complimented his natural scent, both fragrances covering every square inch of the wood-paneled room she'd found a haven in since she was young enough to want to go to her daddy.

Her father still looked the same as he always did. Short brown hair. Pale green eyes. There was something she hadn't noticed before, though—small lines of stress branching out from the corner of his eyes. She paused at the door, suddenly unsure whether she should go in or stay out. He just seemed to have a lot on his mind, and she didn't want to add to that unnecessarily. Turning, she considered going to speak to her mother instead, but she and that female didn't often see eye to eye on stuff. She couldn't imagine them having a heart to heart now.

"Come in, kitten, and close the door behind you," he said, and she jerked back to look at him. "Come on," he added warily.

She padded in, shutting out the noise of the vacuum cleaner.

"Your mother," he started with a heavy sigh.

She bobbed her head. "She's been at it since you left this morning."

He grunted, and the usual secret smile they shared when discussing her mother's cleaning habit was achingly absent. She folded herself onto the sofa, turning her body so her back was against the arm, her legs close to her chest and her arms wrapped around them. She wanted to know what happened at the meeting, but she knew her dad well enough not to push. He'd tell her when he was good and ready.

She wasn't sure how long they sat there for. Him, looking down at the blotter, staring at nothing. Her, staring at him and biting her tongue. It was worse down here than locked in her room with all that silence.

Her dad heaved a sigh. "I suppose you want to know what happened this morning."

She shrugged. "If you want to tell me."

A ghost of a smile appeared on his lips, disappearing just as quickly. "Knowing you, you won't leave until I tell you."

Another shrug. Even though she was burning to know, she said, "You don't have to, Dad." *But I wish you would.*

His elbows hit the blotter, his hands linking as he leaned his chin against them. "I think I do. This concerns you too."

Oh, God. "What happened at the meeting?"

"Katie isn't the first female to go missing."

Her pulse roared suddenly in her ears, her heart hammering against her ribs. Her suspicions had been confirmed, but from the look on his face, there was more. Sucking in a steadying breath, she asked slowly, "And she probably won't be the last either, right?"

"That's my girl," he said softly. "Thinking like a Leo." He picked up his letter opener, a jaguar stretched out along the handle, poised to pounce. Pressing the point to his index finger, he rotated the blade slowly. "There was another girl, Elsie, from California. And a female named Chastity too."

"Jesus." She looked into his dull eyes. "How many more?" she croaked.

He shook his head. "We don't know. There could be dozens for all we know."

"Surely someone's going to report them missing soon."

He dipped his chin to show he was listening, encouraging her to talk like he'd been doing since she'd first shown interest in leadership.

"Holy shit."

He frowned a little, but said nothing about her language, which told her a hell of a lot about his state of mind. Very carefully, he placed the letter opener down onto the blotter and clasped his hands. "Listen, I want you to do something for me."

"Anything, Dad."

His expression smoothed, became remote. "I can tell you right now, you're not going to like what I have to say." He paused, no doubt letting her have a moment to digest his words. "I know you're an independent female, and I hate to do this to you, but I don't want you going anywhere unaccompanied."

She sat forward, bringing her feet to the floor. Wait, that sounded a lot like she was going into lockdown.

"I've asked someone to stop by here tonight, to meet you."

"For what purpose?" Her palms were suddenly sweaty. She rubbed the excess moisture off on the top of her thighs.

He blew out a breath. "He's going to be your bodyguard until all this blows over."

She swallowed, her chest suddenly feeling a little tight. "You can't be serious."

"I'm very serious, Neve. You're not just my only daughter, you're also my only child. I can't leave you unprotected."

"But this is… this is crazy!"

He conceded her statement with a nod. "Maybe so, but I'm not willing to risk it."

"I'll be careful," she countered. "I'll stay home. I'll stay in my room if that's what you want me to do, but please don't let me be babysat like a little girl."

"I'm sorry, Neve, but the answer is no. Look how easily Katie was taken. She was driving from our place to hers. That's only about three miles, and somehow, she got abducted in that time."

She looked around the office, grasping at counterarguments and searching for loopholes. The thing was, there were none. Her father was thinking like a levelheaded Leo should, protecting his most precious commodity—her. There would be no swaying him from this.

"Please," she said—begged. "There has to be another way. There has to be…"

"My decision is final, Neve," he said, his voice taking on that quality all Leos possessed.

She rubbed her brow. "Who? Who's coming to babysit me? Please don't tell me it's that asshat Randall."

"What's wrong with Randall?" he asked.

"What's right with Randall is a better question," she grumbled. "He's barely competent at the best of times."

"That's not true, Neve. I wouldn't keep incompetent cats around me."

Well, he had her there. She just hadn't liked the guy since he tormented her when they were in elementary school together.

"Who is it then? Roman? Taylor?"

If it were one of her two regular sparring partners, it would make the task more bearable.

Just then, there was a knock on the office door. Neve turned her head toward the sound, noting the absence of the Dyson's motor filling the hall. The leather chair creaked as her father stood up and came around the desk to let in his guest. Neve's muscles suddenly felt like they were stretched too tightly on her bones, the tension jacking up her senses.

As the door swung open, the first thing she noticed was the scent of the male on the other side. The next thing was the huge shadow that was cast on the floorboards.

"Sonofabitch," she whispered under her breath.

14

DRAKE

Drake froze in the doorway of the Leo's office, his nostrils flaring as he took in the scent of the female sitting on the couch.

What the fuck is she *doing here?*

"Drake, thank you for coming," Greg said, stepping aside and inviting him in.

"Yeah, no problem," he replied, unable to take his eyes off Neve.

Clearly following his gaze, Greg said, "And this is my daughter, Neve. Neve, this is Drake. He's the captain of the Revenant."

His *daughter?* On instinct, he thrust his hand out. She looked at it for a long minute before sliding her much smaller hand into his. That same frisson of awareness sparked along his nerve endings as skin met skin.

"Nice to meet you."

"Likewise," she replied, pulling her hand free and folding her arms tightly.

"Please, take a seat," Greg said, directing him to a chair stationed opposite a huge oak desk. He sat, turning it so he could see where Neve was parking it.

Sofa.

Got it.

"I suppose you're wondering why I asked you here tonight," the Leo said.

Wondering, yes, but he had a pretty good idea of the why. After the meeting that morning, Greg had lingered long after everyone had left, even his own Shadow. When they were alone, Greg had asked him to swing by the pride house. He said he didn't trust that the Trinity were doing all they could do, and honestly, Drake couldn't have agreed more.

"You want me to watch your daughter," he surmised, shocking the shit out of Greg. "Even if this goes directly against the Trinity's wishes."

Yes, sir.

Sorry, sir.

You were that *transparent.*

His expression of shock only lasted a moment before it was smoothed away into a

business-like calm. "I know this is highly unorthodox, but you have to understand that Neve is everything to me and my mate."

He glanced over at her, trying to gauge how she was feeling about it all. If the way she was glaring at the hardwood like it had just insulted her mother was anything to go by, she wasn't down with the situation any more than he was…

Which was, of course, a lie. He hadn't been able to stop thinking about the female. Her spirit incited him, the spark of her soul inflamed him, and if he wasn't careful, she would brand herself on his soul.

"How do you feel about it?" he asked. Her head jerked up like she hadn't been aware that he'd directed his question at her. She glanced at her dad briefly before settling her green-eyed gaze back onto his face.

"I think it's a terrible waste of your time."

He crossed his leg at the ankle, leaning back in his chair. "It may be, but if it keeps you safe, isn't that a good thing?"

Once more, her eyes made a trip to her dad then back to him. This time, her gaze skimmed down his body, like she was wondering where he kept all the weapons.

Twin SIG Sauers under his arms.

Switchblade on his ankle.

Fucking pissed off black jaguar on the inside.

Check. Check. And check.

"This is ridiculous." To her dad, she said, "Please. There has to be another way."

"I wish there was, Neve, but you are my number one priority. Getting Katie back is of course going to be my main concern right now, but you will always be my number one."

A look of disgust made its way onto her face, her eyes narrowing. She'd been painted into a corner, and he recognized her hate because it was something he fucking despised, too.

"What if Drake doesn't even want to do this?" she asked, standing up from the couch smoothly and beginning to pace. "Isn't he too busy? He's the captain of the Revenant, for Christ's sake."

Everything she said was true. He was too busy. He was so fucking busy trying to get a grip on what was happening to these females that he sometimes couldn't see much else. But the thought of one of his brothers looking out for her instead, spending time with her? That was a huge *fuck no*. He could've asked Sasha to watch her, but she was better at brooding in a darkened room than looking after a female like Neve.

"It would be my honor to do this for you," he said before he could stop the words. "For your father and for the pride," he tacked on.

"There," Greg said. "He's fine with it. You're the only one who's rocking the boat here, Neve."

She stared at him intensely, those green eyes of her piercing through his usually impenetrable armor. The truth he couldn't reveal was that he considered Neve to be his.

He frowned. *Where the fuck did that thought come from?*

"There was one other thing I wanted to discuss with you, Drake." Greg's statement brought his head around.

"Of course."

Greg studied him for a moment, scrutinized him. "Not the Trinity?"

Drake kept his expression neutral. "I don't protect them—that's not my job. *You* are my duty, you and the prides. Always. That's why the Revenant exist."

The Leo nodded, clearly satisfied with his answer. "I attempted to bring this up at the meeting, but the idea of individual prides proactively protecting their females didn't seem to be up for discussion."

"Everyone else is too fucking frightened to challenge the Trinity," Drake replied in a low drawl.

"Yes. Well, *I'm* not going to leave the Black Claws unprotected. I want to have some sort of security plan implemented, effective immediately." Greg spoke in a strong, steady voice. "We need something like an information pack to send out to the entire pride, advising them on how to best protect our females."

"I think that's definitely something we should look into," he replied, sitting forward in his seat. "Firstly, I'd like—" He paused when he heard the office door shut behind him. Neve had stepped out, clearly pissed off that she was essentially under house arrest now.

Turning back to Greg, he continued, "As I was saying, I'd like a curfew to be put in place. All the girls who have gone missing have ghosted under the cover of darkness. Clearly, that's what the kidnappers want. If none of your females are out at night, that should reduce the risk exponentially."

"Agreed," the Leo replied, leaning back in his leather chair and crossing his legs—his ankle on his knee. He scooped up a letter opener that was shaped like a pouncing jaguar and toyed with the pointed end. "I'd also like to have regular check-ins, a number the girls can text to let the Shadows know they're okay."

Drake dipped his chin, surprised by the Leo's accurate evaluation of the situation.

"I can do one better," he heard himself say. "I'll have the Revenant take care of this personally. I'll have one of my team set up a dummy number. Members of the Black Claw pride can text it, knowing they're speaking directly to the Revenant." He paused, unsure how much more to tell the Leo. Finally, he decided on, "As far as I'm concerned, the Trinity have created the environment for these abductions."

"How so?" The Leo's eyes were shrewd, catching every single detail and cataloguing it.

"The distance between the prides and their Shadows is too great. Having that distance is an open invitation to any shifter or human to just waltz on in and take what they want."

"Well, at least we agree on this."

The conversation went on for another hour, until Greg had drawn up a missive that outlined everything they'd discussed. Things were about to get shaken up, but Drake was prepared for the blowback from the Trinity. Greg placed down his Mont Blanc pen and flipped back through the hand-written notes he'd taken.

"Thank you, Drake."

"You're welcome, sir." He stood up and offered the Leo his hand. "I'll swing by tomorrow morning to figure out a schedule with Neve, unless you need me to begin immediately?"

"No, tomorrow will be fine. It's late. She's not going anywhere tonight."

"I'll be around after breakfast then."

"There's no one else I'd trust to watch her," he told him solemnly. "And I know she can be spirited, but she's got a good head on her shoulders. She just lets her heart take over sometimes."

"I'll look after her like she's my own. No, don't get up, sir. I can see myself out."

Drake opened up the office door, expecting to see Neve ready to go for round two, *wanting* her to be there to go for round two, but she was curiously absent. Turning toward the entry foyer, his nostrils flared at the smell of roast lamb lingering in the air. He reached for the front door, but paused when another scent hit his senses, making his blood singe with lust.

Night-blooming jasmine.

Turning his head, he looked into the darkened living room, until he settled his gaze on Neve. He strolled in, shutting the double doors behind him. A small sound of protest escaped her, but she made no other motion to stop him.

He blinked, letting his cat closer to the surface to see through the near-darkness.

"What are you doing?" she asked.

He leaned against the wall beside the door, casually crossing his arms. "Why didn't you tell me?"

"About what?"

He held back the urge to roll his eyes at her. "About who you really are."

"Why would it matter who I was? What would you have done if you'd known I was the Leo's daughter? Treated me differently?"

His hackles rose at the challenge in her voice at the same time as his cock stirred. Damn, this female stoked the fire in his blood.

"It would've been good to know."

She shook her head slowly, her eyes finding her clenched hands in her lap. "Who I am isn't what's important. Finding Katie…" She wiped under her eyes angrily, her back straightening as if she'd mentally locked down her emotions and looked back at him. "Finding Katie is all that matters."

He fought the instinct to go to her, to wrap her in his arms. Which was fucking weird. He never coddled females. He never cared enough to want to…

But Neve got under his skin.

He pushed off the wall and approached, before kneeling in front of her. Very gently, he eased her knees apart and wedged himself in closer. She watched him with skeptical eyes.

"We'll get her back."

"How do you know that?" Her hair fell across her face with the violence of her words.

Slowly, so he didn't startle her, he tucked the strands back behind her ear. She was a cornered animal. Her instinct to bite rather than accept the kindness teetered on a sharp edge. She stunned him when she sucked in a breath as his fingers lingered on her cheek, and he repeated the motion, marveling at the smoothness of her skin.

"I swear to you we will."

His words broke the spell, and she eased back, breaking the contact.

"Why?" she demanded. He frowned. "Why are you taking this so personally? You don't know Katie, and you don't know me."

He could physically feel his expression shutter, her question hitting way too close to home for his liking. Surging to his feet, he yanked open the living room doors and strode out, his boots hitting the floor like thunderclaps.

15

NEVE

Neve blinked at the sudden spill of light invading her retinas, the doors Drake had thrown open still swinging from the force. She sucked in a deep breath, but it did nothing to dispel the adrenaline pinging around her body. Adrenaline and… *want*.

"There you are, Neve," her mother said, appearing in the doorway and dragging her mind away from the Shadow. "Are you ready to eat?"

"I'm not hungry, Mom."

Her mom let out an exasperated sigh. "You need to eat, darling."

"I'm not hungry," she repeated, her words stronger this time. All she could think of was Katie locked away somewhere, scared and starving. Her pulse suddenly became a tangible knocking against her throat. She stood up. "I just need to get out of here," she announced. "Excuse me."

She flung open the front door and walked out onto the porch, planting her hands on the railing and leaning into them. Sucking in a few mouthfuls of cool night air, she looked up to find Drake standing at the bottom of the stairs, his eyes reflecting the light coming from the house.

"What are you doing out here?" she demanded, embarrassed she'd been caught less than composed for a second time in an hour.

"I could ask you the same thing."

She narrowed her eyes at him. "You're infuriating."

His mouth flexed into a sinful smile. "I've never been called that before. Stubborn. Unyielding. *Hard.*" *Jesus.* "All of those things." He climbed the steps, and she turned to face him. "But never infuriating. I think most people would be too afraid to tell me that to my face."

She darted her gaze to his mouth and let out a shuddering breath.

"Why are you out of the house by yourself?"

"I'm not by myself. You're here," she replied sweetly.

"You know what I mean."

She bristled, but kept her anger locked down. "I can look after myself."

"Your father has given me a direct order to guard your," his eyes drifted down hungrily, "*body*, and I'm a real stickler for rules and order."

She glared at him. "I just bet you are, but you should know I'll make your life a nightmare."

His mouth curled into a mocking smile. "You already do, *sweetheart.*"

Shaking her head, she said, "I don't need you here when I'm at home. I don't even know why you're still here, lurking outside the front of my house like a goddamn stalker."

"Your father wants me with you twenty-four-seven, so you'd better get used to seeing my face."

She didn't miss the fact he didn't answer her other question. "I still want my privacy."

"Bathroom and shower breaks. All other times, you're going to think I'm glued to your ass."

Wow. That was an interesting visual, but it wasn't wholly unappealing. He was an exceptional looking male, even dressed in a short-sleeved black Henley and beat to shit jeans.

He folded his arms, his biceps bulging, the strongly corded muscles of his forearms pushing against his skin. "Why are you looking at me like that?" he asked in a slow drawl.

"No reason," she replied with a casual shrug.

"Liar."

She frowned and stepped around him, coming up short when he grabbed her by the bicep.

"Where are you going?"

She shrugged out of his grip. "I need to walk." She sauntered off before he could stop her, but he still followed. She approached the edge of the driveway where the forest inched into existence. Looking out into the darkened trees, she inhaled the scent of pine and loam. Fall was sitting heavily in the air, the promise of colder weather nipping at its heels.

"I need to get out of here," she said softly—mostly to herself, although there was no doubt Drake had heard it, too. She turned back to find he'd moved closer to her without her knowledge. "I need to get out of my head for a bit."

She didn't know how else to articulate her needs, but it felt as if she was trapped inside her skull with the same what-ifs cutting laps through her gray matter. There were only so many times you could examine everything, but then the universal truth remained the same—the past couldn't be changed. What was done was done, and there was only one way to go from there—forward.

"You want to go for a run?"

She nodded, and he sighed.

"Let me tell your father where we're going."

Of course he was coming with her. "Fine," she replied dryly, hooking her thumbs into the waistband of her pants as he stalked away. Dragging them down her legs, her panties followed, and she put them both into the crook of a nearby tree. Her skin broke out in goose bumps as the cool air scrambled to reach every inch of her. Shucking her shirt and bra, she walked a few steps into the forest and let her cat's will roll through her.

Pain licked through her body, starting at her fingertips and working up her arms. When it got to her shoulders, the joints that had already had the *oh-shit* pain treatment began to ache—like the marrow in her bones was taking cover in another part of her body in protest.

Down her torso, the ripple continued, her skin hypersensitive in its wake. Surging further still, it buckled her knees and made her calves ache. When the sensation got to her feet, she watched her toes change shape, turning into her cat's. The long claws that sprouted from the nail beds were long, black, and wickedly curved.

Her muscles began to twitch and cramp, knocking her onto all fours, the pain riding her in relentless cresting waves. Neve embraced it, shutting her eyes and seeing her cat creeping forward. Her eyes flew open as a series of loud snaps splintered her awareness. She blinked, her range of colors falling away until all that was left was desaturated blues and grays.

Behind her, careful footsteps eased over the ground, and she glanced over her now feline shoulder, a long hiss escaping her throat.

"Easy, Neve," Drake said, coming to an abrupt stop, his hands lowered and loose. "I'll wait here until you're done."

She huffed and turned back around, her skin twitching as her fur came in. It felt as if a blanket of ants was being laid down upon her, the crawling, itching sensation dissipating a few seconds later.

She opened her mouth to crack her new jaw and let out a soft chuff to let Drake know she was done. Getting to her feet, she stretched out her body, front legs first, then the rear, her tail swishing as she became grounded in her feline body.

Understanding she should wait so she didn't incur the wrath of Drake, she did her best to ignore the grunts of pain behind her and began washing one of her forepaws. She paid particular attention to the soft fur and webbing between her feline toes. She'd just begun on the other one when he huffed behind her. She turned and blinked. Then blinked some more, something primal and basic warming her blood so quickly, it went from lukewarm to nuclear in a heartbeat.

The giant black cat strolling toward her was bigger than any other she'd ever seen before—even bigger than her father—and she inhaled deeply, taking Drake's dark spiced scent into her lungs. A part of her recognized what he was, what he could be to her, but another part of her was terrified of that reality.

Strong.

Powerful.

Mate.

She shook her head, shifting the traitorous thoughts of her cat away from her frontal lobe. She had to shatter that notion before it could take root. She spun around and bolted through the trees, her pace increasing when Drake let out an angry roar that echoed around the forest.

16

DRAKE

Drake had seen a lot, experienced a lot too, but coming face-to-face with his blood-bonded mate wasn't something he'd either expected or been prepared for. As soon as he'd seen Neve shift, as soon as his cat had seen hers, that was it.

Arnasa.

The word was a sweet whisper in his head. It was something he never thought he'd find. Instinct overrode everything else his human brain came up with and replaced it with just one thing—claim her before another male could. Whether Neve had been conscious of the connection or not, her cat had. He knew because she'd released a bonding scent that marked his brain and seared his soul. Neve was his, and he was hers.

Arnasa…

Males protected their females, but Shadows worshiped theirs.

He let out a furious roar when she turned around and ran, disappearing into the underbrush like a wraith. His desire to protect her was a scream in his head, and the fact she'd run from him triggered his impulse to hunt her down and mark her…

No! That would only scare her.

Despite the internal debate, he took off after her, slamming into the low brush and sliding through the narrow passes between trees. There was no discernable path to follow, but with his mate's scent in his nose, he knew exactly where he was going.

After only a few minutes of running, he burst through a clearing and drew to a stop. Neve was standing in the center—waiting for him—the moonlight filtering down from the canopy to play over her dove-gray pelt. He'd never seen a cat so pale, nor so beautiful. Rosettes appeared near her flanks, the slightly darker coloration complemented by the silvery satin ribbons of her fur.

Making sure to keep a lid on his inner caveman, he stalked toward her, his tail swishing in annoyance. Her ears flattened against her skull in warning as he came closer, his instinct to mark her still warring with the more civilized part of his brain.

Walking down the length of her body, he sniffed her and got a lot of hissing and growling in return. And as he neared her tail, she whipped around without warning and lunged for his throat.

He huffed in amusement as he danced back a step, sweeping her paws out from under her and pinning her to the ground. With his paws on her shoulders, he held her in check as he dropped his head and sniffed at her, rubbing the side of his face against her cheek. He hadn't intended to go in so strongly, but he found himself unable to resist touching her, curious to see if she accepted it or not. It was when her breath stopped heaving in and out of her lungs that he realized she'd frozen in place.

Pulling back, he stared into her green eyes and eased back, shifting his weight from her shoulders. For a beat, she did nothing, but a warning snarl rippled out from her throat, and she swiped at him, her protracted claws catching him on the nose.

He jerked back, the sting an annoying throb rather than an all-out scream of pain, which it could so easily have been. Neve had teeth and fangs, and he'd been awfully close to her mouth. She hadn't bitten him, though, but he had deserved the swipe on his nose.

He concentrated on her, trying to burrow into her mind as he'd tried before. This time, instead of an impenetrable wall, he got flashes of her cat's thoughts. They were base and crude, like a child trying to draw the inside of a computer motherboard, but he sensed the direction of her thoughts—she was attracted to him, wanting him to claim her, but Neve was blocking a lot of the impulses.

With blood slowly dripping from his wound, he jerked his head back in the direction of her house. Her eyes shifted over his shoulder before she bobbed her head and started back. He fell onto her right side, quickening his pace until he was half a length ahead. When they emerged from the edge of the forest, she approached the tree where she'd left her clothes and jumped up, putting her forepaws up against the trunk and pulling the fabric free with her teeth, letting them drop to the ground.

He waited until she shifted back before he got back onto two feet himself. Luckily for him, he was marginally faster at shifting than she was. She was still in recovery from the change—doubled-over and breathing heavily—when he nabbed her clothes and held them under her nose. She glared at him, straightening her body slowly like pain was still licking through her muscles and bones. He was happy to just let her get dressed, but when she drifted her green-eyed gaze back down his body, lingering on his hips, his cock stirred to life, and her body let out more of that delicate scent of hers.

Driven by instinct, he corralled her closer to the tree at her back.

"What are you…" She licked her lips. "If this is about that swipe on the nose, you deserved it." Her words wavered, and he knew how much he was affecting her.

Planting both hands on the trunk of the tree, he leaned in and was rewarded when she tilted her head back to keep holding his eye. His girl wasn't a wilting flower, but then again, he already knew this. He sniffed the length of her neck, feeling her sharp exhale of breath when he did.

"Don't do that again," he growled, opening his mouth over her throat and clamping down on the skin between her shoulder and neck with enough pressure to make her still, but not enough to draw blood. It was the only way she'd understand how serious he was. She couldn't run off on him, and when the human wouldn't listen, the cat would. "Ever."

There was a small hiss before she shoved him away from her. Her eyes said she was pissed off, but her body and the heat it was throwing off said he could do that and more to her and she would welcome him.

Picking up her clothes, he tossed them to her. "Get dressed, *sweetheart.*"

17

KATIE

Everything was off-kilter, including Katie's own innate sense of time. Being left in murky dull light didn't help things, and neither did the infrequent meal times. She sighed and leaned back against the cinderblock wall. The cold seeped in almost immediately, chilling her down to her bones.

"Are you awake?" she asked Elsie. They'd been sticking together a lot more since their last visitor.

"Yeah," came the slow, sleepy reply. Absently, Katie wondered whether they were drugging the water to keep them all docile and compliant. She was certainly suffering from increased lethargy, but with nothing to do but sit in a cold cell, sleeping seemed to be the only real way to pass the time.

"Where do you think we are?"

"Hell."

Katie frowned. "I mean in the country. You said you were taken from California, but I'm from Wyoming."

Her cellmate looked at her with dull eyes. "Does it really matter where we are?"

"I guess not," she whispered back.

Silence fell like an uncomfortable blanket between them. Katie knew everyone was hungry, could feel it like she could feel the desperation or the acceptance that maybe none of them were going to get out of there.

She zeroed in on the cell opposite theirs when a feminine groan cut through the silence. A few seconds later, there was another one, followed by a grunt, and Katie stiffened.

She knew that sound.

Beside her, Elsie straightened as she realized what it was too. Minutes skipped by until the unmistakable sound of popping bones confirmed what she suspected. There was a whispered hush of fur along concrete, of claws clicking on a hard surface, before Katie saw the shadows stir and move as the female in the cell used the last reserves of her strength to shift into her jaguar.

Somehow, her very human cellmate hadn't woken with the noise, but Katie knew the exact moment she did.

A sharp inhale of breath.

A trembling keening.

Finally, the scream.

Around the room, everyone jerked to attention, their heads turning in the direction of the cell.

Another scream.

Shoes scraping along the hard floor.

Katie threw her hands over her ears at the deafening roar that shook the metal bars in their housings.

And then it was a gurgling breath—the death rattle of a human being fighting to live, but dying in the jaws of a hungry jaguar that shared its skin with a frightened young woman.

Once the sound of gasping died off, there was a rip and a gush, carotid blood flowing. She knew by the smell—the woman's throat had been torn out, her blood escaping in a torrent, splashing onto the rough floor.

Unwilling to watch, but equally unable to look away, she forced herself to witness the woman's death. It only seemed right, considering she had been the one to give up her body to feed all of them.

The jaguar split open the human's stomach and started to feast on her organs. Katie should've been horrified, and honestly she was, but that wasn't the only emotion that bubbled up inside her. The most shocking one was jealousy and possessiveness.

She was hungry.

She wanted to be the one eating.

But what did that make her? Just another monster like the human men who had abducted all of them. The scent of spilled bowels and blood permeated through the basement, but the jaguar still ate, gorging herself. Idly, Katie wondered what the men would do when they found them both—one nothing but black fur and a pissed off attitude, and the other imitating a puddle.

She drifted her attention up when boots hit the floorboards above, walking in the direction of the basement door. The jaguar hissed into the gloom, protecting her kill, even though nobody had made a move closer to her. Would they force her to shift back? She couldn't imagine them being okay with a caged weapon—that was if they even knew what they were. Then again, they were all caged weapons, weren't they? Except, instead of being able to function normally, they were all hamstrung by circumstance. Starvation caused weakness, not just in their human bodies, but also in their cats. That female must've used the last of her reserves to shift, but the reward had been great.

Katie squeezed her eyes shut, but it did nothing to stop the sounds of hurried chewing, of bones crunching and muscle ripping. The door to the basement swung open, and a curse floated down the stairs.

Suddenly, light flooded room, and Katie shielded her face with the sudden onslaught. She got her first good look at Elsie, committing the female's face to her memory. If she was right and they weren't getting out of there, she wanted someone to remember her.

Then her eyes went over the massacre that had been committed because there was no other option. Survival was survival, and the will to live was only slightly easier when you had a side to your body that enjoyed the taste of raw meat and spilling fresh blood.

She forced herself to look at *everything*. The human girl's face was a mask of horror. Her death had been terrifying, and it showed. Her throat was missing and blood covered her from her neckline down. The bottom of her shirt was ripped, slashed apart by claws, and her stomach was open and congealing. It had been a quick kill—a merciful kill, really—and the eating had been done with both speed and care, given that no other part of her had been touched.

Listening to it, though, it had been horrific. Seeing it in full color made her realize that although the female hadn't wanted to kill the woman, she did because it was the raging hunger of her beast that had demanded it.

Boots thundered down the treads, coming to a stop. A man she'd never seen before glanced around, his eyes fixing on the cell floor filled with blood.

"God*dayumn*!"

He turned and rushed up the stairs, returning a few moments later with Cowboy. Katie fixed her stare on the little river of blood that was now inching its way to the drain in the middle of the floor.

"Ho-ly shit," Cowboy drawled, drawing out the syllables.

"She ate her. The bitch *ate* her," the other man breathed.

"I think you're forgetting that some of these women *aren't* women, Ricky," Cowboy replied, his tone bored.

Ricky lifted his cap off his head to wipe away the sweat. "Yeah, but I…" He hesitated. Swallowed. "I didn't think they'd *eat* one another."

Cowboy's eyes gleamed as they caught the light, and the sight of it made Katie's shoulders stiffen. They'd *gleamed*, like a cat's. She inhaled to catch his scent, but blood was saturating her senses.

"What's Boss going to say?" Ricky asked, crouching down in front of the cell, cocking his head to the side as he sized up the jaguar still crouching in front of her kill. She hissed at him, her huge fangs stained with blood, red-tinted saliva dripping from her jaws.

"Don't get too close, asshole," Cowboy warned.

Ignoring the warning, Ricky shuffled a little closer, and the jaguar's ears flattened against her skull, her tail swishing impatiently. Her green eyes were fixed on him, filled with the instinct to defend her kill at all costs. Another growl vibrated from her throat, and Ricky laughed, waving his fingers in her direction.

Faster than Katie thought possible, the female swiped at him through the bars, her claws digging into the muscles of his forearm and tearing them from the bone. Ricky's howl of pain echoed around the room as he slapped his hand over the gushing wound. Blood fell freely from between his fingers, dripping onto the floor at his feet.

She jumped when there was a loud *bang*, the sharp smell of gunpowder accompanying the gunfire. The jaguar collapsed in a boneless heap, mere inches from her kill. Stunned, Katie turned her head to find Cowboy holding the gun, smoke still barreling from its end.

Reaching behind him, he holstered the weapon and said to Ricky, "Clean this shit up."

Katie awoke to the sound of her cell door opening. Keeping her eyes shut and breathing even, she waited for whoever had come in to take their pick. She expected it to be her. So far, she'd remained untouched, and it was only a matter of time before that changed. Heavy footsteps came closer, but it was the shocked gasp that made Katie's eyes open.

Ricky was removing Elsie from the cell. His whole forearm was bandaged up, and he held it gingerly at his side as he used his gun as a traffic wand. Katie darted her gaze to Elsie, who seemed to be working on autopilot, moving when told, stopping when told. The cell door shut with a *clang* behind them, and then another across the room opened.

Katie didn't understand what was going on or why Elsie had been moved, but she began to shiver as the reality that she was alone began to sink in. She shut her eyes tightly and prayed for the end to come quickly. Waiting like this was torture. Not knowing was torture. Death would be a release she had no right to hope for.

Some hours later, at least she thought it was hours, the door to her cell opened once more, and she fought the urge to cringe. Forcing herself to remain still, she waited for the hand to reach for her. She waited for the pain and suffering. Instead there was a small *thump*, and the cell door shut. When the footsteps ebbed away and the basement was once again silent, Katie opened her eyes and sat up. On the bare concrete, mere feet from her, was a bundled form.

Katie merely watched her for a moment before getting onto her hands and knees and inching herself closer. She reached out and touched the shock of black hair that was falling out of a set of pigtails. Her eyes skimmed down her body, looking for any signs of abuse, but her clothes were intact, her jeans whole, and her running shoes still on her small feet.

Biting her lip, she reached out and touched the girl on the shoulder, rolling her over onto her back. She got a good look at her face then, the freshness of youth written all over her. Jesus, she was so small, probably only about ten years old. One inhale confirmed she was also a shifter, but where had she come from?

The girl's eyes fluttered open then, slowly, like she was waking from a pleasant dream. That sense of ease didn't last for long, though. As she drew in a deep breath, a frown appeared. She shot up, clutching her head as a headache no doubt spiked in her frontal lobe. She'd obviously been drugged. How else could they subdue a shifter, even one as small as she was? Her eyes widened as she saw Katie then darted around their cell.

"Where am I?"

Katie's eyes slid shut. Even her voice sounded too small for her body. When she opened them, she found the young female's blue eyes on her face.

"Where am I?"

Katie had to clear her throat twice before she could speak. This shouldn't be happening to her. She was too young.

"I don't know," she told the girl honestly. "I don't know where we are, only that we're here, and it's going to be okay."

The girl got busy looking around again, her gaze eventually bouncing back to Katie.

"What's your name?" she asked, trying to distract her from thinking too much.

"Luce."

"Luce," she repeated, smiling gently. "That's a lovely name."

She swallowed visibly, then said, "What's your name?"

"I'm Katie. It's nice to meet you."

Luce skimmed the room again, squinting to see past the shadows. "What time is it?"

Katie shook her head. "I don't know, kitten. And I don't know how long I've been here for either."

Luce hugged her knees to her chest. "I want my brother," she whimpered.

Her brother? Not her mother? Unless she didn't have a mom…

Scooting closer to her, she got within a few inches of her, not quite touching for fear of scaring her. "I know you do, Luce, but since he's not here, I'll look after you, okay? And then when we get out of here," *if* they got out of here, "I'll take you to him myself."

"Promise?"

Katie had to swallow past the lump that had formed in her throat. "I promise." She stared ahead, finding Elsie propped up against the wall in the cell opposite. Her eyes were dead, but she still breathed. Katie would never become like that, she'd decided. She would fight until the end, if not for herself, then this poor young female who didn't deserve to be there. "I promise."

18

JETT

Jett swiped the towel from the arm of the treadmill he was pounding into the basement floor, wiping the sweat from his brow. Picking up his phone, he put the call on speaker so he didn't sweat all over it.

"Jett?" Katya asked. The tightness in her voice made all the muscles in his body seize. What the fuck could've happened now?

"What's happened?"

There was a sob, a sound that cracked Jett's heart clean in two. If their poor excuse for a mother had fucking OD'd on them, *again*, he was going to go over there and resuscitate her so he could kill her himself.

"Tell me, Kat."

A rustle of clothing crept over the line. "I just got a call from Luce's school."

"Is she in trouble?" he asked. "Whatever happened, Luce isn't responsible. She's a good kid. She—" *Doesn't stand a chance.*

"They called to see if she was sick and staying home."

"Is she sick?"

"No. I sent her to school like I always do, but she… she never made it."

Jett's center of gravity suddenly shifted, and he pitched forward, catching himself on the arms of the treadmill. "What?"

"I don't know where she is, Jett. Oh, God… What if, what if something has happened to her?"

Bile rose in the back of his throat, but he got his shit together. "Kat? *Kat!*" When he was sure she was listening to him, he added, "Hey, I need you to keep it together. I need you to…" *Fuck!* "I need you to pack a bag. Pack a bag for Luce too. She'll want her stuff when we get her home. Make sure you grab her unicorn too. You know how much she likes that."

"Okay," his sister whispered. "What then? Should I get a motel for now?"

"Fuck no," he growled. There was only one way he could keep her safe, and that was here at their compound. "I'll come and get you."

"Are you sure?" Katya's voice dropped even lower, but it did nothing to disguise her terror.

"Of course. I'm leaving now. Pack quickly." He hung up the phone and took the stairs out of the basement two at a time. When he hit the kitchen, he prayed Grayson was still at home.

"Looking for me?"

Jett turned around to find just the male he was looking for. "I need to borrow your car."

Without question, Grayson reached into his pocket and pulled out his keys, tossing them at Jett. "Go and do what you have to do."

Jett clutched the keys so tightly, they bit into his hand. "I owe you, man."

"No, you don't. You're my brother. You know I'd do anything for you."

Jett strode forward, grabbing the guy by the back of the neck and pulling him close so their foreheads touched. Just as abruptly, he let go and stalked from the kitchen.

Outside, Grayson's cherry red fast-and-shiny was in the turning circle, already pointed down the driveway. Unlocking things, he got in, barely giving the engine time to really get going before he shoved it into gear and took off down the driveway. He cursed every delay while he made his way through the security gates leading onto the property. His thoughts were a mess, his vision a blur as his sole focus became getting to his childhood home and assessing the damage that had been done.

He barely slowed down once he hit the residential area, and he took the turn too quickly into the trailer park's drive. The GT's rear end kicked out, sending up a plume of dust and gravel as it drifted around the corner. He pulled up in front of the mobile home a minute later and jumped out. Katya was already outside, and she wrapped her arms around him, burying her face into his chest.

"This is my fault," she sobbed.

He rubbed circles on her back, hoping to soothe himself at the same time. His thoughts had been on some sort of sick repeat as he cycled through all the terrible shit that could've happened to his youngest sister. And the conclusion he'd reached? So help the bastard who hurt a hair on Luce's head.

"We'll get her back, Kat. I swear it," he vowed. He looked up at the mobile home. "Where's Mom? Does she know?"

His sister nodded. "I told her right after I got off the phone with you."

"And how did she take the news?"

"Like she always deals with bad news. She shot up with Richard."

"Fuck." Unwrapping Katya's arms from his torso, he put the car keys into her palm and curled her fingers around them. "Get in and lock the doors. I'll be back as soon as I can."

Her nod was slow, like she wasn't quite tracking what was happening. Touching her face softly, he said, "Don't worry, Kat. I'll take care of everything. Now, get in the car. Lock the doors." He'd go insane if Kat was taken from him, too.

Waiting until she was inside the safety of the car, he barged through the trailer door and scanned the living room. It smelled like vomit, and he let out a disgusted growl. Marching through the space, he ignored the new holes in the walls and the new stains on the old carpet runner and pushed into the bedroom. His mom and Richard were on the bed. She was lying on her back, her head on the pillow, one arm dangling off the edge. Beside her was Richard. That bastard wasn't looking too hot, judging by the vomit that was pooled around his head.

Ignoring the male currently tearing apart his family, he focused his attention on the woman who gave him life and stuck his finger under her nose to check she was still breathing. It was a weak stream of air, so he ran his fingers along her throat to take her pulse. Thready at best. Fuck. Rolling her onto her side, he kept her in the recovery position while he pulled out his phone and brought up the details of Doctor Stephen Winchester. The guy must be getting sick of seeing Jett's digits showing up on his screen.

"Doctor Winchester," came the stuffy voice.

"Doc, I need you over at my mom's mobile home."

"Jett? Of course. I'll be right over." He paused then said in a lower voice, "Suspected overdose?"

"Yeah. Hurry." He hung up the phone and glanced over at Richard. The bastard could die for all he cared. In fact, he wished he did die. At least then his mom would have a chance to get clean, because there was no way she could do it with his poisonous influence all around her.

He sat with his mother until Doc Winchester arrived fifteen minutes later. He was wearing his usual tweed three-piece suite, a red tie at his throat, and cufflinks winking at the bottom of the sleeves. He had a pair of wire-rimmed glasses that he doubted he actually needed, and an expression that spoke of his professionalism and discretion. He'd known about Jett's continued involvement with his family for the last seven years.

"How long since she shot up?"

He stood up to get out of the doc's way. "Maybe half an hour."

"Do you know what she took?" He was listening to her chest, his stethoscope plugged into his ear, his brows drawn low as he concentrated.

"I don't know, but it was probably the usual."

The doc grunted, but kept going through his checks. Jett hated that the male had to see this side of his life. Guilt and shame was a noose around his neck, and every time he had to call in the cavalry, he felt like he was less of a male in the eyes of someone as respected as the pride's doctor.

"Her vitals aren't great. I'm not going to—"

His sentence was cut short when Richard began to seize. His whole body shook, foam forming around his mouth. Jett watched with curious disinterest, his eyes locked on the guy, hoping the doctor didn't pull through with his Hippocratic Oath and decide to let the bastard just die. If he did, it would spare Jett and his sisters a whole lot of heartache. Maybe then his mom would become the woman he used to know.

"I need to stabilize him," the doctor shouted, snapping Jett back to reality. As he checked in again, the smells and sounds of the room hit him in the chest. Richard's bowels had released, the scent of his vomit and shit coating the back of Jett's tongue.

"What's happening to him, Doc?"

"Well, if I don't get any Narcan into him in the next few minutes, he's going to die."

Jett thought that sounded like the perfect thing to make his day complete, but he knew the Doc wouldn't be on board with the plan.

"Where is it?" he asked in a hollow voice.

"In my bag," he replied, trying to hold the guy in the recovery position so he didn't aspirate his own vomit and fuck up his lungs. Jett went to the brown leather doctor's bag that looked like it was out of the 1800s. Popping the thing open, he looked inside and found the vial that could bring the bastard back from the brink. He threw up a Hail Mary for at least a little bit of brain damage. Pulling out a syringe, he handed over both to the doc, not at all comfortable with the fact he knew how all of that worked. He watched with that same detachment as the doc filled the syringe, pumped out the air, and jabbed the business end into Richard's upper thigh. It took a few moments for the seizures to stop, but Jett didn't give him any more of his time. His focus now was his sisters.

"I have to go, Doc."

The male looked at him like he'd grown a second head. "Go? But where? Your mother… What…?"

He put his hands up in front of him, motioning him to stop. "I'm sorry. I've spent enough time worrying about her. I have to focus on the females who want to live. Thanks for coming."

Jett walked from the room, feeling like he was floating. Leaving the doctor to tidy up the mess was a low blow, but he couldn't stand to be in that room any longer. Pushing out of the door, he found Katya sitting stock-still in the passenger seat. He tapped on the window, indicating he wanted her to roll it down.

"Where are your bags?" he asked.

"Just inside my bedroom," she replied, reaching for the handle. "I'll get them."

"Nah, I got it," he told her, stepping back inside and walking to the room Kat had shared with Mila. Picking up the two bags, he hightailed it outside and opened up the trunk.

"Did you remember Luce's unicorn?" he asked.

"Of course."

Katya was looking back at the only home she'd ever known when he got into the car.

"What's going on, Jett, and don't tell me it's nothing."

He stiffened, but he forced his fingers—that were trying to strangle the steering wheel—to relax. "Females are being snatched. We don't know who's doing it. We don't know why."

Kat clutched the two sides of her jacket together at her throat. "Luce?" she whispered hoarsely.

"I don't know." He slammed his hands into the wheel once. Twice. And a third time.

Katya was staring at him, wide-eyed. Terrified. She turned her head to look out the window.

"What's going to happen with Mom?"

Honestly, he hoped she died from this episode of drugging. It wasn't fair to think that way, but there was nothing he could do about it. Their mother hadn't just ruined her life, she'd ruined all of theirs too when she decided to bring Richard and his drug habit into their home.

"I don't know, Kat. I just hope this is a fucking wake-up call, and she gets her shit together enough, if not for her sake, then for Luce's."

19

DRAKE

Drake growled down low in his throat as he watched Neve strip off her clothes for him. Her body was curvy, yet strength radiated from the set of her shoulders and the shape of her arms. She was built for him. He pictured himself spearing apart her legs and claiming her as his own. Of course since this was his dream, he did exactly that, pushing his broad shoulders between her thighs and opening her wider for him. Her sex was glistening as she panted—*writhed*—for him, and he was more than ready to give her what she needed.

Palming himself, he pumped once, twice, then brought himself into her soft folds, letting out a hiss when she shifted her hips to take him inside her. He drove himself to the hilt, gritting his teeth as all that warmth and wetness enveloped him.

Heaven.

He was in fucking heaven.

He began slowly, moving at a languid pace that Neve seemed to enjoy, if the sounds of her soft panting was anything to go by. In. Out. Advance. Retreat. He dropped his forehead to hers, staring into those green eyes and deciding he'd actually enjoy getting lost in there.

Lost in her.

Just lost.

Someone thumping on his bedroom door kicked his REM cycle out on its ass, and he was more than willing to give the person on the other side of the door a piece of his mind. He got himself into a sitting position and looked down, his erection punching out from the front of his hips, tenting his boxer shorts like it didn't give a damn it was only a dream.

The knocking came again, and Drake slipped from the bed, cursing whoever it was. As he yanked open the thing, he found Jett standing there, the male's blue eyes hollow, the bags under them looking like they were set up for the long haul.

"What's wrong?"

"I need to talk to you," Jett croaked.

The fact the guy didn't make a crack about Drake throwing wood told him a lot about his mental state.

"Let me put some clothes on," he replied. "I'll meet you down in the rec room." Shutting the door, he found a pair of sweats on the floor and shoved his legs into them. His dick, thankfully, had picked up on Jett's vibe and calmed the fuck down. Pulling a sweatshirt over his head, he opened up the door and walked down the stairs.

He found Jett pacing between the couches and the foosball table, agitation radiating from his body.

"If you keep doing that, you'll wear a hole in the floor," Drake drawled, folding his arms and leaning against the wall. Jett barely glanced in his direction—just kept his head down and eyes plastered to where his feet were striking the hardwood.

He inhaled deeply and got a whole lot of guilt, anxiety, and barely contained anger.

Drake straightened, his senses on high alert. "Jett, man, what's going on?"

The other male looked at him briefly, but didn't stop pacing. It was almost as if he *couldn't* stop moving. Oh, yeah, Drake knew where his boy's head was at.

"Tell me, goddamn it." It was a demand, and he expected obedience from his cat.

"Remember my sister? The one who came here over the weekend?"

Drake saw Jett pumping his hands into fists, one of the tells that his pyrokinesis ability was close to the surface, his emotions running like jet fuel in his veins. "Yeah." How could he forget those blue eyes that were so much older than the ten-year-old girl they belonged to? "Is she all right?"

Jett stopped dead and shook his head. Swallowed. Hard. "She's gone missing."

Just a few words, but Drake felt like his whole world was shifting into some alternate universe. He looked down, expecting to see the floor opening up beneath his feet, but everything was as it should be. It was just his own inner world that had fractured.

"What do you mean?" He had to ask. He had to clarify, because the truth couldn't be a reality.

"My sister Katya called me right after the school called her. Luce didn't make it to class this morning."

"Could she have gone off with some friends?"

"She doesn't have any. Our… personal circumstances are well-known in the school community. There isn't a parent who wants their kid to be friends with her."

"Fucking hell," Drake replied. Not exactly helpful, but the sentiment was fitting. "Okay, we have a pretty good window that tells us when she went missing." He glanced at his phone. "She can't have been gone for more than two or three hours. That works in our favor."

Drake could tell that Jett wasn't tracking the conversation at all. His eyes had gotten that haunted look in them, and he was clearly running through different scenarios in his head. Lord help him when he got to the one where his little sister was tortured, raped, or killed. That kind of thought process could send a male over the edge. After all, Drake had first-hand experience with that.

"Hey, Jett?" When the guy's focus didn't change, he walked up to him and touched him on the shoulder. Jett raised his head with a hiss, his fangs on display, his eyes glittering with red light. "We'll get her back. Trust me on this." When the guy remained mute, he said, "Where's your other sister?"

"Mila lives with her boyfriend, so she's safe."

"You sure about that?"

A nod. "The guy is human."

"You've met him?"

"No, but you can bet your ass I'll be paying him a visit later."

"And Katya? Where is she?"

Jett did look at him this time. "I was going to put her in one of the guest rooms. I hope that's okay. I didn't..." His voice cracked. "I can't lose her as well."

Drake squeezed his shoulder. "Of course. Of course it's all right." He pulled the male into an embrace that ended with a thump on the back. "We're family. We'll handle this together."

Drake's phone rang, and he looked down at the number on the screen. It was the Black Claw Leo. To Jett he said, "I have to take this."

Heading out of the room, he turned toward the kitchen. "Greg, how are you?" he asked when he answered the call. He walked over to the fridge and pulled out some juice. He glared at his hand as a fine tremor shook the carton. Clearly, Jett's news was still working its way through his adrenal glands. "I was just getting some breakfast, then I'll head over."

"Fine, but you should know there's been a development."

He was reaching up to grab a glass when he paused. "Is something wrong? Is Neve—"

"Neve is fine. I'm sorry. I should've thought about that before I called."

Drake let out a breath with confirmation that his girl was okay. "So what can I do for you?"

As he poured his juice, he listened as his Leo said, "I'm going away for a few days—a week, at the most."

"Where are you going?"

"Just over to New York for a business meeting," he replied. "A *human* business meeting, but my mate is coming with me—making a vacation out of it."

"And Neve?"

"Normally, she'd come with us, but she's refusing to leave in case Katie shows up."

He bit back the protective growl bubbling up his throat. "It's not safe for her to be left alone."

"Which is why I called. I know this is highly unusual, but I figured we were already breaking molds, so why not one more?"

"You want her to come and stay with me," he surmised.

"I can't expect you to just stay at my house for a week while I attend to these meetings. You obviously still have work to do, and we can't draw any more attention to what we're doing."

While a part of him was all up for having Neve a little closer, he also thought it was the worst idea on the planet. Ever. With his blooded mate under the same roof as him, he was liable to turn into an overprotective asshole who would tear out the throat of anyone who even looked at her.

Not to mention the need to get inside her at every opportunity.

"What does she have to say about it?" he asked carefully.

"She told me she hated it when she had to negotiate with me because I always get exactly what I want while she's left with nothing."

Drake had to laugh. "When do you leave?"

"Midday, actually. My business partner called an hour ago and told me of a change in the meeting times."

"I'll come and collect her," he replied, figuring he'd let the male know about Luce's disappearance in person. "See you in an hour."

He ended the call and slipped the phone back into his pocket. Stalking from the kitchen, he ran into Jett coming through the front door. He had a bag in each hand and a look of concentration on his face. Behind him, a female stepped into the house. When she saw him, though, the color drained from her face.

Jett looked anxiously between them, like Drake was some kind of wild beast that would maul his sister or something. Instead, he said, "I'm Drake. You must be Katya."

Katya's eyes darted to Jett before bouncing back to him. "Hello." She cleared her throat. "Th-thank you for allowing me to stay."

"Jett is family, which makes you family. You're welcome here for as long as you need." His eyes darted to Jett. "Make sure she understands all the rules."

"Yes, boss," he replied, dropping his gaze to the floor. "Come on, Kat."

They took off up the stairs, and Drake stared after them. He felt like this was the start of some kind of colossal change in his universe, but he couldn't put his finger on the why. Turning back, he grabbed the keys to his Escalade from a dish by the door and stepped outside. Inhaling deeply, he recognized that crispness of the breeze. Winter was well on its way.

Hooray for fucking snow.

Unlocking the SUV, he slid into all that leather and started the engine. It prowled down the drive, eating up the distance between him and Neve. Twenty minutes later, he was easing off the gas and turning down the long drive of the Leo's estate, passing through the security gates and precautions with ease. When he pulled up at the front, he sucked in a breath then let it out. The next seven days were going to be a exercise in fucking restraint.

Rose met him at the door, ushering him inside with soft-spoken words. He glanced around, hoping to catch a glimpse of Neve, but she was nowhere to be found. She was probably protesting somewhere.

"Greg is in his office," Rose told him. "You remember the way?"

"Yes, ma'am," he replied, walking down the hall before knocking on the door softly.

"Enter," Greg called, and Drake pushed into the room. His cat marched forward in his mind as it caught the scent of Neve, and he drank her in. Dressed in dark jeans and a bulky cream cable-knit sweater, she stared at him with disinterest.

"Thank you for coming," Greg said, breaking the tension.

"Of course. I'm here to serve you in any way I can." To Neve, he said, "Are you ready to go?"

She stood up. "Yeah, I am, but I don't appreciate this new level of babysitting. I can look after myself in the house, Dad."

"And what about food? You'll have to leave at some stage."

"I'll order in."

"There's only one place in town that delivers, and you hate Indian food."

She crossed her arms. "Ever heard of Uber Eats?" At her father's flat stare, she muttered, "Jesus. You know I *can* protect *myself*, right? I've been training with Roman and Taylor for nearly two years now. I know how to use a gun, and I know where to hit a guy where it hurts."

Drake bit back the snarl at the mention of the two other males. He sure as shit knew where to hit a guy where it hurt, too. "Where's your bag?" he asked gruffly, giving her an out and distracting himself while he was at it. Rage simmered in his blood, his protective instincts flaring white hot and volatile.

"I'll go and get it," she replied in a huff, leaving the room.

"She's going to be in a foul mood for a few days."

Beating back his anger, he turned back to the Leo. "I can handle her, sir. Don't worry."

"You have my number, so if you have any trouble with her, just call me and I'll lay down the law."

"We'll be fine." He looked around the office. "How did you go with the pride-wide email? Did you send one?"

"Yes, I sent it out last night after you texted me the dummy number. You should be getting texts through by this evening and then again at eight a.m. Twelve-hour check-ins along with a curfew of seven p.m."

Drake nodded, satisfied his Leo was doing everything right. "Fine." He cleared his throat. "Look, there's been a development with the abductions."

Greg's expression shifted from concerned father to concerned Leo. "Yes?"

"Another female has been confirmed as missing."

The Leo eased back in his chair, the leather creaking with the movement.

"Who?"

"Luce Harrison. She's Jett's ten-year-old sister."

"Jesus." Greg glowered at the blotter. "When did this happen?"

"Sometime this morning. She was sent to school but didn't arrive."

"And she couldn't be at a friend's house?"

"Jett's family is shunned."

"The drugs," the Leo murmured, and Drake nodded, unsurprised that his Leo knew about it.

Greg raised his gaze slowly to meet Drake's. "I should cancel this meeting in New York. My pride needs me."

"I think cowing to these bastards will be seen as a sign of weakness. Besides, no demands have been made. We don't even know who's behind this."

Greg slammed his fist onto the blotter so violently, the phone fell out of its cradle and his jaguar letter opener rolled off the desktop. "I want these bastards found and strung up by their balls."

"Understood, sir," Drake replied, seeing the cool return to the Leo. Out in the hall, Neve descended the stairs, loudly dragging a bag with her. "I guess that's my cue."

Greg stood up, straightened his jacket, and offered Drake his hand. "Thank you, Drake."

He bobbed his head. "I'll look after her as if she were my own."

And according to his cat, she already was.

20

NEVE

Neve slammed the car door and dragged her seat belt into place, restlessly tapping her fingers against her knee. She'd overheard the conversation between him and her dad, and she wasn't going to rest until she got some information. The question was whether she was going to get her answers now, or if Drake would make her sweat, *if* he told her at all.

"Are you going to tell me about the latest missing female?" Neve asked, making Drake's mouth thin, his jaw muscle flexing like he was grinding his teeth. "Well?"

"We're not talking about this." Drake's voice was a slow drawl deceptively edged with danger.

She huffed and twisted her body around to face him. "You talked about it with my father."

"He's the Leo of his pride. He needs to know."

She bit the inside of her cheek, tempering her next words. "And my gender is the target of these attacks."

He glared at her before turning his attention to the road once more. "How did you sleep last night?" he demanded.

She blinked at him, jarred by the change of subject, but her brain was already one step ahead. Her body flushed with heat as she recalled the dream she'd had of him, the dream where they'd been a lot less clothed and a lot more intimate. When she'd woken from the fantasy, she'd pinned the reason for dreaming about him on the fact they'd gone for a run together, that after they'd shifted back, she'd gotten a good look at his body.

And holy hell.

Looking like that should be illegal. He was a beautiful male, his body stacked with muscles. She wondered what his chest would've felt like under her fingers or tongue. Lower still, his abdominals were so sharp they threw their own shadows, and she'd had to curl her hands into fists, her nails biting into her palm, to stop herself from reaching for him.

He was dangerous—dangerous for her self-control because she'd never paid too much attention to males and what they could offer, but Drake was… different.

"Neve?"

"Fine," she croaked. Clearing her throat, she added, "I slept fine. Just fine."

His mouth curled into a grin. "That was a lot of fines."

She narrowed her eyes at him. "That's because I'm fine."

"You don't look *fine*." He cocked his head. "In fact, you're angry but also… aroused."

She jerked around to look at him. "I beg your pardon!"

His lids lowered, no doubt picturing exactly what had been running through her head earlier. "Am I wrong?"

Christ, his voice seemed to caress her with invisible fingers. "I'm pissed off." He smirked, and she wanted to slap it from his face. "You're enjoying this a little too much."

"Am I?" he replied in a drawl.

"You're trying to distract me from my first question."

"Is it working?"

She didn't dignify his question with an answer. He was such an asshole.

"Look, I understand why you're angry."

"Do you?" she spat. "I can't imagine you've ever been placed under house arrest and watched every single minute of the day."

"No, I haven't, but that doesn't mean I don't understand how you must be feeling. You're a strong female," he said with a smokey purr. "You like to do things when you want, how you want, and your father has put some pretty big fucking shackles on your delicate wrists and called them jewelry."

Oh, she resented that tone, but she resented the truth he spoke even more. Not bothering to give him a reply, she folded her arms and looked out the window.

"It'll be easier once we get to my compound."

A compound? She wasn't sure if that was just another word for jail.

"You'll have your own room, your own space, and as long as you don't leave the house without telling me, you can have all the freedom you want."

"That doesn't sound like freedom."

"What does it sound like to you?" he countered.

Turning to face him, she said, "Like I'm swapping one cage for another."

She tensed when he reached out and touched her knee, causing her heart to pound. She frowned at his hand, like it was solely responsible for her reaction. As if her whole body was on board with sabotaging her, her brain threw out a fantasy, one where Drake kissed her, his mouth devouring her own like he was a starving male.

"What are you thinking about, Neve?" he asked again, his voice thick—low. When she didn't immediately reply, he squeezed her thigh firmly but not painfully. "What are you thinking about?"

She wasn't about to tell him where her head really was, because that was so far in the gutter, she'd have to scrub her skin raw afterward. She wasn't sure what it was about him, but Drake teased emotions and feelings from her that no other male had been able to do. Sure, he was ornery and irritable, but she realized it was just a front. He was playing the tough guy, but underneath all that was a male who obviously cared, because why else would he be taking this situation so personally, why would he be driving her back to his own house to care for her?

Because that's what your father asked of him, a traitorous voice whispered.

She licked her lips and turned her face to him. "How much further until we get there?"

"Not long. We're taking the next exit."

They eventually turned off the highway and continued up a mountain road that wound slowly up, up, up. Drake slowed the car when they got to a set of wrought iron gates, rolling down the window to punch in a code. The gates swung open slowly, and then they were moving again.

Another set of gates-and-keypad combo later, and they rolled up a graveled circular drive where a yellow Ducati motorbike, a red GT, and twin silver Mercedes GLCs were parked out front. She eyed the cars, wondering how many Shadows lived there and who funded them.

"There are five of us," Drake murmured from beside her. "And shrewd investments in the human stock market keep us well supplied."

It was like he'd read her thoughts. Either that, or she'd spoken the words out loud without even realizing it.

"Come on. I'll show you to the guest room."

Unbuckling her belt, she got out and went around to the trunk to get her bag. But Drake was already there, throwing her duffel over his shoulder like it weighed nothing at all. As she turned around, she stared up at the red-brick mansion that looked better suited in the English countryside rather than the Wyoming wilderness. This was his *compound?* There was even a formal English rose garden planted on either side of the path, box hedges keeping the lavender from spilling out over the path. Did they have a staff here? The idea that Drake tended to the gardening seemed so ridiculous that she almost laughed.

"That's Sasha's pet project," Drake said, gesturing to the garden beds.

"Sasha?"

"I'll introduce you later. Come on."

As she walked up the path, she studied the thick windows, and if they were anything like the door directly in front of her, she suspected bulletproof glass filled the panes. They passed through the door and into a grand foyer that matched the outside façade. Warm honey-colored parquetry floor stretched from wall to wall and into the two adjoining rooms she could see. There was a fainting couch angled in the corner along with a large tapestry that depicted a pride of black jaguars hunting together hanging on the wall above a doorway in the double-height space.

In the center of the foyer was an ornate round table with a tinted glass top. It was bare, but she thought it would look nice with a vase of flowers or maybe a sculpture on there. The round rug beneath it matched the warm tones of the wood, the slightly

Greco-Roman pattern near the outer edge disappearing into floral rosettes.

"That's the rec room," Drake announced, pointing to the room on the left. She peered inside to find more of the parquetry floors as well as a huge TV and foosball table. With those large banks of windows along two sides of the room, though, she thought it looked like a formal sitting parlor, especially as there was a set of French doors leading out into what looked like another formal garden.

"And the dining room that nobody ever uses," Drake continued, walking across the foyer to a room with a large boardroom style table in the center. There were a lot of seats set around it. Maybe this was where the meeting her father had attended had happened? As she turned to leave, she glanced out one of the three floor-to-ceiling windows, gaze lingering on the garden. When the flowers were blooming, it would be amazing to see.

"And the guest wing is up here," he said, gesturing to the grand sweeping staircase in the middle of the foyer. She followed him up, his long, powerful strides taking him up to the landing in only a few seconds. She was still down in the foyer, vacillating between awe and hesitance.

"Are you coming?" His dark voice traveled down to her ears.

"Yeah, just taking everything in," she replied. Seriously, *this* was where the Shadows lived?

Putting one foot in front of the other, she padded up the stairs, reaching the landing where Drake was standing. She glanced to her left and right. There were doors going down the hallway with paintings in bulky guilt frames hanging in between them.

"This way," he told her, leading her toward a room just a little down the blood-red carpet runner. Placing her bag down, he opened the door and gestured for her to go in.

She stepped inside, finding a room that was really not prepared for a guest. The bed was a bare mattress placed into the frame of a four-poster bed in the middle of one wall, and that was it. There was no other furniture except for a small mounted TV in the corner. Drake strode toward one of the only other doors in the room and opened it up, stepping inside.

Neve moved closer and realized that was the closet. She was about to go and check it out when Drake reappeared. They stared at each other for a moment before he said, "The bathroom is through here." He gestured to the other door, and she nodded. "Do you want to have a look?"

"Maybe in a minute," Neve replied, rubbing her sweaty palms against the tops of her thighs. She was aware that it was just him and her in the room then, like her brain hadn't gotten the newsflash until now.

Obviously taking her nerves for fear, he said seriously, "You'll be safe here, Neve. I know you don't feel like you have a lot of freedom or choice right now, but this is for the best."

"You sound like my father."

He couldn't hide his grimace, like the reminder was unpalatable for some reason. "We both want the same thing, so I'll take that." He glanced at the unmade bed. "I'll go and get some sheets and a quilt."

"You don't need to do that," she replied crisply. "This isn't a hotel. Just tell me where I can find them."

"You're my... *guest*," he bit out, and she could've sworn he'd wanted to say something else instead. Pain-in-the-ass maybe? "Let me make you comfortable."

He stalked from the room, leaving Neve to pace for a moment.

Drake was such a confusing male. On the one hand, he was prickly and downright mean, but on the other, he showed her father a level of respect that went beyond a pride member and his Leo.

She turned when he reappeared with a bundle of folded sheets in his hands and a down quilt under his arm. She took them from him before he could protest, the need to stay busy driving her insane. Placing the quilt on the ground because there was nowhere else to put it, she snapped out the sheets and settled them on the mattress.

Drake stepped forward to help her, but she stopped him with a glare.

"No," she barked, then let out a breath. "No, thank you. I don't need your help with this. You're already doing enough."

"I would do anything for you, Neve," he said so softly, she wasn't even sure she'd heard him.

She jerked her head up and stared at him. "Anything except let me out of this place, right?"

"I can't allow you to leave unaccompanied."

She bit back the urge to scream in frustration. Instead, she folded her arms and said sweetly, "What if I climb out the window when your back is turned? What will you do then?"

It was stupid to bait a male like Drake into anything, but her wounded independence was making her act out in strange ways… or maybe it was just Drake who had a habit of needling her and getting under her skin.

"You wouldn't get far if you did," he drawled dangerously.

"Already forgotten how much faster I am than you?" Her voice was practically dripping with honey—a diabetic seizure-inducing amount.

He growled at her. Actually growled. "On four legs, sweetheart.

I can beat you on two."

She huffed and turned around, getting back to making up the bed to keep herself busy.

"Seriously, though, Neve, stay here until I come and get you. It's not safe for you to wander around out there by yourself."

Without looking away from her work, she said, "Why? Have you got a serial killer stashed away down there somewhere?"

"Worse. I've got a cat with very poor impulse control."

She glanced at him out of the corner of her eye and nodded, only to get him off her back. What was that saying? Pick your battles. His heavy footsteps retreated from the room, and she let out a breath. After finishing off making the bed, she wandered into the walk-in closet and unpacked her clothes, hanging them up or tucking them into the drawers.

All that fussing around had only killed twenty minutes. What the hell was she going to do now? She hadn't checked out the bathroom yet. Easing the door open, she felt her brows rise when she saw how opulent it was. She was expecting something that matched the Georgian styling of the bedroom, but was surprised to see it was wall-to-ceiling cream marble. She glanced down at the floor when the soles of her feet warmed as she stood there. She'd been badgering her dad to get in-floor heating in the bathrooms for years.

Lifting her head, she spied the large walk-in shower, a huge sheet of tinted glass the only thing protecting the bathroom from being completely swamped by water when the dual rain showerheads were working their magic.

Beneath the sinks, she found a supply of toiletries in addition to enough towels to keep a football team going. There was also a small arsenal of painkillers, bandages, and saline wash. She figured the first aid stash was more for the Shadows if they got injured out in the field, and even though Drake had said this was a guest room, she wondered who their regular guests were.

Out of the bathroom, she flopped down onto the bed and tried to relax. She hated being confined, or maybe imprisoned was a better word. Drake had said not to leave, and the order made her skin itch. The only male she listened to was her Leo, but even then she liked to push the boundaries to see how far she could take it. Besides, if she had to stare at the four walls for much longer, she'd be liable to throw open the window and make good on her threats to escape.

Sliding from the bed, she opened up her bedroom door and peered out into the hall. There was parquetry flooring running the length of the hall up here too, but the dark red runner helped dampen her footsteps. She headed toward the stairs, leaning over the railing and scanning the large foyer for any movement. When she didn't see any, she eased down the stairs, pausing when she heard two voices drifting out of the dining room. Neither of them belonged to Drake, so she turned to the right and poked her head into the rec room, only to find it empty.

She studied the space, taking in the wet bar at one end and the outrageously large flat-screen on the wall. She was backing out when she ran into something hard and unyielding. Spinning around, she tensed for a fight, but relaxed when she saw a red-streaked, blond-haired male standing there. He smiled at her, and her heart suddenly squeezed in her chest. The smile wasn't friendly—it was predatory, and Drake's words filtered through her mind.

The male's nostrils flared as he took in her scent, his violet eyes glowing with knowledge. She backed up a step, feeling like prey caught in the sights of a predator. She looked over his shoulder for an escape route, even as he walked her backward until her ass hit the back of the couch.

Reaching out casually, he picked up some of her dark hair, rubbing it between his fingers. The muscles in his forearms flexed, making the sienna ink marking his skin dance. The swirls were hypnotic.

"Who do you belong to, huh?" he asked with a small frown. "Bringing females back here is forbidden, so I can't imagine you're Grayson's. Jett's been MIA a lot the last couple of days, so that leaves Sasha. I didn't think she was into females, but I'm happy she is."

She let out a breath, then using her best firm voice, the one she'd used on occasion with some of the cats in her pride, she said, "I don't belong to anyone. Now, I suggest you back off and let me go."

"I can't let you wander around this place without an escort." He stepped closer, pressing his body into hers, his erection prodding at her stomach. "How about you come back to my room with me? I'll take real good care of you."

She fought back the shiver as he ran the back of his fingers up and down her bare arm. Showing weakness to a male like this would be disastrous.

"Mateo." Drake's voice was as loud as a crack of thunder, and no less deadly.

The corner of Mateo's mouth curled up in the corner, revealing sharper than human canine teeth. "Don't worry, Drake. I can share."

"Do. Not. Touch. Her."

When Mateo only leaned in to sniff her hair, a low growl soon become an all-out snarl. One second, Mateo was there, and the next, he was gone. There was a crash, and the foosball table was suddenly nothing more than splintered wood, twisted metal rods, and abandoned plastic players. Drake was standing over Mateo, his shoulders heaving with his breaths, his hands balled into fists at his sides.

Neve shuffled closer, and Drake turned his violent stare to her. Marching forward, he grabbed her by the arm and turned toward the doorway. As he walked past a still-stunned Mateo, he hissed, "Mine."

She glanced over her shoulder, seeing the look of confusion flashing in those lilac eyes of his.

Out in the foyer, he walked her past the round table and the fainting couch, moving into a kitchen that was just beyond an arched door. Once the door was shut, Drake backed her against the wall, covering her body with his and caging her in with his arms.

"Did he touch you? Did he *hurt* you?" he asked, staring at her intensely, cupping her face in his hands.

She pulled his hands away irritably. She hated being coddled. "I'm fine," she replied.

Drake's nostrils flared gently. That was when she noticed his whole body was as tight as a coil. His cat was taking more control, staking a claim on his brain. Even though it killed her, she tilted her head and bared her throat to him. She may have been playing the submissive, but she wasn't stupid—she kept her eyes on his face.

"I'm fine," she said in a low, soothing voice. Reaching for his hands, she placed them on her hips and his fingers dug in almost painfully. "I'm fine."

He blinked, his cat staring out for a long moment before melting back into his mind. Drake sucked in a deep, shuddering breath, his thumbs stroking her skin through her shirt.

"Are you hungry?" he asked, his voice like gravel.

"No."

He let her go and stepped away. "Let me make you something to eat."

"I don't—" Her words died when Drake prowled over to the cupboard and took out a chopping board. She glanced around at the kitchen, finding the modern stainless steel appliances and decor jarring against the overall Georgian design—just like the bathroom in her room.

"Sit," he said, pointing to a set of stools pushed under the island bench. She couldn't help but think they looked like dogs tucking their tails under the glare of their disapproving owner.

She didn't sit.

She folded her arms. "If I'm going to stay here, you need to stop telling me what to do."

Rounding on her, he snarled, "If you're going to stay here, you'll need to start listening to me. I told you not to leave your room."

"You're acting like my father—jumping at shadows that aren't there."

His top lip curled up into a smile. "Shadows are everywhere," he replied. He popped open the seals on the fridge, a wall of condensed air rolling out and hitting his feet. "Sandwich? Turkey? Pasta?" He looked at her over his shoulder. "Something else?"

"I told you I'm not hungry."

"A sandwich it is then." He got busy pulling out some cold cuts and two tomatoes. Sliced cheese. A head of lettuce. A jar of mayo. He worked efficiently, and she had a feeling he lived like this, too.

He cleaned as he worked, constructing half a dozen sandwiches and stacking them up onto a waiting plate.

"Are you trying to make me fat?"

"They're not all for you, sweetheart," he replied, sliding the last sandwich onto the pile. He cleared the chopping board and knife into the sink and pushed the plate toward her. She figured he wouldn't let her go without at least eating one half of a sandwich, so she picked a half up, but didn't bring it to her mouth. Drake kept his eyes on her as he took his own triangle.

"Eat," he commanded.

She heaved a sigh and did as he asked, noticing he only took a bite after she had swallowed her first.

"Who was that?" she asked, propping a hip up against the counter and tilting her head back in the direction of the rec room.

"Mateo," Drake all but hissed, darting his gaze to the doorway. She looked to see if the male had suddenly been conjured, but nobody was there.

"Another one of the Revenant?" She took another bite of her sandwich, the caloric injection much needed as she chewed and swallowed some more.

"Yeah, and I don't want you to be alone with him again."

"Why not? Does he not like females?"

Drake looked positively murderous. "He likes females just fine. He probably likes them a little too much. He was trying to seduce you."

She shook her head. "I highly doubt that."

"Don't underestimate the power of your appeal, Neve," he told her in a prowling growl.

She wanted to laugh. He was acting like she was a freaking supermodel and suddenly the most desirable female around. She was ashamed to say that she'd never had much contact with males other than the ones her parents had approved of. Drake was nothing like the well-bred, well-dressed, well-mannered guys she knew. They looked at her like she was valuable, but he looked at her like she was precious.

"You *are* precious, Neve," he said, stunning her. Damn, he must've read the question on her face.

Clearing her throat, she said, "I haven't had a lot of experience with male jaguars."

He muttered something under his breath that sounded a hell of a lot like *thank Christ for that*. Well, I have, and let me tell you that Mateo was figuring out the fastest way to undress you and have you panting. So do yourself a favor, give me a fucking break, and stay away from him."

She nodded and got back to eating.

In the end, she ate two of the six sandwiches with Drake finishing off the rest. He cleared the plate away and planted his hands onto the counter.

"What would you like to do?"

She felt like someone had pulled her energy plug out, and she was draining quickly. Stifling a yawn with the back of her hand, she said, "Maybe just go back to my room. I thought I saw a TV mounted on the wall in there?"

"You did. I'll come and get you at lunch time."

She folded her arms across her chest tightly, hating how much the being watched like a hawk chaffed. "And what if I want to get a bit of exercise?" she snipped. "Stretch my legs? Do I call you? Do I ring a bell?"

His jaw tightened. "I'm not your slave. You'll wait until I come and get you."

21

DRAKE

Drake's cat was still close to the surface of his consciousness, the animal hissing as it paced within the cage of his skull. It didn't like seeing its mate walk away from it. It also didn't appreciate that Mateo had touched her. Even though she'd denied it, he *knew* the bastard had—he could smell him on her. But what was worse than that? The fact Mateo had been fucking aroused too only made him want to cleave his head from his body and punt it across the room. He grinned sardonically. The bastard wouldn't be able to self-heal that.

A vicious snarl bubbled up his throat, and he pushed out of the kitchen, his feet taking him in the direction of the rec room. When he stalked into the room, he clapped eyes on the guy, and a surge of protective instinct burned through him. He was suddenly deaf and blind to everything else but the male who had threatened his mate.

Mateo turned around and smiled. "Who was that sweet piece of—"

Drake didn't let the male finish his question, choosing instead to pile-drive the bastard into the couch. He recovered first, straddling the male's waist and raining punches down onto his face. His rage fueled him, the sound of flesh hitting flesh a soundtrack going stereo. Behind him there was a shout, and he was suddenly popped into the air—an arm like a steel band locked over his chest—and dragged off his brother.

Drake bared his fangs at whoever had stopped him, his cat spitting and hissing too.

"Drake, come on, man," Grayson said into his ear. His voice was cool and calm, like he hadn't just walked in to see Drake pounding the ever-loving shit out of Mateo. Thanks to Grayson's gift, the anger and protective instincts were drained from him just as suddenly as they'd surged, leaving him blinking at Mateo's bloodied face.

Mateo only stared at him, blood leaking from one nostril and his split lip gushing. "What the fuck, D?" he spat, rubbing the back of his hand over his mouth and looking at the bright red smear left behind.

Drake shook his head and said to Grayson, "You can let me go. I'm tight."

"Are you sure?"

The guy was smart. He could sense the residual rage bubbling in him, but Drake was locking down his cat so he couldn't take over. Grayson's arms finally loosened, but he didn't step away.

Drake rolled his shoulders and unkinked his neck. "I'm fine. Really."

Grayson must've looked at Mateo for confirmation because it was only on his nod that he stepped away.

"What's going on?" Grayson demanded, crossing his arms over his chest. "Usually it's Jett and Mateo I'm hauling apart."

Drake rubbed a hand over his face, suddenly wired and weary in a simultaneous jerk around of his emotions. "I think we need to have a meeting."

Grayson bobbed his head. "I'll take care of it."

Drake walked over to the bar and poured himself a drink, then got one for Mateo, too. He wasn't sorry he'd pounded the shit out of the guy for touching Neve, but he was sorry that he'd lost control.

He handed one to Mateo, holding his eye. "I apologize, my brother."

The guy shrugged. "The cuts are already healing." Grinning in that easy way he had, he added, "Plus, I probably deserved it."

Drake noticed his tattoos pulsing with power, but turned around when Grayson returned with Jett and Sasha. Sasha was in her gym gear, sweat staining the front of her shirt. Her long legs were on display, thanks to the short-cut running shorts, her shoes sporting the same logo. There was color on her cheeks, her usually somber eyes brighter than normal.

Jett, on the other hand, looked like he'd been dragged through broken glass backward. His hair was disheveled, dark crescent-shaped rings under his eyes. Without looking at anyone, he made his way to the wet bar. Sasha pulled up in her usual spot, looking out at one of her gardens through the French doors.

With his drink in hand, Jett's eyes scanned the room. "What the fuck happened to the foosball table?"

Drake cleared his throat. "I have something I need to tell you all."

"You won't be docking my pay to replace the foosball table?" Mateo asked, taking a sip from his glass and hissing when the liquor hit his cut.

He shook his head. "The Black Claw Leo has entrusted me to keep his only daughter safe while he and his mate take a trip over to New York."

He wanted to stake a claim on Neve to make sure none of the others made a pass at her again, but he needed time to figure out if she felt the same way about him as he did about her. He sure knew what she was to him, but maybe she didn't. A blood bond could only be formed if both parties were willing.

"Wait," Mateo said, putting down his glass. "*That* was the Leo's daughter?" For the first time, the male looked chagrined. "Fuck."

"Yeah." Drake scrubbed his knuckles over his head. "Her name's Neve, and since these abductions have gotten all the Leos twitchy, Greg figured it was a good idea to keep her under wraps."

"What did the Trinity say to this request?" Grayson asked, settling down onto the couch.

Drake sucked in a breath and let it out. "They don't know." He stared at Sasha when her head swiveled around, her gray eyes stormy. Turning back to the others, he added, "Greg came to me directly."

Ever the realist, Grayson said, "You're setting some kind of precedent here, D, you know that, don't you?"

"Yeah, I know, but desperate times." He shrugged. "Better to ask for forgiveness than permission."

"Where is she staying?" Jett asked.

"The bedroom next to mine, and I expect you all to treat her with respect."

A chorus of *of course, yeah* and one *natch* went up. His gaze went to Jett, who had returned to the wet bar, hanging onto it like the thing was responsible for keeping him vertical. "What about you, my man?"

Jett's blue eyes ratcheted to Drake's face, but he nodded. "Yeah, I also have a guest."

"You got yourself a female?" Mateo asked with a smug smile, stretching out his legs. "It's about fucking time."

"Yeah," Jett replied softly. "My sister, Katya."

Grayson visibly stiffened as he picked up on Jett's emotions. "Your sister?"

When Jett's jaw tightened, Drake asked, "Want me to tell them?"

Wordlessly, Jett begged him to take the reins. The rawness of his youngest sister's abduction was already wearing on him, and she'd been gone less than seven hours.

"This morning, Jett found out that his ten-year-old sister didn't make it to school. And no," he added, cutting off Mateo's next question, "there's nowhere else she would go."

"And she's only ten?" Grayson asked, disbelief coloring his words.

"Yeah. So that's it. We have two females in the house—the Leo's only daughter and Jett's sister. I don't have to tell you that both are off-limits." He was such a hypocrite because he was already thinking about getting Neve naked and claiming her. He glanced around the room. "Am I understood?"

As a chorus of *yes, boss* rang out around him, he nodded.

"Right. Good. We have to start finding where these girls are going, and we need to do it fast."

"Are there any leads?" Grayson asked.

Drake shook his head. "Besides Luce, all the girls were snatched under the cover of darkness. This last abduction is a change in MO. Whether these bastards are getting greedy or cocky, they've just changed the game. Daylight means potential witnesses, so I think we need to break into the school's security feed to see if she was taken from outside the school itself." He turned to Mateo. "Can you do that?"

"Piece of cake," he replied with a wolfish grin, tipping the rest of his drink down his throat. Being their resident hacker and IT whizz helped on more than one occasion.

"Are the human cops involved?"

"No," Jett replied. "I called the school to let them know Luce turned up at home, complaining of feeling unwell. That should keep them at bay for at least a few days."

"And after that?" Mateo stood up for a refill, his split lip almost completely healed.

"If it takes us longer than twenty-four hours to find her, we'll be cutting her survival rate in half. Another twenty-four hours, and it'll be half again. We *need* to find her and all the others."

"Do you think they're being kept together?"

Drake swirled the vodka in his glass around a few times. "It'll be easier to manage the operation and to keep the unit contained. Multiple sites leads to multiple opportunities for a fuck up by one of them."

"And we have no leads at all?" Grayson asked.

"Nothing." Drake folded his arms. "Once we get some more information, we can move. In the meantime, the Leo set up a text check-in service for the pride. Grayson, you'll be in charge of checking the services twice a day—every twelve hours, starting at eight p.m. tonight. I'll get you a list of names to mark off as they confirm their safety."

"You got it, boss."

"Jett, stay tight with Katya. You have enough shit on your plate right now. Mateo, since you're the computer god, keep your ear to the ground and check the scanners for any chatter about missing women." Drake glanced over at Sasha, who kept her eyes locked on the garden outside. "Make sure to keep your ear on the Trinity, too, Mateo."

"You got it, boss."

"Right. I'll check in with you all later with any official updates we might get from the Trinity."

Leaving the rec room, Drake walked up the stairs, intending to get changed and hit the gym to burn off some of that destructive energy still battering his body, but he found himself outside Neve's room instead. Whenever he got this worked up, the only way to calm him down was a burst of endorphins. Working out or sex were his two outlets, and right now, he could only think of Neve dulling his sharp edge.

Even though it was a bad fucking idea, he raised his hand to knock, but stopped at the last moment, his fist clenching and unclenching with indecision. He sucked in a breath, his hand beginning to shake with the effort to not follow through. After an internal battle that wouldn't have happened if Neve weren't there, he lowered his arm slowly. With a growl in his throat, he reined in his self-control and spun away.

"Drake?"

He turned around again to find Neve standing in the doorway, a towel wrapped around her body as she rubbed another through her wet hair. He practically vibrated with need.

"Did you need something?"

His hungry gaze drifted down, mentally stripping the towel from her body. He prowled toward her, taking note of the scent of her lust as he approached. She backed up a step as he did, retreating into her room. He followed her inside, shutting the door behind him.

She came to a stop in the middle of the room, her chest heaving, loosening the towel around her breasts. He bet she was warm and soft under all that terrycloth. She may even be a little damp, right between her legs. Would she spread those perfect thighs of hers when he slid his hand down to her cleft? Her eyes darted to his mouth before heading south. He felt stripped bare by her, the scent of her lust hitting him square in the fucking chest, like she was a defib machine for his libido. He stopped when there was less than an inch between their bodies, staring down at her upturned face.

He tugged at the edge of the towel, letting it fall to the ground. He watched it lick past her smooth skin before pooling on the ground at her feet. A fine tremor shook her body when he skimmed his fingers across her cheekbone, but he enjoyed her sharp inhale of breath. His gaze focused on her mouth. Would she accept him if he kissed her? Would her lips be soft and pliant? He leaned down, brushing his mouth against hers in a whisper touch.

Pulling back a little, he scanned her face for a moment before she brought her lips to his once more. The flick of her tongue over his bottom lip lit a fuse he had no hope of extinguishing. He gripped her bare waist, a possessive growl creeping up his throat as Neve melted into his touch. Skimming one hand around to the small of her back, he dipped the other down her ribs, over her waist and hips, before finally wrapping his hand around her thigh and hooking it around his waist.

She gasped when his erection prodded at her opening, and she ground against him like a cat in heat. Reaching between their bodies, he found her sex, stroking his fingers through her wet heat and making her squirm. She clutched at his back, her blunt nails digging into his shoulders. He hissed, licking down her neck and leaving her trembling against him.

He needed to be in her.

Now.

Wrapping her other leg around his waist, he picked her up and took her over to the bed. Placing her down gently, he stood back and stripped the shirt from his body. Neve's eyes darkened, her gaze dropping to take in his bare chest. He nearly came when her pink tongue darted out and swept over her bottom lip.

Hooking his thumbs into the waistband of his sweats, he drew them down his legs and kicked them away. As she stared at him, his skin began to grow hot, his cock aching and straining with need. Neve's legs fell open a little, a subtle invitation that Drake was definitely going to be taking her up on.

He crawled up the length of her body, kissing her thighs, her hips, her stomach, between her breasts. Threading her hands through his hair, she kept him in place, writhing beneath him, trying to find that friction she wanted so badly.

"I need to be in you, Neve."

She moaned softly, wrapping her legs around his waist, digging her heels into his lower back. "Then what are you waiting for?" she asked on a breathy moan.

He grazed her skin with his teeth as he made his way back to her mouth, nipping at her bottom lip. Neve shuddered, pressing his lower body closer to hers. His cock rubbed through her cleft, and his hips thrust forward. She made an impatient sound in the back of her throat, angling her hips so that the next pass he made, he was nudging her entrance.

Liquid heat pooled between her legs, inviting him in. She was so ready for him, the thought going straight to his chest, cleaving him with equal parts of longing and need. She wanted him. Just as much as he wanted her. And it was the best fucking aphrodisiac in the world.

Another plaintive moan escaped her throat, a noise that hit him on the most basic level. His mate was desperate, and he *needed* to ease her ache.

"Please." She drew out the last syllable, her body undulating beneath him. His willpower snapped, and he eased into her heat. Her slick channel squeezed around his cock, making his concentration slip. He wanted to take this slowly, but as soon as Neve clamped around him, his cat surged forward, demanding that he mark her. He barely resisted the urge to follow through, forcing his teeth together and clenching them tight until his jaw ached.

He watched her through heavy-lidded eyes, loving the way a flush of color came to her cheeks. The noises she made would be his undoing, though. She mewled like a kitten, gripping his shoulders like she was afraid he would simply disappear if she wasn't touching him.

He squeezed his eyes shut, savoring the sensations, savoring *everything* that passed between them. This was the female his cat had claimed, the female he'd fallen in love with the moment he'd seen her. She was his strength, his weakness, his *arnasa.*

Neve brushed her fingertips across his cheek, and he opened his eyes, seeing her own need reflected. Slowly flexing his hips, he drove his cock inside her, sealing his mouth on hers and swallowed her sweet cries of pleasure. Retreating, he slid back into her, deeper this time. A hiss rumbled through his chest and crawled up his throat.

She arched her back, pressing her breasts against his chest. Breaking the kiss, he latched on to one of her breasts, teasing the nipple with lazy strokes. Neve thrashed her head back and forth, his name on her lips in a prayer. Again, he retreated, gritting his teeth when he returned deep into her heat. Her inner muscles gripped him tighter, tearing away the self-control he forced himself to have.

On the next upstroke, Neve raised her hips, deepening the angle and making his brain fuzz out to white.

"Drake," she whimpered. "I'm going to come."

Yeah, well, he was right there with her. He kissed her again, slamming his lips to hers, his tongue invading the warm, wet recesses of her mouth. Neve's inner muscles began to clench around him, and she moaned, the noise swallowed by their kiss. His thrusts became more hurried then, a spear of heat hitting him as she came apart beneath him. She threw her head back into the pillow, her moans of ecstasy fueling him. A few shallow thrusts later, and he was spilling inside her, marking her as his, even if she didn't know it.

His pistoning hips slowly eased until he was boneless. Rolling off her, he gave her the space to breathe as both of their racing hearts returned to normal. He tucked her against him, stroking her long dark hair back from her face. Her breathing eased into deep breaths that eventually turned into soft snores, and his cat was happy she was so relaxed with him. She trusted him, because Neve wasn't the kind of female who let her guard down so easily.

22

KATIE

Katie ran her hands through Luce's dark hair, pushing it back behind the little girl's ear. She was asleep in Katie's lap, her body curled toward her torso, her legs tucked up to her chest. Every now and then, a shiver wracked her body, and Katie did her best to keep the girl warm.

Luce had fallen asleep hours ago—at least Katie thought it was hours ago. For all she knew, only a few minutes had passed, but time was so strange down here.

Another pass of her fingers through her hair.

Another pass that brought her a sense of calm, even though she felt like she was jumping out of her skin. How was this all supposed to end? Were they going to die down here? Were their bodies going to be buried, or would they burn them?

Burning them made more sense—less chance of discovery by the authorities.

The other question that plagued her was about their captors. They all smelled like they were human, but they didn't seem at all surprised when they found a giant black jaguar prowling around behind the bars instead of a woman. It was almost as if it had been… expected.

Her head tipped back on her neck as the floorboards above their heads creaked. A wave of whispers broke out among the females, followed closely by the sound of clothes whispering against cement as they shuffled into a less visible position. The footfalls moved to the right, farther, farther, farther, until the door to the basement opened.

Katie was unable to look away from the stairs as a pair of boots gave way to jean-clad legs, a Metallica T-shirt covering a broad chest, and a face that didn't just look cruel—it emanated cruelty.

Katie shrank back, even though there was nowhere to go. That hard cinder block wall at her back wasn't going to suddenly envelop her in a warm hug.

The man got to the bottom of the stairs, surveying them like a king would survey his lands. This wasn't the guy in charge, though. He didn't smell like alpha material, but when he was the only one there, he liked to play the part.

"Listen up, ladies. Pack your things." He smirked. "We're going to be moving you very soon."

"Where are we going?" one of the females in another cage asked, her voice hoarse from disuse.

The guy tipped his head back and laughed. "You'll find out soon." He pulled a bunch of cable ties from his back pocket and waved them in front of their faces. "Now, I need everyone to behave themselves. If you do, I won't need to tranquilize you. Again," he added smugly. "This is what's going to happen. My associate is going to be down here in a few minutes, and we're going to escort you one by one up to the van. You'll be blindfolded and bound. You *will not* do anything stupid, like make a run for it, or shift, or fight back, because you *will* lose."

And with that declaration, he moved toward Elsie's cell. Katie watched as he opened things up and stepped inside. Under normal circumstances, she would've called him a fool, but that was when she noticed a gun tucked into the waistband of his jeans. Shifters were strong. They were fast, but they weren't faster than a bullet.

"Stand up," he told her.

Elsie dragged herself upright, leaning heavily against the wall at her back. She'd given up, Katie realized. Just checked out of her body. The abuse was the catalyst, but the starvation was a driving force she couldn't escape. The guy snapped the cable ties on and tightened them before leaving her cell and closing the door. As he moved to the next cage, another set of boots landed at the bottom of the stairs.

Cowboy was here, and he looked like he was in a foul mood. His top lip was curled into a snarl, his eyes narrowing as he looked at all the females. In Katie's arms, Luce began to stir.

"Shh," she whispered quietly, praying that their captors would remain focused on their tasks. "You need to be quiet, Luce."

"What's going on?" she asked, her voice low like she'd sensed Katie's desperation. She probably stank of it, though, so there was no risk of missing it.

"They're moving us."

"Moving?" the girl asked. "Where?"

Katie shook her head. "I don't know. All they said was we were going somewhere else."

She looked up to find Cowboy going into Elsie's cell. Katie's hands flexed and released. Flexed and released. The other female sat there, her eyes glued to the floor. She didn't even make a sound when Cowboy wrenched on her bound wrists behind her back and pulled her to her feet.

He laughed. "Let's see how catatonic you really are," he sneered, grabbing her roughly.

Nothing.

Not even a flicker of recognition. He stepped into the line of her body, nuzzling her neck as his hands disappeared. Katie could only guess where they were.

Still nothing.

Elsie was completely and utterly gone from this basement, her mind setting up the protective barriers that would get her through the ordeal. Only time would tell if she recovered that part of herself again once this was all over.

As Cowboy stepped back, Katie saw that he was turned on, like a woman's denial of him was enough of a catalyst, even though she'd clearly checked out of her own head.

"Come on," he told her, pulling the gun out from the small of his back and holding it against the back of Elsie's skull. They left the cell, and as Cowboy walked past, he leered at Katie. Instinctively, she hugged Luce closer.

On and on it went. The non-alpha made his way around the cells, forcing the women apart before securing them one by one with cable ties around their wrists.

"Where are you taking us?" one of the females asked.

The guy cuffed her across the mouth, the smell of blood tainting the air. "You don't get to ask questions," he growled, jabbing his finger into her face. If she'd been human, the blow would've knocked her down, but because of her preternatural strength, despite the mistreatment, she stood tall, and it looked like that pissed the guy off even more.

"When I get out of here," she started in a slow drawl.

"You're not getting out of here, bitch," he spat back. "Not unless you're leaving in a pine box." Without turning his back on her, he left the cell and closed the door after him.

"Don't tell me the little ladies are giving you trouble, Tom."

Katie turned to find Cowboy standing there with a smug smile on his face. She straightened when she caught his scent, though. Sex was all over him, Elsie's scent was, too. Pressing her lips together tightly, she contained her growl and looked away, hoping to avoid his attention.

"You're a cocksucker, Leroy." Tom seemed to look at him then, taking in the shirt tails that were untucked from the waistband of his jeans. The color rose in his cheeks. "You fucked her, didn't you? You know what the boss said."

Leroy only shrugged casually and tipped his hat back. "Don't worry. I left her breathing in the back of the van."

Tom shook his head grimly then turned to unlock Katie and Luce's cage. Luce sat up, her whole body shaking as she looked at the man stalking toward them.

"Be careful with the little one. She's fresh, so she's still got some strength left," Leroy warned.

"I've got it," Tom replied, his hungry gaze on Luce. Katie stood up slowly, her legs shaking so badly, she thought they'd give way beneath her if she took a step. She moved, though, and they stayed. She put herself between Tom and Luce, holding the guy's eyes.

"Don't you dare think about it," she hissed, her voice becoming a low rumble. Her cat stalked forward in her mind, showing Tom what was lurking beneath the surface. The scent of fear wafted from his body a moment before his expression hardened and he drew out a gun from the small of his back.

He shoved it in her face. "Stand over there," he ordered.

She stared down the barrel and felt her resolve harden. "No."

He took her by the upper arm, his short, stubby fingers digging into her flesh. He marched to the corner, and she didn't make it easy. "Stay there," he hissed.

Katie stayed, sure that Tom wouldn't actually do something against his orders. He crouched down in front of Luce, yanking her arms out in front of her and securing the cable ties. When she winced, a growl of warning came from Katie's throat. Tom glanced over his shoulder at her then stood up, swaggering in her direction.

"Play nicely, or I'll be forced to take your punishment out on her hide."

Katie felt like she'd been doused in cold water. She darted a look to Luce, and she knew in her blood that she would defend that little female until her death. The revelation should've frightened her, but she found it only strengthened her. She would die for Luce. Gladly. But she had to play their games, at least for now.

Like the good little female they wanted, she nodded and kept her eyes down. Tom zip-tied her wrists roughly behind her back, then left their cell, locking the door behind him. He and Leroy shuttled the females upstairs until it was only Luce and Katie left. Leroy's eyes danced with amusement when he re-entered her cell. They'd found the bargaining chip they needed to keep Katie in line, not that she'd been anything but a model inmate since she'd arrived.

She wasn't an aggressive cat by nature. In fact, Neve had often told her she was too soft for her own good, that people would take advantage of her generous nature and her fragile heart. Katie had never seen anything wrong with that before…

Until now.

Luce was moved first, the small girl's wide blue eyes staring at Katie like she was the only thing that could keep her safe. As she was removed from the cell, she began to struggle, which caused

Tom to grab her by the hair and wrench her head back painfully. Katie threw herself at the bars, as pointless as it was, and hissed, "Touch her again, and you'll deal with me."

Tom smiled. "With pleasure, pussy cat."

Knowing he had her attention, he skimmed his hand down the front of Luce's shirt, causing the girl to squirm and whimper. Katie snapped. She slammed herself against the bars, leading with her shoulder. It was stupid, because there was no way the steel bars were suddenly going to give way for her, but the strength of her rage bolstered her.

She could tell her eyes were glowing by the faint pool of light they were throwing off in the gloomy room. Her cat had edged perilously close to the surface, but it wasn't safe to let her out. She probably couldn't shift even if she wanted to. She was too weak now.

Leroy interrupted their stare-off by saying, "All right, Tom. Stop baiting her. Get the kid upstairs already." Leroy unlocked her cell and stepped inside. Elsie's scent still lingered on him, turning her stomach. But this close, she smelled it—shifter. She hadn't recognized it on him previously. Firstly, the scent of food had fogged her mind, then the scent of blood had overtaken her senses. She smelled him now though. For a moment, she was too stunned to do anything other than stare. He was a black jaguar, and he was taking their females and humans alike. He was betraying their species, but for what?

"Why?" she asked, her voice hoarse.

Leroy narrowed his eyes on her face. Like he didn't understand the question. Like she was a fool for even asking.

Her tongue leaded, she demanded softly, "Why?"

"You'll find out soon enough," he replied in a sneer, then took her by the elbow, led her from the cell and up the stairs. She blinked when they came to the top. They were in a well-appointed kitchen with stainless steel appliances and a six-burner stove. The squalor they'd been forced to live in in the basement just didn't make sense here.

"Get moving," Leroy said, walking her through the kitchen and out the back door. She shivered as soon as they got out, the temperature dipping drastically. Or maybe that was just shock. She didn't know. Leroy was leading her to a black van that had been parked at an angle so she couldn't see the plates.

She was taken around the back where the door was open and the chattering of teeth could be heard. She peered inside to find all the women had blindfolds over their eyes. She scanned the interior, looking for Luce. She found her huddled against the wheel arch, her own blindfold stretched tight against her eyes.

There was a noise, and Katie glanced over her shoulder to find Leroy holding her own blindfold.

"No," she whispered.

But it was too late. Her world went black, and then she was shoved into the van, sitting on someone's legs, elbowing someone else in an attempt to get her other senses online. The rear door slammed, the van rocking ever so slightly from the force, then the front doors shut.

The engine roared to life, drowning out the sound of softly shed tears and sniffling. Katie just sat there, waiting for the nightmare to be over.

23

NEVE

Neve pressed the phone closer to her ear, unable to process what she'd just been told.

"I thought you were in New York."

"We were supposed to be," her father replied wearily. "Until I got a call from one of the other Leos, who said they were convening another meeting. This time in California. Your mom and I had to cash in our tickets and get new ones."

"What about your business meeting?" She didn't know why, but a feeling of dread was uncurling in the pit of her stomach.

"I had to reschedule. Larry was fine with doing that. He said he needed more time to prepare anyway."

"When will you be coming home?" she asked in a whisper. "Do you know?"

There was a small *thud* like he had just fallen rather than sat in a chair. Blowing out a breath, he said, "Honestly, I don't know, kitten."

She shifted so her legs were hanging off the side of the bed. "Where are you staying?"

"Tony was kind enough to put us up. We got in late last night."

She traced the lines of the geometric pattern on the comforter beside her, her stomach tightened. "And the meeting starts tomorrow?"

"Yes, although I have no idea what needs to be discussed. Everything that was pressing was discussed on Monday."

"Is everyone there?"

"All the Leos and their mates, yes."

"Mom didn't want to stay home?"

"You remember Tony's mate, Shelly? She's organized for the females to go on a winery tour while the males talk shop."

"That was nice of her," Neve said absently, the quiet discomfort getting heavier in her stomach. She pressed her hand to the spot just below her navel. "Is Mom looking forward to it?"

"Tell her I'm dying to try some new wines!" her mom called in the background.

Her dad laughed. "Did you get all that?"

"Yeah."

There was a heavy beat of silence before he asked, "How's Drake treating you? Is he being respectful?"

She flushed with heat at the memories of what she and Drake had done the day before. She guessed respectful was one word for it. Drake had been a phenomenal lover, but it wasn't like she could say that to her father and Leo. Clearing her throat, she said, "Fine, Dad."

"Are you sure? You don't sound so sure."

She nodded although it was pointless. "He's made me feel very welcome."

"Good," he replied softly. "I can't tell you how much your mother and I appreciate him taking you in this way. It's highly against protocol, and if the Trinity found out, I'm sure they'd have a thing or two to say about it."

"I think your secret is safe, Dad," she replied. "Look, I'm going to go down and get some breakfast. Call me after the meeting?"

"Okay, kitten. We'll talk to you then."

"Love you!" her mom called.

Neve smiled faintly. "Tell Mom I love her too. Talk to you soon."

She hung up and put her phone down onto the comforter. She ran her fingers over the pattern once more, her mind taking her back to the night before. She'd fallen asleep after she and Drake had… *made love*? Maybe not that. She felt like it was more than a fuck for him, though. It had meant something to him, but it had also meant something to her.

She'd tried to resist that low-level vibration that seemed to charge through her body when he was around, but when he'd come to her, his knuckles bloody and smelling of Mateo, it had increased to a level she couldn't ignore anymore. Despite reassuring him that she was fine, he'd clearly taken his questions to Mateo and not liked the answers.

Really, she should've been rolling her eyes at his reaction. She wasn't his. He had no claim on her, but she knew it was a lie. And last night had confirmed it. When she'd woken this morning, her bed was empty but warm, the pillow still smelling of Drake. Her cat seemed content with the knowledge that he had stayed until this morning.

Sliding from the bed, she was still naked, her discarded towel a neat pile of terry cloth in the center of the floor. She pulled on fresh underwear, bra, and pajamas, and opened her bedroom door. The house was quiet, but it was also so big that if someone was in another wing of the house and making noise, she doubted she'd be able to hear it.

She made her way to the kitchen, pausing before the closed door. Pressing her ear to it, she listened. Someone was definitely singing. Badly. She pushed it open and stuck her head into the room. Yup, there was a male dressed only in an apron and some running shorts using a spatula as a microphone as he belted out a disco classic. She leaned against the doorjamb, enjoying the show. He had tanned skin and muscles that were showcased by very little body fat. The strap of the apron looping over his neck was a crisp white, but it wouldn't stay that way, judging by the mess he was making.

He jumped in a circle toward the stove, shaking his hips to the beat. Neve put the back of her hand over her mouth to stifle the laugh. She must've failed, though, because the guy whirled around, his black hair flopping into his face. Shoving it out of the way, his green eyes widened before a blush graced his high cheekbones. Pulling out his phone, he shut the music off.

"Don't stop on my account." She pushed off the wall and sat at the kitchen counter. "You've got some moves."

"Thanks," he said softly. He undid the waist ties on the apron and motioned to take it off, when he realized he was wearing very little else beneath it. He rubbed the back of his neck. "I apologize for my state of undress."

"I hadn't noticed."

"Would you excuse me?"

"Sure." He bolted from the room only to return a few minutes later with a running shirt on. He gave her a genuine smile when he walked back in.

"I apologize again," he said. "You must be Neve. It's an honor to have you in our home."

"Thank you."

"My name's Grayson." He held out his hand to her and they shook. She instantly liked him. His handshake was firm, but not so much so that he tried to crush her hand in his. It wasn't so limp-wristed that she felt like she was shaking hands with a jellyfish either.

"You look familiar," she said.

He shrugged easily, sliding the apron back over his head. "I can't imagine where you've seen me before. Now, what can I get you for breakfast?"

"Oh, you don't have to—"

"Nonsense. You're our guest. Now tell me, will it be waffles, pancakes, or eggs?"

"Pancakes sound good, but only if you're making them for yourself, too."

He flashed her a grin. "Pancakes, coming right up."

She turned when the door to the kitchen swung open and Mateo walked in. No, he didn't just walk. He swaggered like he owned the damned place. She stared at him, wondering if he was going to try and seduce her like he'd done before, or whether Drake's warning had done the job. He glanced at her, his nostrils flaring briefly before giving her a curt nod. He opened up the stainless steel and glass industrial fridge, pulling out a carton of juice.

"Would you like some?"

She glanced around. Was he talking to her? "Oh, um, sure?"

"Thanks for offering, Mat. I'd love a glass, too," Grayson deadpanned.

Mateo snorted and pulled three glasses from the cabinet over the sink. He poured their juice out then returned the carton to the fridge. Each of his movements was precise—smooth. The sienna tattoo on his right arm seemed to writhe on his skin. She tore her eyes away from it when he placed the sweating glass in front of her with an easy smile.

"So I just want to apologize for what happened yesterday."

Wow. Didn't see that one coming. "It's fine," she replied, taking a sip just to keep her hands busy. If she didn't, she'd be liable to fuss with her hair or pull at her pajamas. She glanced down as if just remembering she was in them. Why had she thought that was a good idea?

"It's really not. I'm sorry I got up in your face like that, and I'm sorry if I scared you."

"It's fine." Jesus, was that all she could say? Talk about a broken record.

"It would mean a lot to me if you accepted my apology. I was an asshole, and you didn't deserve that."

She glanced over at Grayson, who had stopped flipping pancakes and was now staring at Mateo. Like the guy never apologized. Or was nice.

"I didn't know who you were," he added.

Oh. "So because I'm the Leo's daughter, I'm suddenly to be treated differently?"

He blinked at her. "No. You're Drake's. I should've realized that last night, but…" He let his sentence drift off before he finished with a shrug. "So, yeah. I apologize. Sincerely."

He took a sip of his juice, his gaze still on her face.

"Accepted. Thank you."

He nodded, an accord struck between them, then took a seat beside her at the island and focused his lavender eyes on Grayson.

"Yo, Gray, you look good with an apron on."

"You should've seen him before," she said, laughing when Grayson's eyes cut to hers. Slowly, he shook his head, mouthing the word *please* to her.

"Oh, do tell," Mateo said, turning his body toward her. "Tell me all your *dirty* secrets."

Grayson was still giving her a pleading look, so she shrugged and said, "Nah. I don't want the guy to spit in my pancake batter."

And that was how it continued for the next however long it took for Grayson to cook them all pancakes. He'd just placed a platter stacked with them into the middle of the counter when Drake prowled through the door. Literally prowled, like his cat was holding the reins on his mind. He was dressed in PT gear, sweat beading on his brow and making the front of his shirt stick to his muscled chest. Neve let out an appreciative breath.

His yellow eyes went from Grayson to Mateo, narrowing on the latter. "I hope you haven't forgotten your manners, M," he all but growled.

Mateo put his hands up, the silent plea for *what the fuck did I do.* "I'm always a gentleman."

"Actually, *I'm* always the gentleman," Grayson said. Drake looked at Neve for confirmation, and it was only at her nod that he relaxed. He strolled over to where she was sitting, standing behind her so closely that she could feel the heat rolling off his body. She inhaled deeply, taking in the scent of fresh sweat and determination, but under that was his own dark spices.

Grayson's expression flickered with confusion for a moment before smoothing out as he said, "Take as much as you want, Neve."

She looked around. "Aren't you guys eating too?"

"Yeah, but only after you and the other female in the house are fed."

She paused for a moment, finally pressing the pancake she'd

speared onto her plate. "Is she one of your mates? The other female?"

Drake's heavy palm landed on her shoulder and a frisson of longing went through her. "Mateo, go and get Jett."

"Sure." He pushed out of his chair and disappeared from the kitchen. Drake still hadn't removed his large palm, the heat of which was warming more than just her shoulder. Grayson was still shuttling pancakes from the pan over to the platter, his eyes lingering on Drake for a moment.

"Eat, Neve," Drake rumbled, finally taking a seat beside her. His large thigh pressed against her, touching from hip to knee. She got busy cutting her pancake and spreading some sweet butter on top. Next came some fruit and a dash of syrup. She felt Drake's eyes on her the whole time.

"You're staring," she said, putting a forkful into her mouth.

He leaned in so his mouth was against her ear. "I love that I can still smell myself on you." His voice was a low growl.

Dammit, why hadn't she thought to take a shower before coming down here? Inhaling sharply, she realized why Mateo had made that comment about being Drake's. He would've scented him on her, and now with his current behavior, he was making sure everyone knew about it.

She turned her head when Mateo returned. He darted his purple-eyed gaze between her and Drake, and she shifted over a little.

"He'll be down in five," Mateo said, planting his ass back down on his stool. He looked longingly at the stack, but made no motion to take anything. Who knew the Revenant were so... courteous.

"Who's the other female?" she asked. "If not one of your mates, why is she here?"

"Her name's Katya," Drake said. "She's Jett's sister."

She tried to keep the surprise off her face. To her knowledge, she was the only outsider to have been brought under the personal protection of the Revenant.

"What's she doing here?" she asked carefully.

"The same reason you're here," Drake replied softly, his yellow eyes like melted butter. "She's under our protection." He opened his mouth like he was about to say something, hesitated, before finally adding, "Her baby sister was taken on Monday morning."

"That's what you told my father when you picked me up." Of course. No wonder he wanted to keep that news to himself for a bit longer. "How old is she?" Her voice was barely a whispered croak, but Drake's cat's hearing was good enough to pick up on the question.

His palm was warm where he placed it on her thigh. "Ten."

She closed her eyes and took a deep breath, her eyes opening once more when she heard voices on the other side of the kitchen door.

It swung open, and a male with sandy-blond hair and blue eyes was leading a dark-haired female inside. Her green eyes widened as she took in the room and all the people.

Jett said something softly into her ear and placed his hand on the small of her back, leading her to the last chair at the island. Grabbing a plate, he loaded it up with pancakes then got her some juice.

"Hello," Neve said, breaking the silence. She cleared her throat. "It's nice to meet you. I'm Neve."

"I know who you are," Katya replied, her voice cautious. "You're the Leo's daughter."

She nodded, adding, "I'm sorry about—"

"I have to go," Jett said loudly, cutting her off.

Katya's eyes widened until even Neve could see the white all around. "Where are you going?"

Jett's blue eyes darted around the room, not settling on anyone's face in particular. "Just to take care of some business. You're safe here." He kissed the top of her head. "I'll be back soon."

24

ASHER

Asher drummed his fingers on the desk he was sitting behind, a phone pressed to his ear and his shoulder cocked at a strange angle.

"Are you on your way?"

"Yeah, we are. Do you have what we want?"

He stroked the cellophane baggies lined up at his elbow like good little soldiers. "Don't I always?"

His question was met with a growl, and without even seeing the male's face, Asher knew exactly what that single noise meant—he was getting desperate for the next hit.

"How long has it been?" he asked softly, knowing he had the guy's balls in a vice. Asher was their only source of *arnastu*, as he liked to call it. He thought it was a nice play on words, twisting their revered word for their blood-bonded mate into something much darker and more addictive.

"Maybe a week."

He smiled. "You must be desperate for another taste of that power then."

Another growl trickled over the line, and this time, the threat was felt like someone had just pressed the muzzle of a gun into the top of his spinal column. Absently, he ran his hand over the back of his neck to assure himself the sensation was just a figment of his imagination.

"We're about three hundred miles away."

"Good. Everything is lining up perfectly on my end. Let's ensure it stays that way."

He hung up, his eyes back on the dozen clear bags filled with off-white powder. To a casual observer, the drugs contained within the cellophane could be mistaken for blow or speed, but if a human were to ingest this, it would have absolutely zero effect. These drugs were specific to shifters, to *Shadows*. Those males were the ones who were bred to fight and protect their Leos and the pride. They were the ones who were blessed with latent powers of increased speed, faster shifts, and super strength. Once these powers were activated, it made them the ultimate super soldier. The downside? Well, there wasn't one…

Unless you were the Shadow.

The drug was addictive, and the more they took, the more they needed it and the less effective it became. It was the perfect Catch-22.

Standing up from his desk, Asher walked the perimeter of his room, studying the large collection of leather-bound tomes—many of them first editions. Reaching out, he reverently touched the gilt script on the spines, his fingertip undulating over the embossed letters. Everything was going according to plan, and by the afternoon, he was going to be the one standing tall.

Outside his office, the grandfather clock began its somber declaration of time. Five chimes. He was going to be late. Taking his suit jacket from the back of his chair, he slid it on and shuffled his shoulders until the fabric settled onto them. Dragging the cuffs down, he made sure everything was in place before strolling from the room and meeting his butler, Reggie, out in the hall.

"Ready, sir?"

"Indeed," he replied, opening up the door and walking outside. He hung back as Reggie opened up the back door of his Rolls Royce Phantom, and he slid into the supple leather that felt like butter against his palms. Once the door was shut behind him, he leaned back into all that opulence and breathed out long and slow. He came from old money, his grandfather owned a number of metal works that profited greatly from the outbreak of the World War—the First that was.

His own father…well, the male he had called *father* had invested well and the *son* had reaped the benefits. Of course, he couldn't have any competition for that wealth, so Asher had done what he'd had to and dispatched his siblings with surprising efficiency. Death by misadventure had been the official ruling, but only he knew the real methods.

As the Phantom sped smoothly out of the Hollywood Hills, he kept his eyes on the window, watching the blur of the passing scenery change from low-lying shrubs and palatial homes to neon signs and human filth. His cat shifted beneath his skin, the animal getting restless with all the noise and smells that were so foreign to it.

Almost two hours later, they arrived at their destination. Like any male of good breeding, he waited for Reggie to open up the passenger door and slipped out of the leather seat. The air was cool, the different altitude making the weather shift, gearing down to a temperature where he longed to have a heavier jacket over his shoulders.

"I shall wait for you here, sir," Reggie announced, standing stock-still beside the driver's side door. Asher nodded. Good help was so hard to find, and he was very glad he had found this human. Glancing up at the house of the Leo, he ducked his head and moved toward the door. In truth, the Yellow Eye Leo was not expecting him. Asher was neither a high-ranking jaguar, nor was he a trusted advisor. He was, regrettably, nothing more than another member of the pride, but all that was about to change.

Raising his hand, he knocked on the door. On the other side, there was a flurry of activity, and he wondered what was going on. A female answered the door, her hair perfectly coiffed, her pant suit well-pressed like she was going out to a day at the races. He bowed, dropping into his formality and breeding on default. He didn't expect to see her, let alone for her to recognize him, so he was stunned when she said, "Asher. How lovely to see you."

"Madam," he murmured. "And me you."

"We were just getting ready to go out."

He rose from his bow. "Oh?"

"Yes," Michelle Scheller, the Leo's mate, said. "The ladies and I are going out on a winery tour for the day."

"How quaint," he replied. It made sense for the males to get their mates out of the house while the meeting was underway.

"Would you like to see Anthony?"

"Ah, yes, please, but only if there is time?"

She stepped back from the door. "Of course. Wait in the living room, and I'll see if he has a few spare minutes."

Asher stepped inside the house and scanned the immediate area. He had never been here before, but then again, why would he ever have a need to? Michelle led him into a comfortable room decorated in creams and tans, the room neither feminine nor masculine, it was just neutral and calming.

"I'll be right back."

Turning, he bowed again. "But of course, madam."

She frowned a little at his address, and he once again cursed his stiff upbringing. His father, and his father before him, wouldn't have had it any other way. He wondered how different his life would've been if his mother hadn't ensnared the male who'd raised him, and had instead stayed with the one who had sired him—his *real* father...

He shook his head.

Any fanciful notions of being happily reunited with his birth father were a fantasy and fruitless. He was a bastard in the truest sense of the word, his mother like a cuckoo laying her egg in another's nest. He didn't know if the whole truth had ever been revealed to his mother's mate, or whether she'd let him continue believing the lie until his very last breath.

He turned around and walked over to the fireplace, the banked fire warming him from his knees down. Now was not the time to think about paternity. Turning his head to the side, there was a dining room through the archway, and beyond that was a kitchen. Judging by the smell, there was a team of housekeepers and chefs preparing food for an army of jaguars. It was just another confirmation that all of Asher's players were coming together as he'd orchestrated.

"Asher?"

He turned at the sound of his name, bowing once more at the Leo. His position afforded respect. It was just a shame the male didn't.

"I thank you for receiving me."

"Sure," he said, gesturing to one of the tan sofas in the middle of the room. Asher sat down, feeling the fine weave of the silk beneath him. At least the Leo had half-decent taste in interior decorating.

"What can I do for you?"

"I wanted to talk to you about possibly allowing me to come and work for you."

Tony frowned. "Ah…"

Inwardly, Asher smiled. The Leo was off-balance, and he was hoping this conversation would do a lot to keep him that way.

"Ah… I'm afraid I'm not following."

"I wish to come and offer my services to you."

"Forgive me, but you've never shown any interest in working for me before. In fact, you've made it abundantly clear that you want to be left alone."

Asher gave him an indulgent smile. "I've decided to be a little more *proactive* in the pride."

"You've also got a larger net worth than the Yellow Eye and Black Claw prides combined."

He waved away the comment. "I don't want to offer my services in exchange for monetary gain."

Tony frowned. "So, why do you want to offer your services?"

Ah, now there was the question. "I have something of yours that I wish to give back—quite a number of *somethings*, actually." Asher took satisfaction in the look of absolute confusion on the Leo's face. Asher thought he looked a little like a basset hound with his dolichocephalic face and droopy eyes.

"I don't know—"

There was a loud knock on the front door, snapping the Leo out of his stupor, but Asher wasn't so ready to let him go.

"I have your females." He said the words so softly that he didn't think the male had heard him until he stiffened. Even his chest seemed to stop moving up and down. When Tony remained mute, he sat forward in his chair, meeting the Leo's eye in smug triumph. "And I have your Shadows."

Tony leapt from the sofa, his face turning red with righteous indignation. "What are you talking about?"

Reaching into his jacket, Asher pulled out the firearm he'd recently obtained and held it down near his hip, yet clearly pointed at the Leo's chest. The scent of the Leo's fear wafted from his pores, making the corners of Asher's mouth tug up.

Victory was going to be so sweet.

"Sit down, Tony."

Tony sat.

"Good, now listen to me and listen well—"

"What do you want?" the male demanded, still angry, despite now having a target in the middle of his forehead.

Asher gave him a condescending smile. "Impulsivity is not a good quality to have in a Leo."

His hands balled into fists at his sides. "You have *no idea* what makes a good Leo."

"Actually, I think I do. You see, I'm planning on becoming a Leo of my own territory."

The bastard had the audacity to balk at that statement.

"You don't believe me?" Asher asked in a deadly voice.

"You can't just say you're going to be a Leo and that's that. You need to be in line for the honor. You need to have the blessing of the Trinity."

He cocked his head to the side. "You have no heir, am I right?" he asked. "No one to pass the mantel?"

Tony blanched but said nothing, and really, that said it all, didn't it? "You need the Shadows to follow you. They're loyal. They'd never defect."

Asher laughed at this statement. "They've already defected. They're mine now."

The male shook his head slowly, like his ears and his brain were playing catch-up and they needed the motion to get his neurons firing.

"I also have the backing of the Trinity. Why do you think you were asked to hold this meeting?" As the Leo's eyes widened, Asher decided to drive the knife home. "Let's just say I can be *terribly* persuasive."

"That's impossible."

"Nothing is impossible. My grandfather taught me that."

"H-how?"

He touched the side of his nose and laughed. "Ah, well, that will remain my little secret."

Over the Leo's shoulder, the leader of Specter came around the corner. With nothing but a small nod, Asher gave the Shadow the order to detain the Leo. Lewis moved with preternatural speed and power—his *arnasa* ability strong, thanks to the powder he'd snorted before coming—and wrenched the Leo from his seat, removing him bodily from the room. Asher watched him go, reveling in the other male's impotence, at his stupid expression and bulging eyes.

25

DRAKE

Drake walked Neve back up to her room, his hand possessively resting on the small of her back. He'd made sure his cats knew she belonged to him, and the bonus that Neve still smelled of him helped confirm it.

"Was there a reason you were marking your territory?" she asked when they reached the landing. She peered over her shoulder at him, her green eyes glowing faintly.

He kept the victorious smile off his face. "Just keeping you safe."

"I thought I was safe here." Her tone was mildly accusatory. "Without the need for overt displays of territorial dick measuring."

Shrugging, he said, "I had to make sure they all knew."

She spun around to face him, color rising in her cheeks. His eyes drifted down her tight T-shirt and flannelette pajama pants. "I don't belong to you, Drake."

He growled softly, his cat surging for a brief moment. "You do, you just don't know it yet," he drawled, stepping closer until his mouth was against her ear. "Or do I have to remind you of what we did together last night?"

"Just because we slept together doesn't mean you own me," she replied sharply. A fine tremor ran through her body, and as much as he wanted to touch her, he held back.

"Why are you looking at me that way?" she asked.

"Like what?" he asked, his voice much lower than normal.

Her tongue darted out as she licked her lips. "Like you want to eat me."

His laugh was slow and deliberate. "Maybe that's exactly what I want to do."

A sharp inhale of breath.

Her delicate scent intensified.

"I don't know what to say to that."

"You don't have to say anything," he replied. "Just come back to my room with me."

"To do what?" she breathed.

He could see she was waging some sort of internal battle, torn between what her cat wanted and what she wasn't willing to give yet. "Let me show you how good we are together."

He waited for her to nod. It felt like an eternity, but eventually she came to some kind of conclusion to her inner monologue. She took his hand. She didn't know it, but she had taken a very important step. He pulled her to his room and shut the door behind them. As if she was nervous, she walked around his room, studying what little furniture he had. He tracked her with his gaze until she stopped at his window. She turned her head slightly when he approached her from behind. She had knowingly put herself in a vulnerable position.

Slowly, he placed his hands on her waist, and when she didn't balk, he pulled her in line with his hips, in line with his raging erection. With her sharp inhale of breath, he knew she'd felt it, felt him and how badly he needed her.

He pushed some of her hair out of the way so he could plant

a soft kiss on the side of her neck. Her ass flexed into his groin, making them both groan. He kissed her again, right over her carotid, his tongue rolling over the pounding vein. So much life and death here. Neve spun around and grabbed onto his shoulders, her fingers digging deliciously deep into his flesh. Yes. More. He needed more. He felt like they'd been dancing around this attraction for weeks, when in reality, it had only been a matter of days. But that was how it went when a male found his blood-bonded mate. Time ceased to make sense, and all they saw was their female.

"Neve," he groaned. He ran his hands down over her ass, the soft flannel of her pajamas warm under his palms. Holding her there, he thrust against her, his cock less than an inch from where it really wanted to be.

He claimed her mouth, kissing her like they were both dying and this was the last contact they were going to have. She opened for him beautifully, just like her body did, and he slid his tongue inside, stroking her and wanting to do so much more. He tilted her head, angling it, giving himself better access. She moaned, and he caught the sound. He broke the kiss and stared at her, holding his forehead against hers.

As much as he wanted to make her hoarse from screaming his name, he knew his focus should be on trying to find the missing females. He'd known when he told Greg she could stay that his focus would be divided. As a bonded male, he wanted to be inside his female as often as he could, and they were walking down a slippery path right now.

Neve touched her lips, her fingers shaking. Drake felt like pounding on his chest like a goddamn caveman. She watched him, her green eyes languid and warm under his gaze.

"Tell me you feel it, Neve." He touched between her collarbones, dragging his hand between her breasts. "The electricity—the *connection*." She had to know it was there. He was absolutely sure her cat did, but it was taking the human side of her a little longer to see.

She nodded slowly, as if she didn't quite trust herself to speak.

"Jesus, I can hardly keep my hands off you."

She laughed in a husky way that made him think of a throat raw from screaming. "I never thought self-control would be an issue for you."

The desire to claim her became a flat-out scream in his head. She would realize it soon enough. "Only when it comes to you, *arnasa*."

Her expression became puzzled over his use of the Shadow word for blood mate, and he kissed her again, lingering on her mouth, teasing small sounds from her throat.

There was a thumping on the door, and he broke the kiss, snarling. "What?" he barked, pushing Neve behind him. Much to his annoyance, she stepped out from his shadow and stood beside him. She folded her arms as Grayson opened the door. Gray darted his gaze from Drake to Neve, his nostrils flaring slightly at the heavy scent of lust piercing the air.

"Sorry, boss, but we have a situation."

"What is it?" he replied, glancing at Neve over his shoulder. Her face was carefully neutral, like she'd slipped on a mask and she was all business.

"I've just checked the texts coming in from the pride's females, and there's one here you'll want to read." Grayson handed him the phone, and Drake took a second to read it.

"Fuck." His voice was a coarse snarl.

"What is it?" Neve asked.

He tilted the screen in her direction, watching her eyes shift over the words.

"I know her," she said, leaning back and wrapping her arms around herself. "We went to school together." She shivered. "I should go and see her."

"Yes, *we* should," he replied, handing the phone back to Grayson. "Can you tell her that we're coming over to speak with her about what happened?"

Gray nodded, his fingers flying over the keypad. A second later, there was a beep and he looked back at Drake.

"She said she has an hour before her mom gets back from the night shift."

Neve brushed past Drake. "Give me five minutes to get changed."

Grayson stepped back and let her pass. A moment later her bedroom door closed.

"Does she know?" Grayson asked.

"Know what?"

"That you've claimed her. Does she know?"

He shook his head, pacing over to the closet to pull out some clothes. "Her cat is aware, but she isn't yet."

"You know there has to be a harmony between the two halves of someone's soul for this to work."

"I know," he muttered a little too snidely. "Sorry." He glanced over his shoulder. "I'm impatient."

The other male shrugged. "Something like this can't be rushed." Grayson walked away, his voice softer when he said, "She's a good female."

He waited for him to say something more, but when there was only silence, he peered around the door to find his room empty.

Stepping back into the closet, he changed into a pair of jeans and a black T-shirt, sliding his arms into his weapon holster last. Opening up his gun safe, he took out one of the two SIGs housed there, checking the clips. Satisfied with both of them, he holstered them under his arms then snagged a jacket, covering up his firepower.

Striding from the room, he waited for Neve out on the landing. When her door opened, he stood a little straighter as she walked toward him with the same fluid grace as her cat had when she moved.

"Are you ready?" he asked, touching her cheek softly. He smiled when she leaned into his touch for a fleeting second. At her nod, they started down the stairs.

"You should know something about Pippa," Neve said, reaching for the front door. "When she was in high school, she was assaulted by one of the seniors. She doesn't trust males easily, so maybe you should let me do the talking."

"Not going to happen," he replied. It was a response that was becoming habitual when it came to Neve.

She gave him a flat stare. "Listen, this whole dominant male/submissive female thing isn't going to work for me."

"You didn't seem to have a problem with it before." Of course, he was referring to the bedroom, and it was a low blow.

The color rose in her cheeks. "We're not talking about that. This female—Pippa—it's more than fear of males with her. It's terror and paranoia all wrapped up in a bow. She won't talk to you. She won't even like that you're escorting me, but that will be my issue to deal with."

"I'm sorry, Neve," he said, unlocking the car and opening his door. He put his foot on the car door sill, one arm slung over the door. "I can't allow it."

"Then you can kiss any information she might have goodbye," she replied, looking at him over the roof.

He bit his tongue. Relinquishing control wasn't something he did easily but, reluctantly, Neve did make a good argument. He didn't know this female, but he could understand that her past may color the way she viewed males. "I'll let you take the lead, but as soon as I sense any danger, it's my way."

She gave him a sharp look but nodded. "Fine."

She got into the passenger seat of his Escalade without another word. He didn't think she'd give in so easily, and was instantly suspicious. He slid into the cool leather driver's seat and strapped himself in. The engine was a throaty growl beneath the hood, which soon turned into a smooth purr as he eased down the drive and waited for the main gates to open.

"What happened to her?" he asked once they were out on the highway.

"I only heard rumors, but they say she was sexually assaulted by a group of friends of the guy who took her to senior prom. She'd been a junior."

Drake's hands curled more tightly around the steering wheel. "Why didn't she fight back?"

"They outnumbered her six to one."

"And she couldn't defend herself?"

"They'd drugged her first."

"What happened to them?"

She shrugged. "They were human. There was nothing we could do. There was no proof to take to the human authorities. It was mostly swept under the carpet. The school denied any wrongdoing, even though the attack happened on school grounds. She didn't want to press charges."

"It shouldn't have happened," he replied coolly.

"It's in the past now," Neve replied, sounding tired. "The side effect is that she doesn't trust anyone of the opposite sex." She turned her body to face him. "What do you think happened last night?"

"Her text was vague, so I'm really not sure. All I do know is that we need to speak with her to see what she remembers."

Neve gave him directions when they got into town, cruising through the nicer neighborhoods until they reached Pippa's house. It was a well-maintained detached house with pristine white siding and a sprawling lush lawn, despite the plummeting nighttime temperatures. The midday sun hadn't quite reached full strength yet, but the flowers in the garden beds turned their faces toward it.

Drake parked the car on the street, not quite in front of the house in case her mother came home early. Neve opened her door, but Drake stopped her.

"Stay there. Wait until I come around."

Before she could protest, he got out and jogged around to her side. There was no way in hell he was going to leave her even slightly exposed to an attack. It was the male jaguar in him… well, the male jaguar and the bonded male. Holding open her door, he scanned the environment.

She muttered something under her breath as she got out and walked up the sidewalk toward Pippa's house.

26

NEVE

Neve tried to ignore the dangerous Shadow at her back, but when he growled at the mailman three houses down, she whirled around to face him.

"You need to back off on the dark and deadly routine."

His eyebrow quirked up. "Dark and deadly?" he asked.

She gestured to all of him. "This. Whatever you're doing right now. Knock it off. If Pippa sees you crowding me, your lip curled up in a snarl, your fangs bared, she's never going to talk to us."

She turned back around, not giving him the chance to defend his actions. She wasn't an idiot, though. For all her grumbling about Drake hovering over her, she understood the whys of it all. He was her mate, and he was functioning mostly on instinct right now.

When she reached the door, she peered over her shoulder to find Drake's expression bland and as non-threatening as she'd ever seen him. It was like saying a hungry bear was bland and non-threatening. Turning back, she knocked on the door and waited. A few moments passed before the door opened a sliver and Neve saw Pippa's pale blue eyes peering out at her.

"Neve?" she asked, opening the door a little wider. "What are you doing here?"

"How are you, Pippa?" She shifted a little to the right, letting her see Drake behind her. "This is Drake. He's…" Telling her he was one of the Revenant was not a good idea. "He's a friend of mine."

Pippa edged back from the door. "What does he want?" The panic was evident in her voice.

"He's here to protect me," she replied softly. "I just wanted to talk to you. Would that be okay?" Neve held her breath, then added, "He'll stay out here if that's what you want."

"Neve," Drake warned, but she ignored him, focusing on Pippa instead. She had to get this female to trust her. She wondered whether she'd done enough to reassure her, but smiled when the other female nodded.

"Okay, but my mom will be home from her night shift soon."

"Okay." Glancing at Drake over her shoulder, she told him, "Wait out here for me."

She slipped inside, banking on Pippa shutting the door firmly behind her. She did not disappoint, cutting off his angry snarl. Turning to take in the house, she blinked at the dim lighting. All the drapes were closed, blocking out almost all the light, and Neve waited for her cat's sight to kick in. Pippa stood in the center of the room, hugging her upper body.

"How are you, Pippa?"

The other female nodded, the movement jerky like she was a marionette puppet. "Fine. Good." Her gaze swept the floor. "Can I get you something to drink?"

"I'm fine, thank you." Knowing she needed to tread carefully, she turned to the photos hanging on the entryway wall. In them, she saw the Pippa she'd known at school, the bright, bubbly, vivacious female who was the life of the party. She found it so hard to connect that girl that she knew with the young woman in front of her.

She came across a photo of Pippa when she was just starting high school. She was wearing jaguar paw print knee-high socks with a short pleated skirt—her signature outfit.

"I remember those socks," she said with a smile.

Pippa barely glanced at the photograph, only tightened her arms around her torso and waited. Clearing her throat, Neve walked into the living room and lowered herself onto the couch. It smelled of Pippa and another female who had the same kind of base scent. It must've been her mom.

"I came to talk to you about the text you sent to the check-in number."

If she hadn't been watching, Neve would've missed the slight tightening in Pippa's shoulders.

"I shouldn't have sent that. I should've kept my mouth shut—"

"No, Pippa," Never interrupted. "You did the right thing." She shuffled closer to the edge of the couch, clasping her hands in front of her. "Can you tell me what happened?"

Pippa drew in a deep breath through her nose then let it go, a visible tremor going through her.

"You can tell me. It will help us to find whoever's behind this."

She eased onto the couch on the opposite wall, making herself look smaller by tucking her feet beneath her body and rolling her shoulders forward. "It was stupid. I shouldn't have gone out there so late, but the light from the security light just reached the curb."

"Gone out where?"

Her arms tightened around her knees. "To put out the trash. I don't normally do it, but my mom asked me to when she left for work…" She shrugged slightly. "She said I have to contribute more to the household, that I can't become a recluse even though

I suffer from agoraphobia. My therapist and I have been working on some stress management techniques but…" She finished with another shrug.

Neve slipped from the couch and settled in beside Pippa, keeping a good foot between them. "What happened?"

Pippa swallowed visibly. "I'd just closed the lid on the trash can when I saw a man walking toward me. He smiled at me, but there was something off about the smile."

"Off how?"

She looked at Neve. "Like he was thinking of hurting me." She turned her head, her dark hair falling to cover her face. "I'll always know that kind of smile."

Damn. Very slowly, so she didn't startle Pippa, she reached out and took her hand. "I never told you how sorry I was that happened to you, Pippa." She wasn't surprised when the other female took back her hand and tucked it under her knee.

"Thank you."

Neve blew out a breath. "So this guy you saw? Was he human or jaguar? Could you tell?"

"H-human," she whispered. "But it didn't mean he was less dangerous."

"You're right," she replied carefully. "Did he say anything to you?"

Pippa shook her head, the ends of her hair slapping her face softly. "He didn't say anything—he just grabbed me, pinning my arms to my sides." She took in a shuddering breath and licked her lips. "I was too shocked to act until a black van pulled up and he tried to shove me inside."

"How did you get away?"

A smile pulled up the corner of Pippa's mouth, a curling of her lip that made Neve shiver. "We were about the same height," she said softly.

Neve said nothing, letting the other female talk at her own pace. She had a feeling if she pushed too hard, she'd shut down.

"I broke his nose."

"Oh?" The word was spoken with calm detachment in the hopes it would help encourage Pippa further.

Uncurling her legs, Pippa placed her feet on the carpet and stared at them. "After… after what happened in high school, my mother suggested I take self-defense classes. I did for a little while, until the female instructor I started with went on maternity leave. Her replacement was a man." She peered at Neve from the corner of her eye. "I never went back after that. But I did learn something."

"How did you do it?" Neve absently wiped off the knee of her jeans, giving Pippa the mental breathing space she needed.

"He had me pinned so my back was to his front. I threw my head back. I heard the crunch. Then I stomped on his foot. He let me go, and I ran into the house, locking the door. I heard the tires of the van screeching as they drove off, then I texted the check-in number."

Her words came out in a long stream, punctuated only by gasping breaths.

"You were very brave," Neve murmured. "Thank you for being able to think clearly enough to text the Leo's emergency number."

Pippa shrugged. "Please don't tell my mom. She'll only worry."

"She loves you. She just wants to keep you safe."

Pippa's nod was that same jerky movement as before. "Do you have any other questions? My mom will be home in ten minutes."

"I just need a description of the man. Hair color, eye color—that kind of thing."

"Both dark. Average build. My height, like I said."

"What was he wearing?"

Her eyes focused on the clock on the mantel. "Jeans. Construction boots. Black T-shirt. Is that all?"

"Yes." Neve stood up. "Thank you, Pippa. I appreciate you speaking to me."

The female wouldn't meet her eyes. "You should go."

Neve walked to the front door and pulled it open. "You'll get in contact if you see the man again?" But Pippa didn't answer. She was staring at the clock, flinching with every movement of the second hand as it made its revolutions around the face.

Neve turned around to find Drake standing with his arms crossed and a thunderous look on his face. Brushing past him, she was brought to a stop when his hand shot out. He gripped her other arm just as tightly, turning her to face him, his yellow eyes more piercing with the power of his cat. His gaze skimmed every inch of her face before dropping down her body.

"I'm safe," she told him, swallowing a lump in her throat. "Nothing happened to me in there." There was a part of her that understood she was talking to his cat rather than Drake.

He didn't loosen his grip, so she got up onto her tiptoes and rubbed her cheek against him. This close, he'd be able to smell her and know she was safe. The feline gesture broke the spell, and his fingers loosened. He let her go and stepped back, still staring at her.

"What did you find out?" he asked in a rough voice.

"I'll tell you on the way back to your house." Without waiting for his reply, she walked to the Escalade and waited for him to unlock the car. When they were both strapped in and Drake was easing out from the curb, he reached out and laid his hand on her knee.

The heat was immediate.

"What did you find out?"

"She was attacked last night while taking out the trash."

Her statement was met by a rush of anger that flooded the car and made her shoulders stiffen. She wasn't usually able to sense things like that, but with Drake, it was like he was hooked up to a nuclear reactor, making every emotion he had unavoidable.

"How did she get away?"

"She'd taken some self-defense classes, so she used some of those skills. She broke the guy's nose. When he let her go, she ran and got away."

Drake flipped on the directional signal with an angry jerk of his hand. "Then what happened?"

"She heard them leave in the black van they'd come in."

Turning back onto the main road that would get them back onto the highway, Drake turned to her. "Did she get a good look at the man? And was he human or a cat?"

"She was quite sure he was human." Neve repeated the description Pippa had given her.

"Hmm, that doesn't give us a lot to go on."

"No, it doesn't."

Drake put his foot down when they got onto the highway, the speed limit increasing as they got out of the town. "Do you want to know what I don't understand?"

"What's that?"

"She got away. Why did she get away when nobody else did?"

Neve shrugged, but it was something she'd thought about too. It didn't make sense. In order for a human to subdue a cat, they'd have to knock the cat out. So why hadn't Pippa been on the receiving end of a tranquilizer or something similar? "From what she said, they just tried to muscle her into the van."

"Which is, I assume, how they got the other females. But trying to get a hissing and spitting shifter to do anything they don't want to do while still fully conscious? It just seems moronic."

"All right, so they would've had to tranquilize the females before they put them into the van to transport wherever the hell they're taking them, so why didn't it happen with Pippa?"

His jaw tightened, the muscle pulsing as he thought. "Either they've gotten cocky and their MO has changed, or I return to my aforementioned statement of them being morons."

She turned her body toward him in her seat, readjusting the seat belt so it didn't cut into the side of her neck. "What if Pippa wasn't the real target?"

Drake's eyes narrowed, but stayed on the road. "What do you mean?"

"I mean, what if they weren't looking for females, but they *happened* to stumble upon Pippa?" Drake didn't say anything, clearly letting her speak. "All the other attacks have been premeditated, or that's what we assume. They'd have to at least be familiar with members of the pride and know *something* about their routine. Pippa has agoraphobia. She doesn't normally venture outside, so really, she shouldn't have been on their radar at all."

"It was an opportunistic attack."

"Right. I think she was very lucky to have even gotten away from them, and

I'm even more stunned that she overcame her fear to text the Shadows."

"We owe her a lot," Drake said softly.

"Yes, we do. She gave us a lot of information. She's also the only female who's been close to one of the abductors and gotten away."

"I'll have Grayson or Jett swing by a few times every night to keep an eye on things."

"Good idea."

Drake slowed the car as he turned onto the private road that led to their house. Neve leaned back against the headrest, closing her eyes briefly as they went through the security checkpoints. She opened them to check the time on the dash. It was well after lunch time now, and she wondered how much longer the meeting her dad was in was going to go for. He said he'd call afterward, but she decided if she hadn't heard from him by five, she would call him.

When they reached the top parking lot, he shut off the engine and sat there for a moment.

"You were right to leave me outside like that. I didn't like it, my *cat* certainly didn't like it, but I realize my presence there would've made her shut down."

She tried not to let him see how much his praise meant to her. "Thank you for respecting her wishes and mine." She opened up her car door and stepped out. She started toward the door, but movement in the front garden caught her attention, and she stiffened at the sight of a female.

"That's Sasha—one of the Revenant," Drake murmured into her ear as he placed his palm against her back. "She created all the gardens around the property."

"She tends them too?" Neve asked, still focused on Sasha.

Drake bobbed his head. "It's… therapeutic for her."

He didn't introduce them as they walked past, but the female's quicksilver gaze fixed on Neve's face.

"Drake," Sasha said, and Neve felt him stiffen. She shivered, the hairs on the back of her neck suddenly standing on end. It felt like her blood had turned to ice in her veins.

"Not now, Sash," Drake warned.

"The sapling needs protection from the oak," she whispered, her eyes liquid mercury. *"Trust in the unbreakable, even when you fear it will shatter,"* she added, looking at Neve this time.

Drake hurried her inside, but Neve still felt cold. "What did she mean?"

"Nothing," he replied. "Sasha was just relaying a message to me."

27

JETT

Jett paused outside the door of his mother's hospital room, indecision playing on his mind. On the one hand, he didn't want to go in there and see his mother laid out from her drug habit. Yes, he'd seen her stretched out on her mattress, her body numb, her mind checked out before, but this was different. This time, she'd gone too far, taken too much, let herself slip into an unconsciousness that usually ended with a body bag.

On the other hand, she was his mom. She was the female who gave birth to him, who had loved him—at least at one point. She was the one who had read to him before he went to sleep, and sang to him when he was scared or sick. But when he looked at her now, all he saw was the empty shell of who she used to be.

Her body was worn down by life, her veins collapsed under the onslaught of drugs that she willingly pumped into her body—all in the pursuit of peace. Inhaling deeply through his nose, he smelled the sharp bite of antiseptic and knew the floor he was loitering on got cleaned at least twice a day.

He glanced to the left and right, seeing more rooms identical to his mom's, but they probably didn't hold the kind of desolate sadness and hopelessness that hers harbored. Behind him was the nurses' station, two RNs working shoulder-to-shoulder with Doctor Winchester heading the charge against illness and mental health issues among shifters.

The building was new—built a few years back for this exact reason. If his mom had been admitted to a human hospital, treatment would have ended with her in a lab being poked and prodded. They had the Leo of the Black Claw pride to thank for that. The clinic serviced Wyoming and most of Montana, and there were plans for two more in Idaho and Utah.

One of the nurses smiled at him, the gesture shuttered like she knew exactly why he was here. It wasn't a damn secret, though, was it? She'd come in OD'ing on a Speedball. Richard, the fuck, was somewhere else in this building, but the Doc wouldn't tell him where. He guessed he had the Hippocratic Oath to uphold. Protecting that POS from Jett only made him angrier. Richard owed him, and he'd take his pound of flesh.

Thank God Katya was safe. If only he could say the same for Luce. His other sister he would pay a visit to after seeing his mom. He needed to make sure she was being kept safe, even if her boyfriend was some cocksucking human.

Right.

The door.

Gotta push through the door.

Letting out a breath, he let himself into the room and abruptly came to a stop. His mom was hooked up to machines, all of them beeping softly—intermittently. He scanned her from head to toe, trying to find what was left of his mom. Her face was different, her eyes sunken, her skin pitted and scarred. Her lips were a pale pink, like even her blood couldn't give a fuck anymore. Lids were shut over eyes the same color as Katya's, and even her height had seemed to change. She was smaller somehow, stooped maybe. A white sheet was pulled up over her too thin body, her arms placed on either side of her torso.

Walking up to the side of her bed, he pulled the plastic chair closer to the rail and sat down. His eyes made another pass, trying to place everything he knew into this moment. His mom had OD'd. She had died. Twice. But the Doc had brought her back both times. He'd told Jett that his mom's body had been through a lot, had endured a lot, and the loss of oxygen and blood supply to her brain had been extensive, so only time would tell if she would recover fully or only partially.

And so here he was. Staring down at her. Hoping she didn't pull through this. That was a horrible thought for a son to have, though. The thing was, she hadn't been a mother to him for a very long time, and that distance had brought with it an estrangement he barely noticed anymore.

"What have you done, Mom?" he asked, suddenly angry. He didn't cry, even though he could feel the tears sitting there, pricking the backs of his eyes. He wouldn't let them fall for her. He had wasted too much already.

"God*damn* you," he said, yet he stayed right where he was. He wouldn't go back without spending some time with her. As he watched, her eyes rolled fitfully behind her lids, her mouth working around the tube that had been inserted into her throat. He stood up, peering down into her face. Her eyes suddenly flipped open, and she stared at him, her eyes so wide, he could see the whites all the way around.

"Mom? Can you hear me? Mom?"

Her eyes were wild, her gaze bouncing around the room, never lingering on one spot for more than a few seconds. She lifted her arms, her hands curling into weak fists.

"Mom!" he yelled. Spinning around, he yelled for the nurse before turning back around. She was trying to bite the tube, the one that was keeping her lungs going.

"Don't bite it," he said, rubbing her arm. "Don't—Fuck!" The machines on either side of her starting blaring. Where the fuck was the—

"Step back, please, sir," the nurse said, all but shoving him out of the way. That was no mean feat. He was a little under two hundred pounds of pissed off shifter, but the female didn't seem to notice or care. He stepped back, pressing himself against the far wall as another nurse ran in and shut all the alarms off. Jett couldn't take his eyes off his mother as her eyes rolled back in her head, her body jerking spasmodically. Her hands were flexing and releasing, flexing and releasing as a seizure wracked her body.

"What's happening?" Doctor Winchester barked as he ran in. He had a stethoscope slung over his neck, his white coat fluttering behind him then settling as he came to a full stop. The first nurse stepped back to allow the doc a better view of things, and that's when it all went to shit.

"She's flatlining!" someone shouted.

A giant bag was attached to his mom's tube, one that inflated her lungs within her ribcage. The doctor took over the motion, yelling at one of the nurses to start chest compressions. As lithe as the cat she shared her body with, she leapt onto the table and started pumping his mom's chest, the sound of her ribs cracking with the force.

"You don't want to see this, son," the doc said, his expression grim. "Wait outside."

Jett didn't even have the strength to fight the order. He simply nodded and moved out of the way. He winced when the door eased shut behind him, his whole body feeling lighter than he anticipated. His legs crumpled beneath him, and he slid to the floor, vaguely aware that he was in the doorway.

Some time later, a nurse approached him and helped him stand, leading him over to a chair she'd placed there. Getting him settled, she pressed a plastic cup of water into his hand, then crouched down in front of him.

He focused on her face. She had pretty eyes.

"How are you doing?"

"F—" He licked his lips and tried again. "Fine." His voice was a croak he hardly recognized. "My mom?"

Her lips pursed, and he knew it wasn't going to be good news. "I'm not sure yet. They're still working on her."

Working on her.

Like she was a car whose engine just wouldn't turn over.

He guessed it wasn't too far from the truth. His mom's engine had stopped, but it wasn't something that could be fixed. She'd chosen her death, and even though it may be slow, it was happening all the same. Poison, after all, would eventually stop a person's heart, and then it was lights out.

No more encores.

He stood up, making the nurse back up or get knocked over. He didn't know where he was going to go, but he knew he couldn't stay there any longer.

"Jett, don't you want to see if your mother—"

"Fuck my mother," he shot back, cutting her off. "Fuck her for choosing drugs over us," he muttered to himself.

Outside the clinic, he turned his phone back on and found a message from Mila. She didn't want him to come and see her, and didn't that just make him want to fuck her over. Walking to his bike, he double-checked the address Katya had given him and started the bike. He probably wasn't in the best frame of mind to be talking to his sister, but damn it, he was going.

It only took him thirty minutes to get there, and as he parked on the street in a middle-class neighborhood, he stared up at the house. It was nice. Flower beds. Tidy lawn. A sealed driveway. Siding not falling off. Mila had certainly moved up from the trailer. He didn't resent her for it. How could he? He'd upped and left as soon as he could.

Getting off the bike, he removed his helmet and placed it on the seat. He walked up that perfect path, glowering at the flowers planted along the length. He didn't know why he was being such a fucking jerk about it, though. It wasn't the flowers' fault for being there. At the door, he knocked then stepped back, his eyes scanning to see the neighbor next door out in the garden pruning the rose bushes. The woman looked at him and smiled, then got back to deadheading her blooms.

When the door opened, he was surprised to see Mila there, her arms wrapped protectively around her stomach. Like she was waiting for a blow to come.

"What are you doing here? I told you not to come."

"I've never listened to what you say."

Behind the storm door, her gray eyes were icy, her face looking more severe with her honey-blonde hair pulled away from her face. That hair color was the only thing they shared, but then again, only getting half your DNA from the same mother would do that. They all had different fathers, but Jett didn't know who Luce's was. His mother had been 'dating' about three males around that time. Honestly, he didn't care. Luce was his little sister, and he loved her all the same.

"What are you doing here?" she asked again.

"Has Katya called you?" A curt nod. "Then you know it's not safe right now."

She actually rolled her eyes at this statement. "I'm fine here. Robby is taking care of me."

He smiled cruelly. "Ah, yes, Robby the *human*, who doesn't know a thing about your real life."

Yeah, he'd totally sneered over the word human, like it was dog shit on the bottom of his shoe.

"He loves me, Jett. That's all I need to know."

He ran a hand through his hair, blowing out a frustrated breath. "You've only been dating for a month."

"Six months, Jett," she hissed. "If you were ever around, you would've known that. But, nooooo, you had to take off and leave us in that *shit hole* with our *shit hole* mother and her fucking *shit hole* drug addiction."

He chewed the inside of his cheek to stop himself from biting her head off. He got it. Abandonment was something they all suffered from, but come on. As if he was the only one to blame. She'd gone and done the same thing—shacking up with the first guy who showed her any sort of affection.

"Look, we can argue about this later, but I have something to tell you."

One brow arched sharply. "Then use the phone and tell me. I don't want to see you, especially not here."

He felt the growl trickle from his throat, but he clamped down on the instinct to bite back. He was wounded, but so was she, and her words stung. He glanced over at the human attending the roses.

"Look, can we go inside and talk?"

"No," Mila replied. "I don't care what you have to say."

"Even if it's about our mom?"

Well, that worked. Like a needle being yanked off a record, she shut her mouth and stared at him.

"What about her?"

"She OD'd. She's down at the clinic. I just came from there."

Those arms of hers tightened. "Is she okay?"

Jett remembered the way her body had gone into seizure, the uncontrolled movements. Slowly, he shook his head. "No, I don't think so. Not this time."

"Was Richard there when it happened?"

"Yeah."

"What happened to him?"

"What do you care?" he shot back, cursing himself a little at the harshness of his tone. "Look, I'm sorry," he replied. "He'd OD'd too. The doc got him back online, but I don't know what happened after that."

Mila's expression hardened. "Because you left, didn't you?"

Jesus. "Mila—"

"No!" she screamed. "Fuck you, Jett. I'm happy here. Robby takes good care of me." She stepped away from the door, her knuckles white as she gripped the edge.

"Mila! Wait! There's something—"

His words were cut off as she slammed the door in his face.

"Dammit!" He wasn't going to tell her that Luce had also gone missing through the door.

Goddammit, was he ever going to catch a break? Turning around, he walked back down the path, waving politely to the woman who was openly staring now. Yeah, he guessed domestic disputes in the middle of the day weren't really par for the course in this neighborhood. She bobbed her head and hustled through the side gate of her yard.

As Jett got back onto his bike, a new Toyota Tundra pulled into the drive and parked in front of the single car garage. Jett waited to see this cocksucker Robby, ready to threaten him with castration if he didn't take care of his sister.

The guy popped the door and got out, his gaze swinging toward him like he had a fucking neon sign hanging over his head.

"Can I help you?" the guy asked, his body tense like he was ready to throw down or some shit. Jett turned toward the guy, visually measuring him. He was about the same height as Jett, but his bones weren't carrying the same kind of bulk. Plus, he was only a human. With cropped brown hair and a matching set of eyes, the guy was as All-American as it got, right down to his Abercrombie and Fitch T-shirt, jeans, and Nikes. He looked like a decent male, too, but Jett was going to ignore that for the time being.

"Yeah. I just came to see my sister," Jett replied.

"You're Mila's brother?"

"Yeah."

The guy rubbed the back of his skull, his bicep rolling beneath his skin as it moved. "Fuck, man, I'm glad you stopped by."

And cue that needle-off-record sound again.

"I'm sorry, what?"

Robby stepped closer until only a few feet separated them. "Yeah, I love Mila, but you and her have some issues to work out."

"I know," he replied, unwilling to dip further into the details that were none of this guy's biz.

"Has she told you a lot about me?"

Oh, gee, only that you were living together after dating for six months. Oh, wait! No, she didn't. He had to hear it from his oldest sister's mouth.

"Just that you treat her well and keep her safe."

The guy nodded, shoving his hands into the front pockets of his jeans. "I do love her, and I want to keep her safe."

"Do you own a gun?"

Jett's question was met with stunned silence. "I don't..." He shook his head.

"Do you know how to shoot?"

"Well, yeah. My old man is a cop. He made sure I learned."

Reaching behind him, he pulled out the SIG Sauer he kept at the small of his back. "Take this."

Robby just began shaking his head. "I can't."

"Look, the numbers have been filed off. It's untraceable. Just take it."

"Why would I—"

"You said you wanted to keep her safe?"

"I do."

Jett gestured for the guy to take the weapon from him. "Then prove it, because I'm sure as shit not going to leave until I know you're protecting her right."

As if on autopilot, Robby came and took the gun, holding it like he knew what he was doing.

Thank fuck for that. "I want your word, my man. You will protect her with your life."

"What the hell is going on? Is she in danger? Is someone coming after her?"

Jett shook his head. Any questions he answered truthfully were just going to blow this guy's mind. "Just look after her, okay? I'm counting on you."

And with that, he got back on his bike, slid on the helmet, and tore away from all that perfection that would never be his.

28

NEVE

Neve had arrived back at the compound with Drake almost an hour before, and Sasha's words were still bothering her as she sat alone in the rec room. She heard people coming and going from the house, but nobody seemed concerned she was hanging out in there.

As she puzzled over Sasha's words, she tried to figure out why Drake had brushed her off so easily too. It was like he was hiding something from her.

"The sapling needs protection from the oak," she whispered to herself. "Trust in the unbreakable, even when you fear it will shatter."

She had no idea what the tree reference was about, nor did she understand the reference to *the unbreakable*. Letting out a sigh, she glanced down at her phone—no calls from her dad yet, but maybe the meeting was still going. She stood up, restless energy burning through her. She hated waiting, but she'd give him until five before she called him.

Five o'clock was more than two hours away. She couldn't sit there for two hours—not without driving herself crazy. She could spend a couple of hours naked with Drake, but she wasn't sure jumping into bed with that male would make things any less complicated.

There was something about him that spoke to her cat, but her more logical human brain was still working hard to beat back the instinct to submit to him. She never wanted to 'belong' to anyone, not like Katie wanted to… not like her mom wanted her to do. Independence was what she craved, and tying herself down to one male was a guaranteed way to not just destroy her dreams, but obliterate her autonomy.

She couldn't deny the attraction anymore, though. If they hadn't been interrupted by Grayson before, she had no doubt in her mind that she would've let him take her again. There was something so *right* about being held in his arms. Even now, she could swear she felt him and how he was feeling. His emotions seemed to brush against her mind, the warmth of his protective streak like a heavy blanket in the winter. She didn't know what it meant, or whether it was reciprocal, but the more time she spent with him, the stronger the sensations were becoming.

"There you are."

She peered over her shoulder to find Drake leaning casually against the wall just inside the doors into the rec room. She took in the swell of his biceps, appreciating the way his shirtsleeves strained. Suddenly, the idea of spending a couple of hours naked with him didn't sound like such a bad idea.

"What are you thinking about, Neve?" His voice was a low rasp that made her squirm.

Forcing her eyes away, she looked back at her phone. "I'm waiting for a phone call."

His whole demeanor changed—honing into a hard edge. "A phone call? From who?" he demanded.

She tried not to let that statement bristle. Letting out an impatient breath, she kept her sharp tongue in check and said, "My father. He said he'd call after that big pride meeting in California."

The air suddenly crackled with pulsing rage, and she rubbed her arms, peering up at Drake as his cat made his citrine yellow eyes glow like coals. When he spoke, she expected his voice to boom, but his words were careful, his tone smooth. It was almost like he shoved that anger back into a compartment in his head in an instant. "What meeting?"

Keeping her words low, and her eyes on his chin, she said, "The meeting the Yellow Eye Leo called. It took place this morning."

His hands curled and uncurled. "I wasn't informed of any meeting." His anger washed against her in a tsunami-sized wave, and she fought not to flinch. "I thought your father was in New York."

"There was a change of plans," she said. She hadn't had a lot of experience with rage like this. Her dad was always a level-headed leader, but she was coming to realize the Shadows were like a whole different breed of jaguar. Everything about them was amplified—their emotions, their rage... their passion.

"When did he tell you about this?"

She watched him as he began to pace. "He called me this morning and told me they changed their flight. They got into LAX late last night." She frowned. "I thought you knew..."

"I didn't." His hands flexed into fists at his sides. "Did he say what the meeting was supposed to be about?"

Neve shrugged. "All he said was that a meeting had been called— all the Leos were in attendance."

"When was it supposed to start?"

"Nine o'clock."

He looked at his watch. "That was over six hours ago."

"I know."

There was a tap on the wall, and Drake turned. Neve peered around him to find Grayson standing there.

"Get everyone in here," Drake barked.

"You've got it," he replied, disappearing like smoke. A tense silence filled the room as they waited, Neve unwilling to break it. Drake continued to pace, doing nothing to reduce the suffocating veil settling over them both. Only a few minutes passed before the rest of the Revenant filed in, all except for Jett. He was MIA, but nobody seemed surprised.

Sasha walked over to the window that overlooked one of her gardens and pushed the drapes out of the way to give herself an unimpeded view. Mateo sat beside Neve on the couch, despite there being a multitude of other seats to take. He even slung his arm casually over the back of the cushion behind her until Drake growled at him in warning. With a blithe smile, he stood up and settled against the opposite wall instead.

Grayson stood at ease by the entrance, and she got the distinct impression that he was the glue that held the team together. Drake, despite being the leader, was often prone to anger, but was tempered by considered and deliberate decisions. Jett seemed too distracted. Mateo, on the other hand, was too flippant about a lot of things to take anything too seriously, although he did have that bad-boy vibe about him too. And Sasha... well, Neve hadn't made her mind up about Sasha yet. There was something incredibly *sad* about the female.

"What's happened now?" Mateo asked.

Drake ran his hands through his hair. "We've been fucked over by the Trinity."

"You say that like you're surprised."

"Shut the fuck up, Mateo," Grayson growled, and Mateo made a theatrical gesture of zipping his lips shut.

Drake let out a sigh, but kept his head bowed. "Neve, can you tell us everything you just told me?"

She swallowed and met everyone's eyes. "My father called this morning and said he wasn't in New York as planned. He was in California at the Yellow Eye Leo's house as his guest." Her stomach churned suddenly, and she pressed a palm just above her navel. "He also said that another meeting had been called—a meeting that started at nine this morning. I've been expecting a call from him to let me know how it went. I haven't received it yet."

"Could he have forgotten?" Grayson asked softly.

Neve turned her head to look at him. "No. If my father says he's going to do something, he does it."

"Have you tried to call him?" This question was from Drake, who was staring at her with his cat's eyes. She shook her head slowly. "Do it now, and put it on speaker."

With a shaking hand, she reached down and hit number two on her speed dial. It rang twice before it went to voicemail.

"Try it again."

She did, squeezing her eyes shut when it didn't even ring this time, a tinny automated woman saying the call couldn't be connected.

"What about your mother's number?"

With shaking hands, she pressed number three and put the call on speaker.

"*I'm sorry, but the person you're trying to call is unavailable...*" Neve ended the call and looked up, the need to act like a fire burning through her blood.

"I need to go there," she announced to nobody in particular.

"Something's wrong. Something's happened—I can feel it."

Everyone turned toward Drake—waiting for his orders. His face was dark, his expression unreadable. "Drake…" Her voice broke. She wasn't above begging if it meant it kept her parents safe.

"No," he said so softly, she doubted she would've known he'd spoken unless she was looking at him.

"What?"

He turned his yellow eyes on her, the muscle in his jaw jumping as he bit out, "You're not going."

Anger made her blood ignite, and she felt her lips peel back from her teeth, exposing her canines. "If you're too afraid to go, I will."

She went to brush past him, but his hand shot out and grabbed her by the arm, dragging her to an abrupt stop. His anger at her statement brushed against her consciousness, but that was not what gave her pause—it was his terror.

A few tense moments passed before he slowly released his fingers from her arm, and she hugged herself. Making demands of him in front of his Shadows was not going to get her anywhere.

"Come with me," she said under her breath, walking from the room. She felt everyone's eyes on her, but she tipped up her chin and kept walking. Drake followed like a shadow at her back, finally pushing through the kitchen after her. Leaning against the countertop, she folded her arms then let them drop to her sides. Being defensive was not a great place to start.

"What's going on?" she asked softly.

"What do you mean?"

"I mean, what's going on—with me, with you. I've been feeling…"

"What?" he croaked when she hesitated.

She fixed her eyes on his. "I can *feel* you—your emotions."

He visibly stiffened. "When did this start?" he asked.

He didn't even blink at her statement.

She moved slowly, giving herself time to think, to wonder *why* he seemed to already know, as she pulled out one of the under-counter stools and sat down. "I'm not sure, but it's getting stronger."

He looked away, staring down at his feet. "You felt my fear just now."

"Yes."

"Then you understand why I can't let you go."

She sucked in a breath through her mouth and let it out, ready to defend her choices, when Sasha pushed through the door. The other female ignored her, her silver gaze on Drake. It felt like the temperature in the room dropped ten degrees, and Neve fought not to shiver.

"Not now, Sash," Drake growled.

She took his arm and spun him around. "Trust in the unbreakable, even when you fear it will shatter. You must go to California and you must take her," she gestured to Neve, "with you."

Drake became incredibly still as he digested the statement. "Have you seen this?" he breathed. He gripped her shoulders, fingers digging in. "*Tell me*, damnit."

Her gray irises rolled like they were molten. "She *will not* shatter, Drake, but without her, *you* might."

29

DRAKE

She will not shatter, Drake.

Drake scrubbed his face as Sasha left. The very idea that he would willingly take Neve into what would undoubtedly be a very dangerous situation made him break out in a cold sweat. She was his strength and his weakness all rolled up into one. Yet even as fear gripped his heart, he knew that to live without her and not touch her would surely kill him, too. She was his *arnasa*.

"Pack a bag," he croaked. "I need to go and speak to the others." He pressed against the kitchen door to leave, but paused, letting out a shuddering breath. "Can you feel what I'm feeling right now?"

"You're terrified," she murmured. "But resolved."

He tensed when she touched his back, right between his shoulder blades and over the skull of the Grim Reaper. "Thank you."

Slowly, he turned around to face her. "I would do anything for you, Neve…even if it terrifies me." Leaning down, he kissed her, lingering there when she kissed him back just as fiercely. Breaking away, he touched his fingertips to her cheek. "Pack for a couple of days. Grab the first aid kit beneath your sink as well as mine."

He left her in the kitchen, stalking back into the rec room where his team still waited.

"Orders, boss?" Grayson asked.

"We're going. Mateo and Sash, you're coming with us. Grayson, I need you to stick around for damage control. Jett will have to stay to look after his sister and to get his head back in the game. Tell him what's happening when he gets back."

"Yes, boss," Grayson replied.

Turning to Mateo and Sasha, he added, "Get packed. We're leaving in thirty."

Returning to his room, he pulled out an overnight bag and shoved some clothes inside. Unlocking his gun safe, he pulled out his SIGs and grabbed the extra clips. His eyes settled on the length of chain he kept in there, and he grabbed that too. He added a few blades to the mix just for good measure, then shut things up.

He changed into a pair of jeans, a black tee, and his duster to cover up the weapons he was carrying. Out on the landing, he found Sasha and Mateo waiting.

"Armed?"

Mateo grinned and pulled back the side of his leather jacket to reveal a holster loaded with twin Berettas. Drake didn't have to ask if Sash was protected. She preferred to fight with her hands, although she was known to carry a lot of knives on her too. They all turned when Neve came out of her room, her hand wrapped tightly around the handles of her bag.

"Are you ready?"

She gave him a curt nod. He knew better than to offer to take her duffel, so he motioned for Mateo to go down the stairs first. Sasha pulled up the rear behind him and Neve, and when they got to the foyer, Grayson was there to meet them.

He held out his hand to the male. "If we're gone longer than three days, do *not* come after us. Do you hear me?"

Grayson nodded stiffly, but the skin around his eyes was tight. He didn't agree, but he'd follow his orders. "I'll do what I can to trace these females while you're gone. Mateo managed to pull some feeds from the school's security system."

"Good."

Outside, Drake led Neve over to his Escalade. "Mateo, take the van in case we need to move injured jaguars."

Their van was a refitted Mercedes Sprinter panel van, which had a few extra pieces of kit added—blacked-out windows, bullet-proof panels, and a cache of weapons that the military would envy. Mateo stepped in closer. "You think this is body recovery?" he asked in a low voice.

Jesus, he hoped not. "No. I just want to be prepared. Follow behind us. We're going to push through until we get to California. Text if you need to stop for gas or to change drivers."

Mateo held out his fist, and Drake pounded it. "Is it wrong that I'm looking forward to potentially whooping ass?"

Drake's smile was fierce. It had been too long since their last physical fight, and he was looking forward to it too. "Stick to the speed limit. We don't need the human authorities sniffing around when we have an arsenal in the back of that van."

He helped Neve into the Escalade, then placed their bags into the back. When he got into the driver's seat, Neve asked, "You're not planning on stopping?"

"No," he replied grimly. He wasn't surprised that she'd overheard the conversation. He just hoped she didn't catch his reasoning for taking the van. "We'll drive through the night."

Drake pulled on his seat belt, dragging the nylon strap across his body. Such a simple thing—a length of man-made fabric strengthened to reduce the chance of a trip through the windshield. Although it seemed flimsy, it was strong, doing what it had to do to save lives. He wanted Sasha to be right. He wanted the tentative thread of his and Neve's bond to be the same. After she'd told him she could feel him, his emotions, he realized their mate bond was strengthening. The only thing they'd need to do was complete it now, but that required a blood exchange, and he had no idea how she would react.

His female was headstrong, resistant to anything that bound her to someone else. In order for their mating to work, though, he needed her to need and want him. He needed her to bend to him without breaking her spirit. He rolled through the security check-points and got out onto the highway. Checking his rearview mirror, he made sure Mateo was still with him before he mentally settled into the thirteen-hour drive.

"What does it mean?" Neve asked quietly about an hour into the trip. "Why can I feel what you feel?"

He blew out a breath. He couldn't avoid answering her question for the next twelve hours, and he didn't want to lie to her either. She had a right to know, and he had a feeling she'd appreciate having all the facts before she made a decision.

"A mate bond has formed," he said, glancing at her to gauge her reaction. Her face was impassive, but she was listening. "It's fragile at the moment, but your ability to feel what I feel is a good sign."

Neve crossed her arms tightly over her chest. "Can you feel what I'm feeling?"

He smiled slightly. "Not in the way you described. I can decipher the scent of your feelings, but that's got nothing to do with the bond. That's something distinctive to Shadows."

"And other shifters too, right?"

He conceded her statement with a nod. "To a degree. Shadows have been born with stronger senses of smell than the average shifter. It gives us…an edge."

The night was drawing in around them, and he flipped on the headlights. "There's something else you probably don't know about me and the other Shadows."

"You're smarter than the av-er-age bear?" she quipped in her best Yogi Bear voice, her mouth quirking up in the corner.

He chuckled. "My team…" He wondered how to tell her. He'd never had to explain this part of his life to anyone before. He hadn't even known *he* was different until he'd begun training with the Trinity a decade ago. "We're Shadows, yes, but we're called the Revenant because we have extra abilities—abilities the regular Shadows don't have."

She turned her body toward him. "How did you get them, these extra abilities?"

He touched the center of his chest. "I was born with them." She tilted her head to the side, inviting him to continue speaking, and he blew out a breath. He was standing on the precipice of a cliff. Would he fall, or would Neve throw him the rope he needed? "I can read thoughts, get into people's heads, manipulate memories, and feed them images."

"What kind of images?"

He shrugged, shifting his hands around the steering wheel. The leather was warm beneath his palm. "It depends on what the situation calls for…"

"The butler," she said suddenly, her eyes widening in sudden understanding. "The butler at Charles's place wasn't going to let us in that night, but he changed his mind."

"That was me," he said carefully. Dipping inside someone's head and thoughts was invasive, and he only ever did it when absolutely necessary. Yes, at the start, he'd done it to Neve, but he soon realized why he couldn't get much more than blips and flashes. She was immune, and as soon as their mate bond was sealed, she would be completely closed off to him.

She was quiet for a moment, obviously coming to the conclusion he feared the most. "Have you done it to me?"

"Neve—"

She rounded on him, her anger a harsh sting in his nose. "Have you?"

He shook his head. "I can't get clear images from you."

"What do you mean?"

"I get flashes from you, and really only when you're in your cat's form."

"You've never…manipulated me into thinking something else?"

He knew exactly what she was asking of him. "What you feel for me is real, Neve. I can't change emotions, all I can change is memories and read thoughts. If they're tied to strong emotions like hate or love, it becomes harder to change them. Once our mate bond has been sealed, my abilities will intensify and a few extra abilities will evolve too."

"Extra?"

He reached out and put his hand on her knee, stilling her fingers, which were furiously plucking at the threads on the rip on her knee. "Stronger. Faster. Shifting more quickly with far fewer side effects."

She was staring down at his hand when she asked, "What about the others? If you can read minds, what about the rest of your team?"

"Grayson can manipulate emotions by touch. Jett has the ability to create fire."

"What about Mateo?" She glanced over at him and frowned. "Hey, put the fangs away. I only asked a question about the male."

Drake took a deep breath and apologized for his reaction. "My cat is a little territorial when it comes to you."

"Noted." A small smile flexed her lips. "But I still want to know."

"You've seen Mateo's tattoos on his right arm?"

She nodded.

"He can heal with his touch. Only that hand has the power."

"Why not the other?"

He shrugged. "Honestly, all of our powers are…" Unpredictable wasn't the right word. "Unexpected."

"What do you mean?"

"Well, Mateo is a player who only cares about when he'll get laid next. Him having the power to heal seems pretty wasteful."

"How so?"

"Willingness to heal implies compassion, of which I'm not sure Mateo has."

That seemed like a pretty accurate evaluation. "And Jett?"

"Jett's a loose cannon. His abilities require great restraint and control, but he lets his emotions rule rather than his head."

"And you?" she asked, her thumb rubbing over the knuckles of his hand. He kept his eyes on the road. If he drew attention to it, she'd make a big deal out of it.

"Me?" He smiled. "I might be the only one where it makes sense. I like control and order. Rearranging someone's thoughts is as a controlled environment as you can get."

"You haven't told me about Sasha's ability."

His index finger tapped against the steering wheel. "Sasha has the gift of premonition."

Neve stopped stroking for a moment, then resumed. "Premonition," she started softly. "Like she can see the future?"

Turning his head in her direction, he replied, "She can see how people will die."

30

NEVE

Neve watched the sign for the California border pass by her window. They'd been driving for nearly ten hours. She should be exhausted. She'd been awake for almost twenty-two hours straight, but she kept turning things over in her mind. She had a lot to think about too—her cousin, her parents… and then everything Drake had told her. All of it had been told in confidence, an exclusive sneak peek behind the curtain of mystery the Revenant kept around them.

She hadn't even heard a whisper about special abilities among the group of jaguars who were the most feared and revered members of their society. After getting to know some of them a little better, she could see how each of their abilities molded their personalities.

"You should sleep."

She looked over at Drake, at his strong hands gripping the wheel. "Why didn't you let me drive?"

He shrugged, the movement gracefully rolling through the muscles beneath the fabric of his T-shirt. He'd taken off the duster at their last stop, revealing the weapons holster across his shoulders and back. The leather was black and well-worn, but his guns looked brand-new.

"I'm not tired," he replied, eyeing her with interest.

"Me neither," she whispered. Aside from everything else that her gray matter was chewing on, there was also the discussion they'd had about their relationship—if that's what they could call it. She had to know whether a mating between them would be like her parents and every other shifter couple she knew of. Would they be on equal footing, or would the balance of power tip to him?

"What are you thinking about?" he asked.

"You said before that our mate bond needs to be sealed." She noticed the subtle tightening in his jaw. "Can you explain that to me?"

"You sound like you're actually considering it."

She caught the surge of hope that welled in him. "I'm making an informed decision. My father taught me to get all the facts first."

He was quiet for a moment. "The mate bond is sealed with an exchange of blood." He shrugged his broad shoulders. "Once that's done, the bond grows and strengthens. The only thing that will break it is death. And you should know that forming a mate bond with a Shadow holds very little risk for the *arnasa*."

"*Arnasa?*"

"What you are to me. It means *breath*. Our *arnasa* breathes new life into us." He shrugged as if his words embarrassed him, and she sensed it in him too. "At least that's what I've been told."

It was going to take her a while to get used to this. "Are there many Shadows who've found their mates?"

"No." Sucking in a breath, he repositioned his hands on the steering wheel. His eyes shifted to the rearview mirror briefly, and she glanced over her shoulder to see the black Sprinter four car-lengths behind.

"You have to understand that we aren't like regular shifters, Neve. We're something else—something more."

"Believe me, I've noticed," she muttered dryly.

He glanced at her, holding her gaze for a long minute before a small smile curled up his mouth.

"Okay, so if you bond with…me, you get faster and stronger?"

He bobbed his head. "Yes, but it's not that simple. It's very risky—bonding ourselves to one female—and a lot of Shadows aren't willing to accept it."

"What do they risk?"

His eyes darted to the rearview mirror again. "In order to gain our powers, we have to concede a part of ourselves to our mate." She frowned, but he continued, "Regular mate bonds and relationships give the power to the male, but for Shadows, it's tipped the other way. *You* would hold the power in the relationship, and for a lot of males, especially dominant males like Shadows, they aren't willing to give up their control. Our bond sparked the moment I saw you in your cat's form. Whether you accept it or not, I'll always be yours. *Always*."

31

DRAKE

Drake wished he hadn't spoken his last words aloud. Neve had closed herself off to him, and he let her. Clearly, she needed time to digest everything. The fact that she'd listened without denial was a good sign, but it was still early.

As they closed in on the Yellow Eye pride house, his cat began to shift and stir beneath the cage of his skull. Neve's anxiety levels, which had been cruising along at a steady simmer, had spiked to a roar when he told her they were only about twenty minutes out from their destination. He took her hand, trying to calm her, to prepare her for what they might find.

"You need to know—"

"I know," she replied sharply, cutting him off. "It could be body recovery." She peered at him with her luminescent green eyes. "I overheard your talk to Mateo before we left. I know…" She swallowed. "I know we could find something very bad here."

Drake pulled out his phone and called Mateo.

"Boss," Mateo said. "Did you know that Sasha has *never* watched *Die Hard*? Like ever—Oww."

"I hope she used one of her blades to shut you up," he growled.

"She did," he muttered. "What's up?"

"We're closing in on the pride house. There's a fork in the road in about a mile. It cuts behind the property on a fire trail. I want you two to come in from the rear. Stay out of sight until you rendezvous with us at the front. Come in from the west. Stick to the trees. I don't know what to expect, but I'm counting on a shit storm."

"Roger, boss."

He hung up and gripped the steering wheel tightly. When they passed the split in the road, he watched Mateo peel off to the left in the rearview mirror. A few minutes later, Drake made the turn up the long drive of the Yellow Eye pride house. A huge colonial style home emerged from between the trees, its white siding offset by dark green shutters. A low box hedge trimmed to within an inch of its life ran below the windows. The large parking lot was filled with cars—at least a dozen—all parked in neat, orderly rows like some bellhop from a ritzy Hollywood hotel had been getting his Tetris on.

Drake did a three-point turn, facing down the driveway in case they needed to make a quick escape. Shutting off the engine, he waited for a moment. No shots were being fired at the car yet, which he would take as a good sign. The back of his neck itched, though. They were going in blind, and his need for control was screaming at him.

"Are you ready?" he asked.

"Yes," she whispered.

He saw the way her spine straightened. *That's my girl.* Reaching across, he wrapped his hand around the back of her neck and pressed a hard kiss to her mouth. She fisted his shirt in both hands, clinging to him for a moment before releasing him.

He pulled away and reached for one of his SIGs, handing it to her. She didn't even hesitate, palming the weapon and studying it.

"Do you know how to shoot?"

"I've been training with some of the other males in the pride for a few years now. I can take care of myself."

He let out a breath, relieved that she wasn't a complete liability. "Only use this if you absolutely have to," he told her solemnly. "The first shot is the hardest. You have to pull the trigger all the way back to disengage the hammer. After that, the trigger movement is much shorter. I hope you don't have to use this, but I'd rather you were armed than not."

There was steel behind her eyes when she replied, "Okay."

"I'm going to get out first. I want you to stay behind me the whole time." He waited until she nodded. Taking out his other SIG, he held it against his thigh and popped open his door. He slid from the seat, his eyes jumping from the covered porch to the dozen windows spanning both levels at the front of the house, as well as the three dormers on the roofline. He saw no movement, but the scent of copper was in the air.

Movement from the left side of the house drew his attention, and he raised his weapon only to let his arm fall to his side once more. It was Sasha and Mateo. Sasha had shifted, Mateo was still on two feet. With his free hand, Drake motioned for them to stay low and make their way around to the back of the building. Mateo nodded and took off, Sasha moving faster than him and disappearing around the building.

He waited for a few moments then opened Neve's door. "Ready?"

"Yes."

No hesitation. Pride flowed through him. He realized Neve was a soldier. Sure, she may not have much formal training, but it took more than training to become a soldier. It took balls of steel and determination. It took the ability to make fear your bitch, and Neve had all those qualities in spades.

He stepped back to let her out of the car, using himself as a shield. His shoulder blades tightened as the sensation of being watched brushed against his skin once more. Turning his head, he did another quick scan of the surroundings, focusing more on the trees that lined the long driveway.

Neve held the SIG down near her thigh, her finger resting just outside the trigger guard, her gaze scanning the area.

"Stay close." His words were just a breath, but she nodded. "If I tell you to run, you run, okay?" Pressing the keys to the Escalade into her hand, he met her gaze. "If I tell you to leave me and get out, get your ass into this car and drive."

Although he could see she didn't like his orders, she bobbed her head and he let out a deep breath. He couldn't forgive himself if she got hurt.

"Do you think anyone is still in there?" she asked.

"I don't know. If they are, they already know we're here."

Drake began walking toward the front door, trying the knob. It was unlocked, and he eased the door open. He waited a beat, then slipped inside with his gun raised. Neve was following at his back, close enough that he could feel the heat of her body. The scent of blood hit him a moment later, a wall of copper and salt that staggered him. Neve gasped, and he had to fight the urge to send her back to the car. If she was even considering becoming his mate, he needed to treat her like the independent female she was.

Following the muzzle of his gun, he took in the entry foyer. There was blood everywhere.

In everything.

On everything.

The more he looked, the more the house revealed its gruesome secrets, a macabre peep show that burned into his brain. There were at least three bodies in the first room to the left. The jaguars who were bleeding out weren't the only broken things. Every stick of furniture was splintered or destroyed completely. Cushions were eviscerated, the couch frame shattered, the rug soaking up all that blood like a hungry sponge.

"Jesus," Neve croaked in a hoarse whisper.

Keeping her close, he checked every corner of the room, but there was nothing left that was a threat.

"Do you recognize them?" she asked.

Drake took a knee and rolled over the first male who had died face down. His head canted off to the side with the movement, revealing more than just a broken neck. It looked as if someone had tried to take the head from his shoulders. Tendons and flesh stretched and snapped with the weight of the head, but no fresh blood seeped out. They'd been dead for a number of hours already. Jaguar shifters were tough, but Shadows were tougher, so whoever had done this was strong.

"It's…" He cleared his throat. "It's Tavaris, the Red Paw Shadow captain."

He shook his head. Tavaris was an excellent fighter. He hadn't even drawn a weapon, so whoever got the drop on him must've taken him by surprise. Looking ahead at the next body, he knew who it was already. He would've recognized that red hair anywhere. Still, he rolled the male over, coming face-to-face with Elian's death mask of terror. His throat had been torn out, but there were absolutely no defensive wounds from what Drake could see. The guy didn't even get the benefit of a warrior's death.

The remaining body belonged to Van, Shadow captain of the

White Fang pride. His stomach had been opened up, his intestines looped around his neck like a necklace. The sick fuck who killed him even dug his heart from his chest and placed it in Van's slack hands.

The Red Paw, Gray Fur, and White Fang Shadow captains were all dead. He looked across the floor, passing over the broken furniture and bodies, trying to piece together the scene.

"What's that?" Neve asked, pointing. Drake frowned at the upturned plate on the ground. He eased the coffee table out of the way and picked it up, studying the greasy, perfectly formed circles on its surface. Absently, he ran his thumb through the slick patch. Bringing the digit to his nose, he inhaled.

Belladonna. The tang of unripened tomatoes was unmistakable.

"Fuck. They were poisoned—incapacitated with nightshade."

Neve's mouth was a grim slash. "They ate them?"

"They can be mistaken for blueberries very easily," he murmured, looking for more evidence that he was right. "It looks like they'd been baked into muffins."

"Nightshade is bad, right?"

"It disrupts the nervous system, which would explain why there aren't any defensive wounds on any of them."

"They were slaughtered like animals," Neve breathed.

A familiar sharp, short ascending whistle sounded from their right, and Drake turned. Mateo appeared in the foyer with Sasha. Sasha's feet and forelegs were slick with blood.

"There was a human, a cook or something, who was still alive," Mateo reported.

"Were they able to tell you anything?"

"He just kept muttering 'they forced me.'"

Drake looked back down at the dead Shadows. All their clothing was intact, so they couldn't have shifted in a rush, and the injuries weren't consistent with claws and teeth. The cuts to Van's stomach were surgical-neat, and no jaguar in cat form had the kind of dexterity needed to break someone's neck and nearly decapitate them.

"Where else have you been?"

"Just the kitchen. The back door opened into it. We came here through a hallway that led to the foyer."

"We have to clear this floor, then we can go upstairs." He looked at Sasha. Was this what she'd seen? Did she know they were going to be too late?

Mateo said, "We'll check the east side of the house. Rendezvous in two in the foyer?" The pair slipped from the room, and Drake turned to Neve.

"How are you doing?"

She swallowed before saying, "I'll be fine."

Giving her a firm nod, he led her through the archway that connected the living and dining rooms. The large table was unmarred by blood and had been set for about two dozen people. Everything was perfect from the highly polished flatware, the pristine china plates, and the creamy white candles that were lit and throwing off a cheerful glow in the center of the table.

"Two chairs are missing," Neve said softly, pointing to the spaces at the far end. She walked around to the other side of the table and looked around. "Why is there no blood or bodies in this room?"

Drake shook his head. "I have no idea." Staring at the white door on the opposite wall, he said, "Come on."

Stepping around the table, he pushed it open and did a visual sweep. The kitchen looked worse than the living room did. There was a pile of bodies that had been stacked against the back door, but Mateo had obviously moved them when he and Sasha had entered. On the other side of the room, propped up against the bottom cabinets, was a dead man dressed in chef whites that were soaked through with blood from the stomach wound.

One of his own knives lay abandoned beside him.

He must've been suffering for hours.

To his left, there was another door. He was about to push through it when the sound of gunfire exploded through the house. Shoving Neve behind him, he brought up his gun and nudged open the door. This was the secondary entrance into the kitchen that was linked by a hallway. There was a feline hiss, and then the sound of bones breaking. A jaguar screamed, the sound vibrating through Drake and hitting him square in the chest, making him stumble back a step. Neve gasped, and her hand—which had been on his shoulder—suddenly fell away, and he spun around and caught her before she hit the ground.

Her face was screwed up in pain. "Sasha?" she rasped. "I think I felt…"

He frowned. She shouldn't have been able to feel that. It was him who had the connection to his cats…

The bond.

It was growing stronger.

He eased her down onto the ground and pressed the gun firmly back into her hand. He could feel Sasha suffering, and it was tearing at his cat. "I need to check on her," he told her softly. "I'll be back in two minutes."

Her hand shot out and gripped his arm. For the first time, he saw true terror in her eyes. "Don't leave me."

Cradling her face in his hands, he kissed her mouth softly. "Do you trust me?"

She nodded.

"Trust that I will be back then."

"If you're not back in two minutes, I'm coming out to beat your ass for lying to me."

He smiled at her fiercely, then stepped from the kitchen. As quietly as he could, he crept down the hallway, keeping the wall at his back. Another shot rang out, followed by a very human grunt. He came up behind the staircase that took up two-thirds of the foyer, using it for cover.

The sound of a hand-to-hand fight echoed around him, and he peered around the edge of the staircase to find Mateo fighting with another male. Drake recognized him as a Yellow Eye Shadow and tried to recall his name. He raised his gun, the muzzle following the action, but he couldn't get a clean shot.

The Yellow Eye cat threw a punch, and although Mateo dodged it at the last second, it still caught him on the shoulder and spun him around like a top. He fell to the ground in a jangle of limbs, blood from multiple cuts on his face making him almost unrecognizable.

The other cat moved with preternatural speed, straddling Mateo's hips and throwing punch after punch, his arms pistoning faster and faster, until they were nothing more than a blur. It was almost as if...

Mateo's head kicked back into the tile each time, his skull making a dull *thump* with every strike. There was bloodlust in the other male's eyes, his intention to kill Mateo like a neon sign for anyone who wanted to see it.

This was his opening. Drake took aim and squeezed the trigger. The recoil kicked into his shoulder, but the bullet found its target. The Yellow Eye went rigid then fell backward, his brain matter spraying the ground behind him like a gruesome fireworks display.

Drake emerged from behind the staircase, keeping the weapon trained on the Yellow Eye male.

"Mateo?" he hissed, tapping the guy on the shoulder with the toe of his boot.

His violet eyes opened and rolled to the side, his mangled mouth opening and sucking in a shuddering breath. "Sasha."

Drake's head jerked up, his eyes settling on a form in the dark adjoining room. All the drapes had been closed, and as he got closer, he stopped.

That was when he saw the rest of the bodies.

32

NEVE

Neve had done her best to ignore the pile of bodies she was sharing space with, but it was hard to avoid looking at the chef sitting opposite her. His mouth was slack, frozen. His eyes were still open, but they'd gone opaque in the short time since his death.

Bang!

Without thinking, she leapt up, fumbling when Drake's gun slid from her grip. Wrapping her fingers more tightly around the grip, she eased open the same door Drake had disappeared through, looking around before stepping out into the hall. Everything had gone quiet, except for a short rasping sound. She found out what that was when she got to the staircase. Mateo was on the ground, his hands resting on his chest as he sucked in air. Beside him was a dead male. She turned her head to the left and saw Drake crouched down in a darkened room.

She halted a few feet from the double-doors, her shoulders tightening until it was almost painful. The smell of blood was so prolific, her olfactory senses weren't just saturated, they were drowning. Someone made a strangled sound, and Drake glanced sharply over his shoulder, his fierce expression melting away.

"Neve."

She hardly heard him, just walked forward until she was on the threshold of the room. Reaching out with a shaking hand, she flipped on the lights and stared at the death on display. Haltingly, she walked into the room and fell to her knees, staring at the Leos and their mates discarded in that darkened room.

Her gaze fell on a female only a few feet from her, a ragged sob climbing up her throat. She pushed it down, inviting the cold numbness to take over.

Drake's concern washed against her like a warm caress. "Do you know her?" he asked.

"It's Michelle Scheller, the Yellow Eye Leo's mate." She began to stroke the hair from her face. The only wound she had was a small bullet hole between her eyes, the flesh around the entry point turning the surrounding skin necrotic.

"I don't understand. My mom said all the females were going on a winery tour while the meeting was taking place. They aren't supposed to be here with the Leos." She forced herself to look around, to see the faces of the Leos who'd died beside their mates, who'd *died* protecting their mates. But where were *her* parents?

"I don't know," Drake replied tightly. "But we're going to find out."

He helped her up, his free hand holding hers. There was a low groan, and she saw Sasha in her cat form lying on the ground, doing her best to keep one of her legs very still.

"Broken leg," Drake replied, crouching down beside her and stroking her head like she was just a house cat and not a hundred-sixty-pound killing machine. Sasha purred a little and blinked up at him slowly.

"Mateo," Drake called. "How are you feeling?"

Mateo sat up slowly, his face a patchwork of drying blood and already forming bruises. "Like Mike Tyson and Ronda Rousey's lovechild cut their teeth on me." He glanced down at the dead male beside him and grinned. "Thanks for not missing, boss."

Drake grunted. "Can you do anything for Sash?"

"Only the superficial—"

"*Neve! Run!*"

Before the words could stop echoing around the foyer, Neve's blood turned to ice. Her mom. That was her mom. Neve's pulse jammed into her throat at the sound of absolute terror in those words. She was moving before she knew what she was doing, running out of the room, only to be slowed down when Drake grabbed her wrist.

"Let me go," she gritted out, yanking her arm back hard. She stumbled away as Drake released his fingers, and she frowned. By the look of frustration on his face, he hadn't expected to do that either. She turned and ran up the stairs, taking them two at a time. Drake followed behind her, his fear for her life blanketing her, suffocating her with its strength.

At the top of the landing, she looked in both directions but had no idea where the sound had come from. Her head wrenched to the left at the sound of twin gunshots. The scent of blood hadn't been as pervasive up there until that sound. Now, it was strong enough to coat the back of her tongue.

She rushed forward, Drake yelling her name in warning. She wasn't listening, though. Her parents…

The double doors flew open with such force that she jerked back a step and fell onto her ass. She looked up at the male standing between the jambs, the expression on his face making her heartbeat thrash in her ears. Covered in blood from head to toe, his lips pulled away from very human teeth as he fixed his attention on Drake.

"Lewis?" Drake asked.

The other male—Lewis—held out his hands as if presenting himself. Gore covered nearly every inch of his skin, and Neve felt her stomach turn. His skin seemed to shiver then, and he shifted between one breath and the next. How was that possible? Unless he was one of the Shadows who had found his blood mate?

"Fuck!" Drake shouted, throwing his hands up to protect his face as Lewis leapt. Neve scrambled to her feet and ran into the bedroom he'd just exited, keeping her eyes on Drake as he tried to wrestle the cat off him. Drake managed to get his legs underneath Lewis's stomach, and he kicked out, sending the other male sailing through the air and crashing into the wall. The drywall crumpled under the force, sending dust into the air.

Drake slapped a hand to his neck as he staggered into the room and shut the doors.

"Let me see, dammit," Neve demanded, trying to pull his hand out of the way to see how badly he was injured.

"I'll be fine," he replied weakly, grimacing. His knees buckled, and he fell to the ground. His hand fell away from his neck, revealing the gaping wound that had been inflicted with claws.

"Drake?" She slapped his face, rousing him for a moment before he lapsed back into unconsciousness.

Desperately, she looked around the huge room. It smelled of Michelle, and she realized it was the Yellow Eye Leo's master bedroom. Shoving to her feet, she went looking for the bathroom to get a towel to press against the wound, but her world came to a sudden stop as her eyes passed over the alcove by the dormer window, and saw two figures slumped over in matching chairs—

the missing dining room chairs.

The blood drained from her face as an inhuman sound was wrenched from her throat. She crouched down at the feet of her parents, reaching out to touch her dad's knee. They'd been executed, and if she hadn't hidden in the kitchen, she could've saved them. Tentatively, she reached out and touched her mom's cheek with the tips of her fingers. Warmth lingered there, but even now, she could feel it was leaving her body, draining from her just like her life was.

The door to the bedroom suddenly shattered apart, and she jumped to her feet in time to see Mateo wrestling the feline Lewis. They rolled into the room, coming to an abrupt stop when they crashed against the foot of the bed. She rushed to Drake and pulled him out of the way. She had to get out of there. Grabbing Drake under the arms, she waited until the doorway was clear, then dragged him out onto the landing. Mateo and Lewis were still twisting on the floor, blood spraying and clumps of fur flying.

Lewis swiped his paw against Mateo's torso, the sound of skin ripping filling the room. Mateo dropped like a stone, his legs jerking up to his chest as another layer of blood was added to the bouquet. Neve's breath was whooshing out of her lungs, but she couldn't seem to catch it, to slow it.

Lewis spun around to face her, his gold eyes glittering with so many promises of earth-shattering pain. Lowering his body down to the ground, he prepared to pounce. Remembering all her training, she lowered her center of gravity too, shifting her weight to remain balanced. The other cat's eyes darted to Drake, his lips peeling back in a feral snarl. Neve hissed back, baring her hopelessly blunt human teeth.

"If you want him, you'll have to get past me first."

He leapt at her a moment later, aiming for her throat, but she twisted around, taking the brunt of his claws and teeth on her shoulders and back. Her back was suddenly blazing with acid fire, ribbons of agony tearing down either side of her spine. He rode her down to the ground, leaping off to attack again. Crawling the few feet to Drake's inert body, she threw herself over him, protecting him. With her head bowed and her breath whistling past her clenched teeth, Neve tried to get her feet back under her, pausing when she heard a growl of warning.

With blood streaming down her back, soaking through her shirt, she peered up to find Sasha standing over her and Drake, protecting them. Her leg wasn't working properly. She wasn't putting any weight on it, and it seemed to be misshapen. The two jaguars hissed and growled at each other, circling just a few feet away.

Neve jerked back when Drake reached out and touched her shoulder, his fingers coming back bloody. He touched them to his mouth, his tongue darting out to taste her blood. He swallowed roughly then collapsed back.

"Drake?" she whispered.

His hand shot out and pulled her closer, their mouths brushing in a kiss that made her lips tingle. She tasted copper and felt a physical connection to Drake that hadn't been there before. No, that wasn't right. It had been there, it just hadn't been as strong as she felt it now. It was almost like hearing a car alarm going off from a block away to hearing it right outside your house. It was loud and intrusive, and the power that flowed through him and into her would've knocked her on her ass if she wasn't already there.

"Blood to blood," he groaned. "Knife…right ankle."

"What?" she asked in a hiss, but he was out again. Neve closed her eyes as the sound of battle raged around her. Sucking in a breath, she could almost see a golden thread coming out of her body, from her heart, connecting her to Drake. From Drake, there were another four threads, each a different color. A silver one was linked to Sasha and a deep forest green one connected him to Mateo. Two others—a royal purple and sky blue—disappeared above them, obviously connected to Jett and Grayson. As she looked down, she found a silver thread was sprouting, as well as a forest green one.

They both stretched out from her chest, creeping toward Sasha and Mateo. She was jolted with awareness as they connected, and Sasha turned to look at her sharply. The distraction cost her, though, and Lewis attacked. He forced her backward until she was on top of them, crushing them. Neve struggled to breathe. Something hot dripped down onto her face, making her to turn away to stop it getting into her nose.

Sasha suddenly went slack, her muscles turning to lead, and Neve had to beat back the panic that she was going to die this way. The weight was suddenly lifted away, and Neve sucked in a deep breath. She blinked up at Lewis as he stood on two feet once more. His clothing was shredded, revealing patches of his skin that was just as bloody as the rest of him. Reaching down, he grabbed her by the back of the shirt and hauled her off Drake like she weighed nothing at all.

Pressing her lips into a tight line, she held back the scream as every terrible twist and turn of her torso made her whole body tremble in pain. She needed to get away from him, needed to lead him away from the others, but she also needed a weapon...

Knife. Right ankle. Drake's words filtered through her mind.

Gritting her teeth, she kicked her legs out, throwing her weight around and trying to knock him off-balance. Her body torqued painfully to the left, and she felt his grip on her shirt slip. Finally, she tipped him off-balance, making him curse as he let her go. Landing heavily on her hands and knees, she scrambled over to Drake and wrenched up the leg of his pants. Her fingers had just brushed the hilt of the knife when she was hauled away.

Neve screamed in frustration, twisting around until she was on her back and facing her enemy. The claw marks on her back were on fire as she was dragged across the carpet, but she used that pain and channeled it into her fight. Lewis dropped her at the top of the stairs, his bare foot on her hip.

"Enjoy the ride," he sneered, kicking her off the edge and sending her tumbling down the stairs. She tried to protect her head as she rolled, but judging by the black spot bursting into her vision, she knew she'd failed. Sprawled at the bottom of the stairs, she took a minute to suck in air before finally pushing herself onto her knees. Lewis was slowly walking down the stairs like he had all the time in the world. Drawing on a strength she didn't know she had still left in her, she pulled herself up and started toward the living room. Her right ankle ached with each step, but she had to keep moving.

Pausing at the door, she left bloody handprints on the wood before stumbling into the chaos. She searched the three bodies they'd found when they first arrived, patting down their bodies to find a weapon. She found a knife on the body of the redhead then froze at the sound of Lewis's voice from the doorway.

"So kind of you to come here so we didn't have to travel to you, Neve," he told her with a smile that would've been cheerful under any other circumstances. Right now, it just looked downright evil.

Keeping the weapon hidden behind her, she stepped away until her back hit one of the dining room chairs. He came to a stop in front of her.

"You know, I'm starting to get a taste for shifter meat." A feline snarl came out of his throat as he shifted into his cat in an instant. He leapt at her, knocking them both into the table. China plates and flatware rained down on them, the candles toppling over and extinguishing with the force. Fetid breath that stank of blood and rancid meat blew over her face in a steady stream as his razor-sharp teeth grazed her cheek. Just like she'd practiced in training, she jammed her forearm between Lewis's throat, shoving him away and giving herself the room she needed to work with the blade.

It was only a second, but she repositioned the knife in front of her, driving it forward while using the momentum of his own pounce to bury the steel to the hilt in his stomach.

His roar of pain was so close to her ear that it nearly deafened her.

Forcing Lewis backward, she purposefully fell with him and twisted the blade deep into his gut. Hot blood spewed over her hand as it escaped his body, running down the sides of his abdomen. Still, Lewis snapped his teeth at her, weakly snarling in her face.

"Fuck you," she breathed then struck again, driving the blade through his heart this time. And again. She was lost in a frenzy, her arm moving independently of her body as she avenged the death of her parents.

Lewis's body finally went slack against her, and she shoved away from him with what little strength she had left. On shaking legs, she righted herself, brushing shards of wood and china from her clothes. The handle of the knife, now slick with his blood, tumbled to the ground at her feet.

33

NEVE

Both Neve's ankle and knee on her right side were screaming as she pulled herself up the stairs. With the battle over, the adrenaline drained out of her and her whole body went limp. She dropped to the ground at the top of the stairs, dragging herself over to Drake. His chest was still rising and falling shallowly, and if she concentrated, she could visualize their golden thread. She also saw Sasha's and Mateo's connected to her chest and Drake's.

Sasha whined when she saw Neve.

"I'm going to get us out of here," she said. Working as quickly as she could, she limped to the bathroom and grabbed as many towels as she could find. Pressing one to Drake's throat, she was relieved when he lifted his hand and held it weakly in place.

She rolled Mateo over onto his back, moving his hands out of the way. She was expecting to see his intestines being held in position, but all she saw was a wound that looked as if it had been healing for weeks rather than minutes. He blinked up at her with his violet eyes and gave her a half smile. "I'll be fully healed in a couple of hours."

"Good to hear," she said. "Are you able to walk?"

"I'm sure I can manage that if I take it slowly."

She gave him a curt nod. "Good because I could use the help." Glancing back at Drake, she said, "Do you have enough juice to heal him a little bit?"

He flexed his fingers. "I might be able to." Getting up slowly, he shuffled over to Drake and practically collapsed beside him. Reaching out with his right hand, he hovered it about an inch over the throat wound and shut his eyes. For a moment, nothing happened, then a warm yellow glow began emanating from his palm. Drake groaned, his body relaxing. Even a little color started to come back to his skin, going from a grayish tint to a pallid white.

The glow faded out after only half a second, and Mateo squeezed his hand into a fist. "I've taken away some of his pain."

She pulled the towel away from his throat and found that the bleeding had slowed but not stopped. "Okay. It'll have to do." Walking around to the top of his body, she slid her hands beneath his shoulders and hauled him up. She cursed when his full weight hit her, but she gritted her teeth and dug in, getting him in a fireman's carry.

Over her shoulder, she said, "Have you got Sasha?"

There was a grunt and a small indignant hiss, and when she looked back, she found Mateo cradling the other cat like a lover. They moved down the stairs together, that feeling of 'wrongness' she'd felt before gone from the house. Outside, she popped open the rear door of the Escalade and tried to get Drake inside without hurting him any more than he already was. Leaving him half hanging out of the car, she limped around to the other side and opened the opposite door. Positioning her knees on the seat, she hooked her hands under Drake's arms and braced herself. She blew out a breath and began to pull, shuffling him inch by inch into the car.

"Need a hand?" Mateo asked with an easy smile. He lifted Drake's feet and helped maneuver him into the car. He was taller than the width of the backseat, his knees bent to fit him in there, but it would have to do.

"Thanks," she replied, walking back around the car. "How are you feeling?"

He glanced over at the house then back at her, his eyes morphing to an odd shade of violet-green. "Thankful?"

She knew exactly what he meant. Neve looked down as she shoved the toe of her boot into the ground. "I want to take my parents' bodies with us." Peering up, she expected to see a look of surprise on Mateo's face, but he just looked resigned.

"It's only right," he replied. "But I'll need some help."

Leaving Drake and Sasha outside, Neve walked back into the mausoleum that was the former Yellow Eye Leo's house. The smell of death was a perverse punch to her senses, and she took a couple of deep breaths through her mouth to stop the worst of it from tattooing onto her memories. Mateo led the way up the stairs, a hand pressed to his stomach like his injuries were still hurting him.

At the top of the stairs, Neve's steps slowed, then stopped outright on the threshold of the bedroom where her parents had been murdered. Mateo, as if sensing her hesitation, turned around and approached her. His warm hands gripped her upper arms to hold her steady. She hadn't even realized she was swaying.

"You can wait outside if you need to."

She shook her head. "No. They're my parents, and I'll honor them in doing this."

He gave her a nod and stepped back, his expression so unlike what she expected of him.

Straightening her spine, she walked farther into the room, determined. Her parents were just how she'd found them, her father on the right, her mother on the left. Walking behind them to untie the bindings, she hissed when she discovered they were coated in silver. That explained why they hadn't tried to escape— the pain would've been excruciating.

Ignoring the way her fingertips burned, she teased the knot apart until the rope finally fell away. Her fingers and hands were raw, blisters already forming between the patches of skin that had been burned off. With the back of her hand, she wiped away the tears that had been silently falling since she'd started her task and looked up at Mateo.

"Give me your hands," he said softly.

She did, shutting her eyes when his palm started to glow softly. Warmth spread through her, from her fingertips to her wrists, the burning sensation inflicted by the silver slowly easing away. When she opened her eyes, all she could see was slightly pinked up skin.

"Thank you," she murmured.

"You're welcome."

She returned her attention back to her parents. They'd both been shot in the back of the head, executed for what appeared to be no reason at all.

"Why did this happen?"

"I don't know," Mateo replied. "We'll find out, though. Drake won't rest until he has someone's head on a platter."

She bobbed her head and walked around so she was standing in front of her parents. She lifted her mother up, easing her onto her shredded shoulder. The pain lashed at her, but she gritted her teeth and took the burden. Mateo did the same for her dad, grunting a little with the weight of his charge. Together, they left the bedroom and went down the stairs once more and out the front door.

Mateo paused halfway to the van. "Do you smell that?"

Honestly, all Neve could smell was blood and death, but she turned her face to the side and inhaled more deeply. The wind was blowing at their backs, bringing the smell of—

"Gasoline," she breathed.

Mateo cursed and started running to the van. Neve followed in her limping gait, placing her parents side by side in the back.

"Get to the car! Drive!"

She hobbled back to the Escalade and hit the *let's go* button. The engine roared to life, and she hit the gas, the five thousand-fifty-pound steel cage and engine block surging down the drive. Neve kept her attention split between the road in front of her and the rearview mirror. She saw the van tear out after her, then a split second later, the pride house exploded in a fireball that engulfed the house and parked cars. The van swerved with the force of the impact, but the Escalade was buffeted from the worst of the blast. Her side mirrors showed nothing but intense red flame and black smoke.

As they came to the end of the drive, she didn't bother stomping on the brakes, she just yanked on the wheel and sent the Escalade into an *oh shit* turn that kicked out its rear end. Thankfully, the road was quiet, and her crazy driving was only witnessed by a couple of cows at the side of the road.

And Mateo. She peered into the rearview mirror and saw him grinning and letting out a whoop. Shifting her mirror down, she checked on Drake and found his yellow eyes focused on her. But it wasn't the man staring out at her—it was the beast.

"What happened?" he asked, his voice lower, more graveled, than usual.

"Someone blew up the house."

His eyes glowed brighter. "Your parents?"

"We got them."

Drake's eyes shut once more and unconsciousness took him. The wound to his throat was still bleeding steadily, but it wasn't as bad as it had been before Mateo had healed him. She got onto the highway where Mateo slid out of the lane behind her and surged forward. He guided the van past her then changed lanes so he was in front.

She followed him for a few miles then got off at Little Lake when he did, desperately trying not to think about the two bodies in the back of the van. He pulled into a run-down motel that looked like it had gone out of business in the seventies. He parked in front of the reception office and got out. Neve stayed in the car with Drake, waiting for Mateo to come back out again. It was only a few minutes later that he emerged swinging two sets of keys around his index finger like he hadn't just fought for his life, moved dead bodies, then fled for his life.

Neve rolled down the window as he approached. "Room twelve," he told her. "Park rear end in."

She double-checked the room numbers as she went, finding that number twelve was at the end of the row. After parking the car, she glanced over her shoulder at Drake. He was still motionless. There was a tap on the window, and she jerked her head around. It was just Mateo.

"I got adjoining rooms," he said, handing her a key. "I need to re-break Sasha's leg to stop it from healing badly, and Drake's wound will need to be attended to."

"Can we spare the time?" she asked, thinking about her parents in the back of the van.

"Unless you want Drake bleeding out in the back of his own car."

She bit her lip. "How long will we need?"

"At least six hours. Sash is going to be fucking pissed off with me, so the longer she has to recover, the better. Same for Drake. They need rest. Come to think of it, so do we."

He had a point, but the idea of her parents in the back of the van didn't sit well with her. She opened up the door to her room and took a quick look around. There was one king-sized bed and a few pieces of worn furniture to fill out the room. Stripping the bed down to the mattress, she tore the shower curtain off the rail in the bathroom and laid it out flat on the bed. Back outside, she opened the rear door and recoiled at the fresh blood that was pooled on the leather seat beneath Drake. Jesus.

"Mateo!" she called. "Help me."

Together they moved him onto the bed, and Neve stripped the shirt from him. Scanning his body for any other injuries, she found some shallow cuts on his abdomen. Shifting her eyes up, she ran her fingertips over the strange mark over his heart.

"It's our Shadow Mark," Mateo said softly, startling her. He handed her a medical kit. "When you're finished with Drake, come next door."

Neve nodded, then opened up the kit and looked over everything. She needed to close up the wound, but she needed to clean it first. It wasn't as if he was going to die of infection or anything, but it would certainly speed up the healing process.

Opening the bottle of hydrogen peroxide, she slowly poured it first over the cuts on his stomach and then onto his neck wound. His eyes shot open as soon as the fizzing began, the muscles and tendons in his neck and jaw standing in stark relief. Working as quickly as she could, she grabbed the gauze and mopped away most of the solution and fresh blood.

The wound on his neck was large—large enough that even she knew it would need stitches. She rummaged around in the kit again, finding the surgical thread and needle.

She could do this.

Drake needed her to do this.

Opening the box, she prepared the needle and let out a breath. Squeezing the two sides of the wound together, she inserted the needle and pulled it out the other side, pulling the thread firmly, but not until it was too tight. She'd had some first aid training, but anything more than finding someone unconscious and putting them into the recovery position was out of her league.

She continued to sew Drake's throat up, finally putting a knot into the thread and cutting off the excess. Taking a large pad of gauze, she pressed it into place, then tidied up. Draping a sheet over his body, she went and washed up.

After checking on Drake once more, she opened up the connecting door to find Mateo staring down at Sasha, who was now fully conscious again. Sasha turned her boxy feline head Neve's way and growled.

"She won't let me treat her," Mateo said, sounding wounded.

"Do you know why she'd do that?"

He shrugged. "Probably because she's in pain, and I'm only going to cause more of it."

"How long before the damage is permanent?"

"She could have nerve damage right now, and the longer we

wait, the more likely it is that it'll stay that way. She'd be deformed, and the Trinity wouldn't allow it."

Wouldn't *allow it*. It sounded like they'd rather put her down like a stray dog than keep her alive. Kneeling down, Neve looked into Sasha's eyes.

"We need to do this," she said, and the other female blinked. Pain bled into her stare—pain and…acceptance. "You will let Mateo do this." She forced power into her voice like she'd heard her father do to younger, less experienced jaguars.

After a tense moment, she blinked again, more slowly this time, and Neve nodded. To Mateo, she said, "Okay. I'll hold her down. You do it, but be fucking quick about it."

Positioning herself over the top half of Sasha, Neve kept her eyes on her feline's face but away from her teeth. A wounded jaguar always reacted badly.

"On three," he said. "One…"

Snap!

Sasha jerked under Neve, almost dislodging her, but she rebalanced herself and stayed on. A low keening noise filled the room, and Neve felt Sasha's pain like a sledgehammer to the chest. Looking up at Mateo, she watched his reaction, wondering if he felt it too, but his face was a mask of impassivity as he worked to set Sasha's leg. When he was done resetting the bone, he wrapped the leg in a crisp white bandage, securing a splint in place.

He wiped the back of his hand across his forehead. "That should do it."

"When will you know if it's healed properly?"

"By the time we get back to Wyoming, we should know." He paused, then added, "Will you let me treat you?"

The muscles twinged suddenly. "I'm fine."

"No, you're not. You had a jaguar tear through your back. Let me clean the wounds and bandage them, otherwise Drake will skin me alive for not taking care of you."

Reluctantly, she nodded. "Okay."

He gestured to the bed, which he'd stripped down to the bare mattress. She lay down, tensing when she felt Mateo's hands under the hem of her shirt. Something cold pressed against her skin, followed by the *snip, snip* of a pair of surgical scissors cleaving her shirt in two. He sucked back a hiss when he pulled the two sides apart.

"Are you in pain?"

"More than you could know," she replied in a soft voice.

To his credit, Mateo didn't say anything more as he cleaned the deep gouges and bandaged them up. When he was finished, warmth flooded her, starting in her shoulders and trickling down either side of her spine. She closed her eyes as Mateo took her pain away from her, letting out a deep breath as the last slivers of it drained away from her body. A moment later, something was dropped beside her head—a clean shirt.

Heaving herself off the bed, she stripped her own bloody shirt from her body and murmured, "I should go and check on Drake."

As she reached the doorway between the rooms, Mateo called, "Hey, Neve?"

She turned to look at him, rubbing her arms as she suddenly grew cold.

"Thank you." His words were heavy, so much meaning wrapped up in them.

Bobbing her head, she turned around and walked back to her room.

34

KATIE

Compared to the previous location, Katie's living standards had gone up exponentially. The cell she was in was at least one and a half times larger than the last, with a few metal platforms set up as beds. There was also a stainless steel toilet against one wall with a small, in-built sink on the top. Having a proper flushing toilet was something she'd never take for granted ever again.

Luce was still with her, the small female unwilling to let go of her hand, even though they'd been left alone in this new location for a while now.

In the cell beside her, Elsie had been placed with another female who had chocolate-brown skin and pale green eyes. She looked so out of place here with her movie-star looks, high cheekbones, long lashes, and full lips.

"What's your name?" the other female called out, and it took Katie a moment to realize she was talking to her.

"Katie. You?"

"Leesa."

Katie glanced around at the other cells. Unlike in the last place, a light was on all the time. There were only about five feet between hers and the cell on the opposite wall. The other women and females were either asleep or staring dully into the middle distance. They'd checked out already, but Katie wasn't ready to give up just yet. If they moved them once, they would do it again, and that would give them an opportunity to escape.

After all, when you had nothing left, hope was what you worked with.

"Where are you from, Leesa?"

"Nashville."

Tennessee? She almost choked. Was that where they were now? The weather seemed drier here, but she didn't think they'd gone that far into the south.

"What about you?"

"Wyoming," she replied.

Leesa gave her a tight smile. "You're a long way from home."

"I think so, yeah. Do you know where we are?"

The other jaguar shrugged her slender shoulders. "I don't know. We were moved about twenty-four hours ago."

"We?"

Leesa's mouth thinned. "Me and the two other girls who'd survived. One human, one cat. The human died on the way over."

"And the cat?"

"Kohbi. She's over there."

Katie followed where Leesa gestured, finding a young female with blonde hair sitting against the wall of the cell opposite them. She was in with Elsie, both females looking lost in their own thoughts—or nightmares, as it were.

"She's not in a good place," Leesa murmured. "One of our captors took a liking to her, and it got…physical."

Katie nodded. "The other female in there with her, Elsie, she suffered the same. I didn't see it happen, but one of our guys took her, too."

Leesa darted her pale-eyed gaze to Luce. "Let's pray they don't go after anyone else."

Katie couldn't deny the thoughts had gone through her head on more than one occasion, but she was going to protect that female to the best of her ability.

"Do you know what they want?"

Katie still couldn't figure that out. It made no sense to have so many females in one spot. It was a disaster waiting to happen actually, because all it would take was one shift, and there would be a jaguar caged in and pissed off. If viability was actually the aim of all this, maybe they wouldn't meet the same fate as the other female who'd shifted in their original location.

Which was why she supposed they kept them so underfed.

Weakness was their only advantage.

"Katie?" Luce whispered.

"Yeah, sweetheart?" she replied, breaking free of her thoughts and stroking the girl's dark hair.

"Are we going to," *hiccup*, "get out of here?"

"Of course," she replied without hesitation. Framing Luce's face in her hands, she said, "We'll get out of this, and I'll return you to your brother."

"Do you swear it?"

Katie felt as if she'd been cut off at the knees. There was such fragility in that voice, but the question was one that had required strength to ask. Being able to rely on anyone else in this kind of situation was tough. Shifter nature, like human nature, was to survive, and the will to live was burning bright in Luce's eyes.

"I swear it, Luce. I *swear* I'll take you back to him."

Luce's chin wobbled with the declaration as she tried to hold back the tears that were sitting just below the surface. Katie drew the girl in closer, resting her chin on the top of her head, vowing silently that she would protect this gentle soul with her last breath if she had to.

There was an electronic *beep* then, and the mood in the room shifted from wariness to all out fear. The scent of it—like burning hair and gasoline—filled the room. Opposite her cage, there was a small hallway that led into darkness. There were no lights down that far, and she thought it had been done on purpose. Psychological warfare was best waged with darkness.

Luce pressed herself more closely to Katie's side, burying her head against her knees. Absently, she stroked the young female's hair again as the sound of heavy footsteps drawing nearer made her heart rate accelerate. The vague outline of a man appeared, and as he stepped into the light, she recognized him as one of their original captors—Tom.

He stood just inside the room, swaying a little as his feral gaze swept over them, the scent of his lust and the stringent sting of alcohol sharp in Katie's nostrils. She knew what he was down here for, and it wasn't just for a chat. He prowled in farther. She took in the large knife he had on his belt. She hadn't seen him with any other weapon other than the gun he'd wielded when they'd moved them.

He stopped on Katie, a cruel smile forming on his lips. If she thought her heart was galloping before, it was strapped to a rocket now. He got closer, flicking a glance to Luce, who was still taking cover.

"That's who I want," he drawled, pointing his finger at Luce. Moving to a small electronic pad attached to their cell, he pressed his index finger against it, causing another *beep*. The door slid open on soundless tracks, and Tom stepped inside. She watched that wide-open space behind him, wondering how long it would—

The door started to slide shut once more. Five seconds. That's how long it stayed open. Tom moved closer, his heated eyes fixed on Luce, and Katie shuffled her legs around until she was covering the girl's body. When he reached for them, she bared her teeth and hissed, the sound coming out of her throat not at all human.

Tom stopped then, sensing that he wasn't dealing just with a female, but with a pissed off jaguar. Slowly, he reached for the sheath on his belt and popped off the clip.

"You don't want to get between us, bitch," he said, pulling the knife free of the leather and holding it in front of him. It was a big blade—at least a foot long—with serrated teeth near the handle. It smelled of oil and old blood. A feline growl bubbled up from her throat.

"Think about it. You're unarmed. You're too weak to shift, and I'd have this buried in your neck before you could finish getting furry." He said the last word like it was abhorrent to him. He twisted the knife around, letting it catch the light, but Katie wasn't budging.

Tom struck her across the cheek with the back of his free hand, the force of it combined with her own growing weakness throwing her backward. Her teeth snapped together when her back hit the wall of the cell, the base of her skull throbbing in time with her racing pulse. She blinked the black spots from her eyes, her vision clearing in time to see Tom reaching for Luce, dragging the girl up and onto her feet. Luce tried to resist, pulling away, trying to twist free of his grip, but he only held on tighter, his nails dimpling her skin and his knuckles turning white. With a hard yank, he pulled her into the line of his body then slung her over his shoulder.

"No!" Katie screamed, crawling over to his retreating form. "Take me."

He was about to put his index finger to the reader on the inside of their cage when he stopped and peered at her over his shoulder. "What did you say?" His words were a slow crawl, cold and calculating like this was *exactly* what he was hoping would happen.

Tears spilled down her cheeks. "I said take me. Leave her. She's too innocent."

Tom seemed to be weighing her words then shook his head. "Nah, I like virgins, and this one," he slapped her on the ass and squeezed, making Luce whimper, "is ripe for the picking."

Katie closed her eyes, finding a reserve of strength inside her she didn't know existed. She couldn't let this happen. She *wouldn't* let this happen. "Take me. I'm a virgin, too."

Well, that certainly got his attention. He considered her for a moment. "Nah, you'll fight me. The kid won't."

Katie stood up, despite her spine and ribs screaming. Despite the way her whole body shook, whether it was rage or fear, she didn't know. "I promise not to fight back. I'll do whatever you want, just give me your word that you'll leave her alone."

She'd heard the expression before—make a deal with the devil— and now she knew what it meant. She was condemning herself here, but it was a bargain she made readily and gladly if Luce didn't have to live for the rest of her life with the trauma of being raped.

Tom dropped Luce to the ground and gestured for her. "Come on then. Show me that you're worth my time."

She bobbed her head, turning to find Leesa staring at her with wide eyes. Katie shook her head, letting her know it was okay, that this was her choice, but somehow, that didn't stop the pain from spearing through her. She was about to lose her virginity to a human man who had captured and tortured not just females of her species, but also humans, for apparently no good reason.

Walking stiffly, she kept her chin up and stepped through the door. As she passed the front of the cell, Luce was at the cage's side, reaching out to her. Their fingers brushed and, Katie shut the door in her mind that contained all her emotions. She couldn't feel this. She couldn't harbor this memory. She didn't want it, so she was going to lock up everything that was good and put it in a box in the back of her mind where nobody else could touch it. She would survive this, and she would recover.

Because she had to.

Because she made a promise to a little girl who wanted to return to her brother.

Because she could shield a female from the horrors of this world.

Willingly.

35

DRAKE

Drake woke with a start, the pain ripping through his chest the only thing that could be responsible for the cold-cocked wake-up call.

"Neve," he croaked, his eyes wide as he looked around the strange room with a water-stained ceiling. The whole place smelled of disinfectant and mold, old cigarette smoke and stale sex. His cat shifted uneasily beneath his skin. Being injured and in a strange place would make his jaguar pricklier than usual. He couldn't afford to be left defenseless and weak, though. A sheet fell off his arm as he lifted it. He winced as his shoulder let out a scream—he didn't even know when he'd hurt it—but he felt his way along the bandage across the front of his throat. Tearing it off, he ran his fingertips over the neat stitches there.

"Drake, stop. You need to leave them alone. Jesus." Neve pulled his hand away, and her cool touch was on his skin, smoothing the non-stick bandage back into place.

He blinked rapidly, unable to believe what he was seeing. "I thought I lost you," he whispered reverently, reaching up to touch her face. "Are you okay? Are you hurt?"

"Shhh," she said softly, leaning into his palm. The mattress dipped, accompanied by the crackle of plastic. He inhaled, taking in her natural jasmine scent—a scent that was layered in blood. At least not all of it was hers—a lot of it belonged to Lewis. If she was sitting here, it had to mean that the bastard was dead.

"I'm fine." Her voice was just a whisper, but there were shadows in her eyes. He would give anything to take them away from her. Anything.

"How…" His mouth felt like it was stuck to the roof of his mouth. Swallowing, he tried again. "How are Sasha and Mateo?"

Neve glanced over her shoulder, her head tilting to the side as if she was listening. "Mateo's fine. He had to re-break Sasha's leg. Sasha…she's resting."

There was something in her expression…

"What is it?"

She rubbed her chest, grimacing. "When we re-broke her leg, I felt her pain like someone had shoved a dagger through my heart."

He sucked in a breath and let it out slowly through his nose. "It's the bond, Neve."

It had worked. Initiating the blood exchange had been a ballsy move, but one that had been driven by desperation and the desire to know that she would be all right, that she would survive. By doing so, he made sure the strength of his Shadows bolstered her and kept her going.

"How are you feeling about that?"

"You mean do I hate you for doing it without my consent?" she shot back. Relief washed through him when she shook her head. "No. I don't hate you. I understand why you did it. I just wish it could've been under different circumstances."

He brought her hand to his mouth, kissing her palm. "I know, sweetheart."

She rubbed at her chest, clearly still remembering the severity of Sasha's pain. "Are the…" She hesitated. "Are the sensations always so strong?"

He nodded. "For me, yes. When my team and I were assigned together, they swore a blood oath to me. I can feel them, but they can't feel me like you can."

"Makes sense. Mateo wasn't affected like I was," she murmured. With her head bowed, she asked, "And the colored cords?"

He kept the surprise from his face. He wasn't expecting that to transfer to her, too. "It's my connection to them. Since *we're* now connected, it makes sense that you can see them in the same way I do." He kissed her hand again, lingering there to inhale her scent. "Tell me what happened after I passed out. I need to know everything."

Her slender shoulders rose and fell in a shallow shrug before she unloaded the story on him. He listened in stunned silence as she told him how she'd fought Lewis, killed him, then got all of them out of there. Not only that, but she'd had the strength to go back into the house to collect her dead parents, which could have cost her and Mateo's lives, had they not gotten out of there before the blast. By the time she was done, his forearms ached with how tightly he was squeezing his free hand into a fist.

He could've lost her.

"Your cat spoke to me."

He stilled. "Oh?"

"In the back of the car. He asked if I got my parents out."

"He was worried about you. We both were."

She nodded, but stayed quiet. To stop himself from thinking about his cat coming out so far, he cleared his throat and asked, "Where's Mateo?"

"Here, boss," came his tired reply from somewhere across the room. Tilting his head up, he sucked in a hiss when the stitches on his throat pinched. Mateo came forward and touched him on the foot with his right hand. The aches and pains in his body washed away a few moments later, but the pain from deep tissue injuries still lingered.

"Have you called Grayson?"

Mateo pulled away and went to lean against the wall, folding his arms. The male looked worn out, like he was soul weary rather than just sleep-deprived.

"Not yet. I was waiting for you to wake up first. What do you want me to tell him?"

"Tell him we're returning home with the Leo and his mate. Tell him to have Doc Winchester there with an ambulance. Tell him…" *Everything has changed.* "Tell him whatever happened in California has destroyed the structure of the prides. We need to be ready for the blowback."

"Got it."

The question now was, what was the blowback, and how did all these events and pieces fit together? Each and every pride was a rudderless ship lost in a tempest without their Leos and captains of the Shadows. Add to that the stress of females disappearing, and he was left with no doubt in his mind that the two incidents were connected.

Where is everyone?

Drake paused, tilting his head a little to the side. "In here, Sash," he called out, turning when Mateo made a strange noise.

"How did you…" He glanced at Sasha, who hobbled into the room. She hissed at Mateo before coming to sit on the ground at the foot of the bed. Mateo looked back at Drake. "The bond," he breathed. "When did you complete it?"

He rubbed his thumb over Neve's knuckles, more to soothe himself than her. "When I was bleeding out on the floor."

The other male's face lit up with recognition and a smile. "Oh, was that when I was trying to stuff my intestines back into place?"

Drake grunted, then said, "Since I assume you're no longer trying to jam your intestinal tract back into your abdomen, are you feeling up to getting us all some food? Sash will need the calories to help her heal."

"I saw a fast food joint a few miles up the road," Mateo replied, sounding a little miffed about being sent as an errand boy. "I'll be back in about twenty."

The other male slid from the room silently, like the Shadow he was.

"I need to take a shower before we eat," Neve announced, getting up. She glanced back at the bathroom then said, "I'll use the one in the other room."

He nodded, watching her go like he was never going to see her again. He guessed he could blame it on the bond. She was his mate, and he would protect her at all costs.

Turning his attention back to Sasha, he asked, "How long have we been here?"

Maybe an hour, she replied, her internal voice sounding so different to the one he was used to listening to with his ears. He realized it was probably because the cat was more in control in this form, and he sensed that she wasn't as morose as the human.

"Is the pain bad?"

She shook her boxy feline head. *It's nothing I haven't endured before.*

"Did you know?" It was weird having a conversation with someone lying flat on his back. He couldn't even see Sasha to judge her expressions, even if they were more feline. When she said nothing, he added, "Did you know that was going to happen?"

I saw your death, she replied softly. *I never saw Neve's—that's how I knew she had to go with you.*

Jesus. "What about our bond, hers and mine?"

It's fragile, but I feel it. She's bound to us in the same way as we are to you. You did the right thing.

Can you hear me now, Sasha? He sent the mental message cautiously. He was used to seeing inside people's heads, to listening and twisting memories when necessary, but he'd never spoken to someone like this.

Sasha sighed. *I can hear you, but it's faint. Your bonding abilities will continue to grow, but like your bond, you have to give it time.*

"Do the same rules apply to the faster shifts and extra strength?"

I think so. She hesitated. *But I don't know for sure.*

About the same time Mateo returned with the food, Neve wandered through from the other room, running a towel through her damp hair. Drake inhaled her scent, feeling the tension bleed out of his muscles. Mateo placed half a dozen bags onto the small desk in the corner, then selected one and threw it to Neve.

"That should be enough for you two. I'll start unwrapping Sasha's."

They all ate in companionable silence, Sasha the first to finish her dozen burgers.

"We should all get some rest—at least a few hours before we get on the road," Drake announced when they were all done. Mateo mumbled something about taking a shower first and disappeared into the other room with the trash from their meal.

Neve stared down at the shower curtain on the bed. "I'm

exhausted, but I'm not sleeping on that," she said. "Think you could move over to the chair without hurting yourself too much?"

Glancing in the direction she was pointing, he nodded and braced himself to move. His whole body hurt, but it wasn't because of a specific injury. It was more a general ache of his muscles, which he took as a good sign. From his spot, he watched Neve remake the bed with the same precision as when she'd first seen her room, snapping the sheets out to cover the mattress with a no nonsense efficiency. Once she was satisfied with the bed, she nodded at him.

"Get back on then."

He kept the slight grin to himself as he stood up and shuffled over to the edge of the mattress. Letting out a groan, he relaxed back into the pillows. The mattress dipped when Neve joined him, her body curling into his. He'd just closed his eyes, when the mattress dipped once more and Sasha's scent invaded his senses. She curled up on his other side, her head coming to rest on his hip. Reaching out, he scratched her behind her ear.

"Fuck, I hate being last in," Mateo muttered, making Drake crack his eyes open once more. The other male settled on the end of the bed, lying against Drake's feet. Although natural jaguars were solitary animals, shifters tended to seek the comfort of their fellow cats when they were hurt. Drake let out a content sigh and finally fell asleep with the scent of his pride and his mate in his nose.

36

JETT

Jett hung up the phone and stared at the screen until it went dark. He sucked in a breath just to make sure he could still do it—still *breathe*—because he felt as if his chest was crumpling under the pressure of the news he'd just received.

His mother was dead.

And now he had to tell his sister.

Raising his hand to knock on her door, he hesitated. How was he supposed to break this to her? Was it a rip the Band-Aid off kind of thing, or was it something that required kid gloves? Exhaling sharply, he sacked up and knocked.

Katya was there a moment later. "What's wrong?" she asked softly when she saw his face.

"Can I come in?"

She stepped back, wrapping her arms around herself. "You're scaring me."

Fear. She was doing better than him. All he felt was hypoxic. "She's dead." The words came out of his mouth before he could soften them. Kat stared at him with utter desolation in her eyes, and somehow, she looked a decade older all of a sudden.

"Luce?" she croaked, tears already streaming down her cheeks.

Grim, he shook his head. "Mom."

With a ragged sob, Katya broke apart and fell to her knees. Jett joined her on the ground, wrapping his arms around her and just holding her.

"What are we going to do?" Katya whispered into his chest.

He rubbed her back, hoping to soothe her. Their mother may have been an addict, but she was still their flesh and blood, even if she'd chosen chemicals over their love.

"Mila needs to know."

Kat pulled back, swiping the tears from her cheeks. "I'll call her."

Jett shook his head. "No, we need to do this face-to-face, and we need to do it now."

"Okay," she replied, standing up unsteadily and going to the closet and pulling out an oversized sweater that was so old, it had tears in the sleeves.

He stood up, his knees protesting. "You need new clothes," he told her stupidly. How had he never noticed this before? Everything about his sister signposted their poverty. Well, that was going to end today. He could support her and Mila and Luce. He'd do what he should've done all those years ago.

"We didn't have the money to spend on new clothes," she replied softly, ducking her head.

Lifting her chin, he said, "No more, Katya. You don't have to be embarrassed anymore. It's…over. All of it. I'll look after you and Luce." Somehow, he'd make it all work, he'd stretch the pittance he was paid and make sure they were taken care of.

"And Mila?" she asked. "I know you two don't see eye to eye all the time, but she still needs you."

"I know." And didn't he feel like an absolute dick for not seeing it earlier. "Are you ready to go?"

Grabbing her purse, she walked toward the door with her shoulders back and her chin high. Following her out, Jett said, "I just need to grab my keys from my room."

In. Out.

Down to the front door.

Stepping outside, he got bitch slapped by the cold wind. Normally, he wouldn't be taking Katya on his motorbike, but the trip was a short one, and he wanted to have her close to him.

Walking over the pea gravel, he flipped open the compartment on his bike and pulled out the second helmet he kept in there and tossed it to her.

Katya's brows rose. "Are you serious?"

"Yeah. Hop on."

To her credit, she did just that, sliding in behind him once he was settled on the bike. She put her hands on his shoulders and pressed her body close, letting out a squeal when he started the engine and rolled them down the drive. She loosened up as they went, her grip easing off, her body losing some of that rigidity.

Twenty minutes later, he pulled up in front of Mila's boyfriend's house, killing the engine and taking off his helmet.

Katya climbed off the back, wrapping her arms around herself while he lowered the kickstand and set the bike on an angle. The front door opened then, and Katya started toward Mila, who was standing on the stoop. Looming behind her was her boyfriend. Jett made sure to keep eye contact with the guy, waiting for him to nod, to acknowledge that unspoken agreement.

"Kat?" Mila asked. "What's going on?"

His sisters embraced in the middle of the front lawn while he watched from the curb.

Robby stayed standing in the doorway, a frown forming between his eyes.

"She's dead, Mila," Katya moaned. "Mom. She died. She—"

A ragged sob escaped her, the sound of it tearing at Jett's self-control. He eyed Mila, wondering if she would accept his comfort now, despite everything they'd been through. Damn it, he had to try. He approached her slowly, giving her time to retreat if she wanted to. She stunned him, though, when she opened up her arms and invited him into the embrace.

So they stood there, the three of them, hugging each other, hugging what was left of their family. Mila squeezed Jett's shoulder as if trying to convince herself that he was real and he was there. They cried together, mourning not just the loss of their mom, but perhaps their childhood too. They'd reached a place none of them had expected to be, but were there nonetheless.

Katya was the first to pull back, but she kept her arms twined with them, one wrapped around Mila and the other around him.

"Come back with us, Mila?" she asked softly. "Come and stay with us at Jett's house, at least until we get Luce back. I can't stand the thought of losing another member of my family."

Mila stiffened. "Get her *back*?" She turned to look at Jett. "Where's Luce?"

He could feel both his sisters staring at him. "I tried to tell you last time." He sucked in a breath. "She was abducted, but we're doing everything we can to get her back."

Mila folded her arms and took half a step back. "She's ten." Her words were a bare whisper.

"I know," Jett replied just as softly. "We'll get her back, though." His hand curled into a fist, stifling the flames trying to leap from his palm. "Even if I have to raze the entire country to find her."

A pall fell between them until Katya said, "So, will you come back to stay at Jett's house?"

Mila's expression looked pained. She glanced at the door then back at Katya. "I'm sorry, Kat. I can't. I belong here now."

"But… But…"

Mila just shook her head. "I didn't get to choose who my mother was. I didn't get to choose what kind of life I wanted, but I can choose this. He's a good man. He looks after me." She looked to Jett. "He's keeping his word to my brother."

Jett's stared at the guy, and when he nodded, Jett returned the gesture. He could leave Mila here, knowing that Robby would protect her just like he would.

"Come on, Kat," he eventually said. "We should go."

"But you could come back." Mila spoke quickly. To Jett, she said, "You could come back whenever you want to see me."

"I—" He cleared his throat. "I'd like that."

"Good," she replied. "Good." And with that declaration, she turned around and ran back to the house. Her boyfriend wrapped his arms around her, planting a kiss on the top of her head.

"What now?" Katya asked as they wandered back to his Ducati.

Sliding on his helmet, he said, "We go home."

37

NEVE

Neve stared out the passenger side window, gazing at her reflection. She, along with Drake, Mateo, and Sasha had slept for nearly five hours in the end, leaving the motel a little before dark. Drake had been moving a lot better after resting, and although Sasha wasn't favoring her leg as much, she'd still remained in her cat's form. Neve could understand why—shifting with a broken bone was the definition of insanity.

In less than an hour, they'd arrive at the Shadows' compound, and her parents would finally be laid to rest on their pride's lands. Her heart felt heavy, like it would simply drop out of her chest if her ribcage wasn't there holding things in place. Drake reached out and took her hand in his, bringing it to his mouth and placing a kiss in the center of her palm. His compassion and love was a warm light heating her body, and she found herself relaxing.

Her mate did that.

Her mate, who loved her and protected her, even when he was mortally wounded, his cat making sure she was safe. Her mate, who let her make her decisions for herself and gave her opinions thought and consideration.

Drake cleared his throat. "Have you thought about where you

want to bury your parents?"

She nodded. She'd thought of nothing else for the past twelve hours as they drove back to Wyoming. "There's a meadow out the back of our...*the* pride house." As much as she wanted to think of it as hers still, it wasn't. It was not her home anymore, not with her parents gone. "They used to have picnics under an oak tree in the middle of it. They'd be happy there."

"Sounds perfect." He kissed her hand once more, but kept his eyes on the road.

Eventually, he said, "I really am sorry if I rushed the blood bond."

She shook her head. "No, you were right to do it. I don't regret it at all."

He grinned at her, and she decided she liked it when he genuinely smiled. "Good, because I've known I wanted to bind myself to you since the first time I saw your cat."

As much as she wanted to just be happy and content that she'd finally found her mate, there was something still bothering her, and the longer she tried to ignore it, the more the idea would fester.

She didn't want it to fester.

"Do you want to know what terrifies me?"

He glanced over, looking at her through his dark lashes. "Knowing you, it would be losing your independence in our relationship."

Giving his hand a squeeze, she extricated herself and rubbed her palms over her knees. "I fought my parents so hard to not be pigeon-holed into a role. As the Leo's daughter, there were certain expectations of me, but I wasn't ever happy conceding and condemning myself just to be someone's mate, someone's mother."

"And I wouldn't want to break that spirit either."

She gave him a sharp look. "You say that now, Drake, but what about five or ten years from now? What if you get tired of waiting for me to conform into the female you want?"

"*You* are already the female I want."

Shaking her head, she drummed her fingers on her thigh. "I want more from my life than just being someone's mate."

"You know, you've told me all the things you *don't* want to be, but you haven't told me what you do want."

Neve was quiet for a moment. "I want to be a Leo."

Drake was momentarily stunned into silence.

"I see my aspirations have scared you," she dryly. Shrugging, she added, "I won't apologize for it. You're the only person who knows. Clearly, it's never going to happen, so you can forget I mentioned it. With my father gone, my uncle will step into the role until the pride can vote on a new Leo."

"Neve," he said seriously. "You can do whatever you put your mind to. I'm not going to tell you that you can't, because that would be hypocritical."

"In what way?"

"Well, a lot of jaguars would say that females can't make good soldiers, but all you have to do is look at Sasha to see that that's a load of shit."

She gave him a small smile. "Like I said, it doesn't matter anyway."

"If it's important to you, of course it matters. Look, I can't promise I won't overreact when you're in a dangerous situation, but there are some things I can promise you."

"What are they?" she asked hesitantly.

"I will always love you, and I will always support you. So, if you want to become the Leo of the Black Claw pride, then I will do everything in my power to make that happen."

"You don't think it's a stupid idea?" Her question was a whisper, the truth of his words meaning more to her than she could articulate.

"'Do not follow where the path may lead. Go instead where there is no path and leave a trail.'"

Grinning, she said, "Ralph Waldo Emerson."

"I think if you want to be Leo, forge the path yourself. I think you're stubborn enough to break all the molds."

"Drake?"

"Hmm?" he replied, his eyes on the road.

"I love you."

His eyes were molten as he said, "I love you, too."

When they reached the gates of the Shadows' compound, Neve's heart was trying to claw out of her throat. As Drake guided the car up the drive, efficiently rolling through the security checkpoints, she craned her neck to see if the pride's doctor was there with the ambulance to take her parents away.

Her fingers curled around the door handle when she spotted the dark blue Ford E-350 Emergency vehicle parked in the drive. It looked like all the other Wyoming ambulances with the large picture of some native wildlife emblazoned on the side, but the signage stated it belonged to a private medical facility.

Drake wrapped his fingers around the back of her neck, stroking his thumb over her carotid, slowing her pulse with each sweep. "You're not doing this alone. I'll be by your side the whole time."

She blew out a breath and nodded. "I know. Thank you."

He brought the car to a stop at the far end of the turning circle and shut off the engine. Neve opened her door and glanced over to see the Mercedes van pulling in behind them. With Drake by her side, they walked into the house to find Grayson and Doctor Winchester sitting at the large table in the dining room.

"Neve," the doctor said, standing up and coming toward her. He took her hand, shaking it slowly. "I am so sorry for the loss of your parents."

"Thank you," she replied stiffly. "What's going to happen to them?"

The doctor shifted his gaze to Drake briefly. "We'll take them to the morgue and prepare them for burial. Have you thought about…?"

"The meadow behind the pride house," she supplied. "How soon can we bury them?"

He bobbed his head. "Within the next forty-eight hours."

"Fine. Thank you." Turning to Drake, she said, "Now, if you'll all excuse me, I think I need to lie down for a little while."

38

DRAKE

Drake never took his gaze off Neve as she went. His mate was hurting, but he fought the urge to chase after her. She needed some time to herself—especially now.

"Thank you for coming, Doc," he said. "Mateo will help you with the Leo and his mate."

"Ah, yes, of course," Winchester said, taking his cue. Drake showed him from the house, then returned to the dining room.

Grayson gave him a wan smile. "How are you holding up, boss?"

He ran a hand through his hair. "Honestly, a lot of shit went down, and I'm still trying to process it all."

"Mateo said as much. Who do you think was behind the attack on the Leos?"

Pulling out one of the chairs, Drake sat down and clasped his hands in front of him. "Lewis could've been working alone, but what would his motive be?"

"Or he could've been working with the whole Specter team. But like you said, what was the point? What did they stand to gain by killing all the Leos, their mates, *and* the captains of the Shadows?"

Grayson grunted. "Nothing. They destroyed the hierarchy of the prides in the attack, creating anarchy until new Leos can be elected. It also leaves a vacuum in the Shadows' ranks."

"Which would make them the muscle for whoever's calling the shots."

"But who does that leave us with?" Drake leaned back in his chair, tilting his head back until he was looking at the ceiling. "The Trinity. They're the only logical choice."

Grayson exhaled on a steady stream. "That's a dangerous theory."

He acknowledged that with a nod. "Yes, but if it looks like a duck and quacks like a duck, why would I call it something else?"

"And what would they have to gain from an attack like this?"

Now that, Drake had no idea. "Fuck if I know, Gray, but I can guarantee I'll find out. For now, we have to notify the prides of the deaths." Drake stood up and stretched out the kink in his neck. "Where's Jett?"

"Upstairs," Grayson replied, his words careful. "Something else happened while you were away."

His word were grave, his expression somber, and Drake braced himself for more bad news. Seriously, what else could go wrong? "Just tell me."

"His mom died."

"Fuck." He ran a hand through his hair. "How's he holding up?"

Grayson looked in the direction of the foyer. "As well as can be expected. He wants Katya to stay here rather than return home."

"What are your thoughts on that?"

Grayson's shoulders lifted slightly in a shrug. "I think the prides are fractured and we should look after our own, since we currently don't know who's friend and who's foe."

Drake smiled despite himself. "The sapling needs protection from the oak."

"What?"

He shook his head. "Just something Sasha told me." He clapped Grayson on the shoulder. "We can talk more after I sleep."

"You got it, boss."

39

KATIE

Katie was shivering, although it had nothing to do with being cold. Weaving on her feet, she tried to cover as much of her body as she could, but was forced to drop her arms when Tom snarled at her. She'd promised him no trouble, and if she wasn't true to her word, she had no doubt he would punish her by punishing Luce.

Tom continued stalking around her bare body, making all sorts of grotesque statements and noises. He was like an animal in heat, the smell of his lust and the raw alcohol on his breath making her feel sick to her stomach.

He could've taken her quickly, but humiliation was the name of his game.

Stopping in front of her, he reached out and ran his finger across her collarbones, between her bared breasts, down her stomach, until it reached the place she had not shown to any male before.

He smirked at her.

Taunted her with that flex of his lips.

"I bet you really are a virgin," he drawled.

Pressing her lips together more tightly, she kept the promise she'd made to herself—she wouldn't cry. She wouldn't give him that satisfaction.

He shoved her forward with a hand between her shoulder blades. Her face made contact with the wall first, then her body. She was instantly chilled to the bone. Behind her, Tom pressed himself against her, a fetid blanket of his lust and anticipation covering her. She was sure there was a special place in hell for men like this.

He hadn't bothered to take her far. They were only a few feet from the cells and the other women, but the hallway gave them some measure of privacy. Tom was still fully clothed—yet another symbol of the power he wielded over her.

Pinning her arms above her head, he dragged his free hand down her back, over her ass. Pushing aside the revulsion, she gritted her teeth and thought about what she would do if she got free. She lost all her bravado, though, when Tom kicked her legs wider.

The sound of a zipper being drawn down made her pulse race and her mouth dry. This was actually going to happen. She was going to lose her virginity like this. Better her than Luce, though. At least she had the mental capacity to digest this violation.

Tom caressed her ass once more, running his hand between her legs. She tried to stay still, to not pull away. Resistance would only make him work harder to hurt her more. Then there was something else there at her opening, something blunt and thick, and terror made her throat constrict.

Instead of letting the fear control her as she had before, she tried to think about what Neve would do. She'd probably lull the guy into a false sense of security then nail him to the wall for touching her uninvited. But Katie wasn't her cousin. She was not violent. She was a gentle soul...

But maybe she could change that.

She'd realized that if she or one of the other females didn't get themselves out of this mess, then it was very likely they were all going to die there, and she had no intention of dying here.

Not today.

Not tomorrow.

And certainly not when she was the apex predator in this situation. Even as weakened as she was, she still had a spitting, hissing black jaguar inside her body, and *she* was her best weapon. Katie abhorred violence, but the human and the cat weren't always so in sync. *She* had been fantasizing about ripping their captors' throats out for days now. *She* had been showing Katie just how easy it would be.

All she needed was the opportunity.

She was stunned when he released her arms, his hands coming to rest on her hips, his fingers digging in to the point of pain. Slowly, so it didn't rouse his suspicion, she lowered her arms and placed her palms against the concrete wall she was being pressed against. Tom leaned forward, placing his nose against her neck—just below her ear—and inhaled. Katie let out a slow breath then threw her head back, nailing him in the nose.

There was a crunch, followed by a howl of pain. Tom released his hold on her hips as he was no doubt holding his injured nose. Satisfaction curled in her stomach, the feeling both foreign and so familiar that she realized her cat had edged closer to the surface.

Tom was still bent over at the waist, cupping his hands over his nose. He was too busy cursing her to see where her eyes were fixed. Darting forward with as much speed as she could muster, she reached for the knife that was still attached to his belt. She managed to pop the top clip off, but cried out in frustration and pain when she was shoved away. She'd almost had it—her fingertips had just grazed the hilt.

Landing in a heap on the bare floor, her sweat-damp skin stopped her from skidding too far. There was a collective gasp, and she looked up, behind her, to the side. She was in the center of the cells with nowhere to run.

Tom was coming toward her now, blood gushing from his nose, over his lips and chin. She smiled when she saw the deep cut on the bridge of his nose. Scrambling to get to her feet, she edged backward as he prowled toward her. His face was twisted—a mask of rage and frustration.

"Think you can outsmart me, huh?" he snarled, wiping the back of his hand over his mouth to clear it of blood. With a cocky sneer, he pulled the knife free and brought it up to show her, twisting the handle until there was that flash again—that light, that spark…

Katie had retreated until her back collided with the closest cell, her bare shoulders pressing into the cold steel. Tom—thinking he'd caged her in—lunged for her. She side-stepped him, but he still caught a blow on her shoulder, the pain radiating out like a spiderweb from the strike. He swung back around, anger amplifying his features, making him look monstrous.

"I'll make you bleed for that," he threatened, charging for her again. Once more, she side-stepped him without getting hit, using the advantage of the alcohol and rage in his system against him. Again and again, he lunged and she darted out of the way, maneuvering them around the perimeter of the cells.

Over his shoulder, she caught Leesa standing at the front of her cage, her fingers curled around the steel bars. There was a look of dark satisfaction in her eyes. After a moment, she nodded, and Katie knew what she had to do.

She let him catch her that time. Sucking in a wince when he grabbed her by the upper arm and spun her around, she barely had time to brace herself before she was slammed against Leesa's cell. Her face made first contact with the bars, her hip bone on the left taking second place in the race to Agonyville. Pain exploded across her cheek, and her eyes watered from the impact.

Something sharp was pressed against her neck, and the scent of blood flooded her senses. She tried not to move, to breathe. Leesa came into her line of sight, the determined look still shining in her eyes.

"Stay back," Tom barked in warning, the scent of his anticipation riding on the back of the blood. "Stay back or you're next."

She felt him fumble with something behind him and realized he'd re-holstered the knife when he stretched her arms above her head with both of his hands. Kicking her legs apart, he pressed his hips against her ass. Katie bit her lip hard as her mind worked, trying to come up with the next step in the plan.

"You're going to regret playing with me. By the time I'm done with you—"

Tom's words were cut off by an inhuman scream, the smell of blood going from a trickle to a torrent. The anchors of his hands were suddenly gone, and she spun around to find him writhing on the floor, holding the backs of both his ankles. He turned his eyes to her—eyes that were burning with a new level of rage...

And perhaps also fear.

His gaze shifted over her shoulder, and she turned to find Leesa holding the hunting knife dripping with Tom's blood.

"It's not over yet, Katie," Leesa said, handing the knife over to her, hilt first. Katie looked down at the bloody weapon. "You have to finish it," she said.

Katie's eyes widened. "What?"

"I only cut his Achilles. If you want us to get out of here, you have to kill him."

She swallowed. "I can't." She wasn't a murderer, the mere thought of taking someone's life abhorrent to her.

"Katie? Katie, look at me." She did, compelled by the power in Leesa's voice. Keeping their gazes locked, she spoke very slowly— deliberately. "He was going to *rape* you. He was going to rape that little girl. He's responsible for terrorizing us, and now he's the only way we can get out of this."

Katie knew the words she was saying were true, but to kill him? *Kill* him? Once more, her thoughts went to Neve. She wouldn't have any qualms about taking out a threat. She was so strong, so sure about what she wanted. Her world was black and white with very little room for grays. Katie was staring at one of those gray areas now.

"He would've done worse to you," Leesa said, pushing the knife in her direction. "You have to do this. We're all relying on you to get us out of here."

Katie's gaze flickered over to Luce, her protective instincts flaring. The young female was huddled up against the wall, her face buried into the top of her knees. She wouldn't look, and Katie knew that was all the permission she needed. If Luce didn't witness her doing this, then she could go through with it.

With shaking hands, she took the knife and turned back to Tom. He was trying to get up, but his ankles were folding beneath the weight. The guy's brown eyes widened as he saw the intent on her face.

"No," he begged, trying to edge away from her. "Please."

He had never listened to their pleas, so why should she? She glanced back at Leesa, finding the female's eyes glowing gold with her cat, anticipation a stroking caress along her skin. She couldn't get too close to Tom. He still had two functioning arms, and he would use whatever weapons he still had in his arsenal.

She had to be quick, though, to strike then move away before he could react. Leaping forward, she slashed at his torso, cutting through cotton and flesh, past the muscles and into the protective abdominal sac that housed his stomach. She'd watched enough movies to know that stomach wounds could be fatal if left untreated and were severe enough.

Tom's scream vibrated around the room, and she heard the other females shift closer to the bars, closer to the smell of freshly spilled blood and meat. Katie felt the pull too. Hunger. It burned through her, but she knew she wouldn't be able to live with herself if she ate Tom too. Her cat hissed in protest. She had no such qualms, and if Katie wasn't terrified to let her out without losing control, she would have. But right now—with her jaguar half-starved, and her human side terrorized—shifting now would end in her harming more than just Tom. She would not be able to control her ravening cat.

His torso was suddenly stretched taut in front of her, one of his arms being held through the bars by Elsie. Elsie's cellmate grabbed his other arm, pinning it under her knee by the wrist.

"Do it," Elsie said in a dead voice that matched the dullness in her eyes. "Do it."

"I've got his leg," Leesa said. Katie turned to see her straining against the bar to grab Tom's injured leg by the cuff of his pants. He was too weak to fight off their holds, she saw it in his face, saw the realization that dawned on him.

He was going to die by the hands of the females he'd been charged with brutalizing.

Easing down beside him, she brought the knife up to his chest, her hand shaking violently.

"Do it," Leesa commanded softly at her back. Katie hesitated a moment, reluctant to take that next step. If she'd left him to die from the stomach wound, she could easily brush it off as self-defense. What she was contemplating was murder.

She would be a murderer.

How was she supposed to live with that kind of stain on her soul?

How was she supposed to live with herself?

"Do it."

Katie spun around, her wide eyes finding Luce standing at the front of their cell. Her hands were gripping the bars, her blue eyes flashing gold as her cat stalked closer to the surface. She was shaking too, tears streaming down her face.

"Do it," she repeated. "Make him suffer."

She turned back to Tom, whose eyes were so wide now that she could see the whites all the way around. She lifted the knife once more and didn't hesitate. She drove the metal down, knowing that the protective cage of his ribs was going to try and divert her. She put all her strength into it, feeling the resistance of bone but pushing through it anyway. Blood—red heart's blood—welled, and Tom's body went slack. As she witnessed the last moments of his life, watched the spark drain out of his wild eyes, she knew she'd done the right thing.

Leaving the knife in place, she stood up on shaking legs and looked around, wondering how to get everyone out of there. Clothes were a must. Normally, nudity wasn't an issue for shifters, but she felt particularly vulnerable right now, and doing brave things required clothing. Tracing her steps back to the hallway, she grabbed her torn and dirty shirt and pulled it back on. Next was her underwear and jeans. When she finally pulled her glittery Keds back on, she stared down at the gray satin laces that were stained with blood and dirt. She couldn't help but draw parallels between herself and the shoes. Sure, they had their practical uses, but the reality was they were frivolous and pretty. Now they were stained from an experience out of their control.

"Katie?" Leesa called out. "Are you okay?"

"Fine," she replied softly, her gaze still on her shoes. "I'm fine."

"Find out how you can get us out of these cages," the other female urged.

Walking slowly, she approached the only door in and out of the basement, finding another fingerprint scanner—the same as on their cells—attached to the wall.

"There's another scanner," she told the waiting females. "On the door."

Leesa cursed.

Katie came back into the room, her eyes falling on Tom's slowly cooling body. Sucking in a breath, she walked up to him and gripped the knife still sticking out of his chest. Yanking with all her strength, she pulled the blade free, stumbling back with the force.

"What are you doing?" Leesa asked.

"Getting us out of here," she replied, determined to survive. Pulling him arm back through the bars of Elsie's cell, she laid his hand out flat on the concrete floor, splaying his fingers wide. Placing the knife just above the first knuckle of his index finger, she started to saw, breaking through the skin, tendons and bone. Bile bubbled up the back of her throat, the visceral scene bringing a roll of nausea that her cat didn't even blink at.

When the digit was finally free, she picked it up and prayed the scanner didn't also rely on body heat or a pulse to work. She placed Tom's finger against the reader on Leesa's cell, watching the static red light turn into a blinking green one. There was a click, and the cell door opened on well-oiled tracks. Leesa ran out, wrapping her arms around Katie.

"You did it," she breathed. "Thank you." They broke apart, and Leesa turned to the other females in the cells. "Quick, get the others out before someone comes down here to check on us."

Katie opened the cells, accepting thanks and gratitude from all of the females. Luce wrapped her arms around her waist and refused to let go.

"Stay with Leesa for a minute, Luce," she told her as she tried the scanner by the main door. She held her breath as she waited for the red light to go green, then held it a little longer as she waited for the alarm to be raised.

She let out the breath. "Clear," she croaked. Leesa was the first around the corner, Luce tucked closely at her side. The others followed behind her, their untrusting eyes darting around. Katie indicated that she would ascend the stairs first, adjusting her grip on the hilt. As she crept forward, she felt her pulse throb through her. She smelled the scent of her fear, but also Tom's blood on the blade and her hands.

On the landing at the top, there was another reader. Putting Tom's finger to good use, she waited for the blinking green light then eased open the door an inch. She sniffed the fresh air rushing to get in and didn't smell anything other than cigarette smoke, stale food, and alcohol. Inhaling once more, she tried to decide whether the scent of her captors were strong enough to indicate they were still in the house.

They couldn't sit there forever, though. As her dad would say,

"Shit or get off the pot." There was no use waiting for them to get caught—not after everything she'd sacrificed. She looked down the stairs and motioned for Leesa and the others to come up. If they went out as one, there was a good chance a lot of them would escape.

"On three," she breathed. "One. Two. Three."

Katie was out the door first, the knife held out in front of her. A few steps into the hallway, she realized there was no sound coming from anywhere in the house. She lowered her arm and took a good look around when they came to the living room. The place was barely furnished, just an old couch and an upturned milk crate being used as a coffee table. The carpet was stained and smelled of mold, and the paint on the walls was peeling. On the table, there were empty booze bottles and food containers, and the desperation for food almost had her stopping to cram whatever was left in the bottom into her mouth.

"We need to check out the rest of the house," Leesa said quietly.

The other females were still huddled together, their fear like a separate entity in the house. The living room was safe as far as they could see, so she told them all to wait there while she and Leesa began another sweep.

"Don't leave me," Luce whimpered, clutching at Katie's shirt. She eased her hands away and kneeled down so they were level.

"I promise I'm coming back," she told her softly, running her fingers over her unbruised cheekbone. "I promise. Then I'll take you back to your brother."

Standing up, she turned around and inhaled deeply to sift through the other less pervasive scents. At least two other men and one male had been in the house recently. The strongest scent belonged to Tom. The other scent was Leroy's, but it was faint, like he hadn't been there often or for any real period of time. The third male was a stranger to her, although he was a shifter.

Together with Leesa, she crept down the shallow hall, eyeing the closed doors that were on its perimeter. Leesa pulled up in front of one door, nodding at Katie decisively before opening it.

Tom's scent rolled out, causing Katie to take an unsteady step back. The guy was dead, but it was like his ghost was still in the house with them. The next room was completely empty, save for a couple of folding chairs and a cheap card table. The carpet in here had been torn up, revealing slashes of unvarnished floorboards. The only other door was a bathroom that would've been original to the house, which placed it as a seventies build. The toilet, sink, and bath were all a gaudy avocado green, the color clashing against the brown starburst tiles on the floor and walls.

"I think it's empty," Leesa murmured, looking longingly at the bath. Katie would've killed to take a shower, but now wasn't the time. They weren't out of danger yet.

They rejoined the others in the living room, and Leesa peered past the too bright lime green, orange, and yellow diamond-patterned drapes.

"It's getting late."

Katie peered around the other side, stunned by what she saw. They were in a suburb, a white-collar one, judging by the BMWs and Mercedes parked in driveways. How had nobody noticed what was happening in this house?

"There's a car pulling up next door," Leesa said, her voice betraying her giddiness. "It has...*fuck*. They're New Mexico plates."

They were in New Mexico?

"How in the hell are we going to get out of here?" she asked, not expecting an answer to just leap out and present itself. There wasn't a car parked in the house's driveway, nor was there one on the street.

Leesa turned around, her eyes scanning the room. She approached the brown couch, sliding her hands down between the cushions. Her frown turned to a look of triumph when she pulled her hand free, and she held up a cell phone. It must've been Tom's. She picked it up and swiped a finger across the screen. Internally, Katie prayed that the guy was a dumbass who didn't believe in password protecting his devices.

"Bingo!" Leesa said, flashing the device her way.

"Who are you calling?"

"First, my parents, then my cousin. He lives in New Mexico, although I don't know where we are specifically right now. Thank God for Google Earth, huh?"

She wrapped her arms around Luce. "We're going home," she said. "We're going to get you back to your brother."

After Leesa gave her cousin the details of their location, the phone was passed around the group so everyone could contact their respective parents or mates. Katie waved the phone on each time someone offered it to her. She had no idea who to call. Her parents would've been sick with worry, but she was ashamed for them to see her. She had done something unspeakable. She was tarnished, and she didn't want to bring that to their house. When it was finally her turn, she dialed Neve's number.

"Hello?" her cousin said suspiciously when she picked up.

She felt like her throat was closing up. Katie tried twice before any words came out, and when they did, it was a croak. "Neve?"

"Katie? Where are you?"

With those words, a rough sob escaped her throat, and she finally let the tears fall.

EPILOGUE

LEROY

eroy whistled through his teeth. Hot da*yum*, Tom had been torn open, his intestines falling down his sides. The scent of death was still cloying, so he couldn't have been taken down any longer than a couple of hours ago. Crouching down beside his former colleague, he ran a finger through the puddle of cooling and congealed blood on either side of his torso and brought it to his mouth.

Hmm, terror and death.

"Are you quite done?" someone drawled from behind him. He turned around slowly, readjusting his Stetson as he grinned at the shifter standing stiffly at the mouth of the hallway. Asher looked all wrong standing in the basement, his bruised purple smoking jacket clinging tightly to his tense shoulders. His blond hair was perfectly styled and coiffed, and if Leroy didn't know what lurked beneath his skin, he'd call the guy a dandy to his face. As if sensing his thoughts, Asher's eyes flared a brilliant green, a sure sign that the male's jaguar was close to the surface.

"What happened?"

Leroy looked down at Tom. "Looks like Tom lost control of the situation."

Asher gave him an irritated glare. "Clearly," he drawled. "But what I want to know is how he managed to get himself killed. They were all secured behind bars."

Leroy shrugged and resettled his hat, staring at all the wounds. Whoever got him had showed no mercy. "My guess would be he tried to get one of the females to submit to him—"

Asher hissed, the sound more feline than human.

He put his hands up in surrender. "Hey, *I* didn't do it, and it wouldn't be the first time he took one of them," he lied. Tom was jealous as fuck that Leroy'd gotten some action.

"You *allowed* one of your men to be alone with them?"

He snorted. "Of course not. The guy probably snuck down here while he was drunk and I or the others were sleeping."

Asher took a few steps forward until they were standing nose to nose. The scent of his cologne tickled his sinuses. "That stops now," he growled, his eyes flashing green. "These females aren't a commodity so easily secured—yes, we collected the first lot easily enough, but that was because they weren't ready for it. Now they're on high alert." He looked away, his eyes shifting from cell to cell to cell. "How many did we lose?"

"Nine—four humans and five shifters."

He turned those cold, dead eyes to him. "If you ever want more *arnastu*, it would be in your best interest to acquire some more humans."

"I thought we only needed the shifters. Why are you so pissed there are no humans?"

Asher roared in frustration, his face morphing into a terrifying mask of rage. "Without the humans, there's no drug supply!" He tore his gaze from Leroy and said more calmly, "What about the other locations?"

He shook his head. "We centralized to this one."

"Zero? We have *no* females left?"

Leroy shrugged and rubbed at his nose. It was tingling again. He needed another hit. How long had it been since his last one? Less than twenty-four hours.

Asher bared his teeth at him. "You need more?" he asked with a sneer. "You can get more once you get those five females back."

MARKED BY SHADOWS